DELTA FILE

Dale Dye

"Shake Davis is back! Author Dale Dye gives us action, guts, and a fitting Memorial Day tribute to the glory of our warrior's past. A gripping tale of pride and commitment to the courageous values that made America great."
—Mark Greaney, #1 *NYT* bestselling author of *One Minute Out*

"Locked and loaded with action and mayhem: oh-man does Shake Davis deliver! From stem-to-stern, Dale Dye's *Delta File* is filled with all the guts and twice the glory. Read it today!"
—Rip Rawlings, bestselling author of *Red Metal*

"The Skipper Dale Dye dreams in the language Gunner Shake Davis speaks. Give me more…"
—Tom Hanks, actor, author of *Uncommon Type*

"Dale Dye proves himself once again to be as good a storyteller as he was a soldier during his own distinguished military career, bringing his stalwart Shake Davis back to the grounds that define him to this day on a Conrad-esque journey into the heart of darkness….Dye manages to combine the pacing and plotting of Stephen Hunter with the angst-rattled soldier's sensibility of Phillip Caputo. He hits the bulls-eye dead center, resulting in a tale as riveting as it is relentless and not to be missed."
—Jon Land, *USA Today* bestselling author of the Caitlin Strong series

Also by Dale Dye

BANGKOK FILE
SEA HUNT
AZTEC FILE
HAVANA FILE
CONTRA FILE
BEIRUT FILE
CHOSIN FILE
PELELIU FILE
LAOS FILE
RUN BETWEEN THE RAINDROPS
PLATOON
OUTRAGE
CONDUCT UNBECOMING
DUTY AND DISHONOR

DELTA FILE

DALE DYE

WARRIORS PUBLISHING GROUP
NORTH HILLS, CALIFORNIA

DELTA FILE

A Warriors Publishing Group book/published by arrangement with the author

PRINTING HISTORY
Warriors Publishing Group edition/May 2020
All rights reserved.
Copyright © 2020 by Dale A. Dye
Cover art copyright © 2020 by Gerry Kissell

ISBN: 978-1-944353-31-5
Library of Congress Control Number: 2020937480

The name "Warriors Publishing Group" and the logo
are trademarks belonging to Warriors Publishing Group

PRINTED IN THE UNITED STATES OF AMERICA

10 9 8 7 6 5 4 3 2 1

Here's to Kenneth, Vivian and
Dale Dye, a colorful family trio cut
From Southeast Missouri cloth.
And here's to that damn old
Gar fish still hanging in Schindler's Tavern.

Oyo Province, Nigeria

They lowered the old woman's body into the loamy soil and made the sign of the cross. There was not much more they could do. At least she died peacefully of old age and infirmity. These days that was a rare blessing. The priest from Lagos would not be available to say the requiem mass for a day or two, but God in his mercy would understand. It was necessary to get a dead body into the ground as soon as possible. The Nigerian climate corrupted quickly, and it was dangerous for the living to delay burial of the dead. There was enough disease already ravaging the land and such precautions were necessary.

Jambon Imbasa prayed silently, standing in a light rain while other men from the village shoveled dirt onto the canvas shroud that covered their latest loss. Off to the right of the new grave were two others, a young man and his wife, finally at rest after nearly a year fighting the AIDS virus slowly destroying their systems. And beyond those graves were three more, even more recent. Young men killed in a Boko Haram raid. They tried to run for the forest, but they were too slow. It had been two long days before the rebels left and the villagers could return from hiding to bury those men.

Jambon Imbasa was a leader, a relatively educated man, but he had no answers for the Ibo people who relied on him for advice and guidance. And now he would have to make the long walk to Ibadan and use the phone to call the good Father in Lagos, who was also of the Ibo people, asking him once again to come and say the mass for the dead. Jambon Imbasa could only wonder as they all did why God seemed to be punishing them.

There was a truck parked near the center of the village when his people returned from the burial. A visitor? They didn't have many. The village had been carved down to just five or six extended families now. But the man standing in the shade of a banyan tree wore the amulet of an Ibo leader. Jambon didn't recognize him, but perhaps he was from the family of the dead woman they'd just buried. He looked healthy and prosperous in nice clothing. Perhaps he could offer a ride in his truck to Ibadan. Jambon approached him with a friendly wave. When the stranger spotted the symbol hanging from Jambon's neck, he smiled and waved back.

"I am Samuel Imshana from Lagos," he said, offering a hand. "I'm sorry for your loss."

"Thank you, sir." Jambon shook the extended hand feeling the bite of a large ring that looked to be a diamond set in gold. "We have had too many in recent days."

"So I've heard," the man said, leading Jambon toward the shade near his truck. The rain had stopped and heat from the sun emerging from the clouds was intense. "I have come to offer you and perhaps some others a great opportunity." He waved a hand at the small cluster of ramshackle homes that lined the village street. "An opportunity to leave all this for a better life."

"A better life?"

"Yes, a better life and a good job—in America. It won't be easy, but it is possible for those who qualify and wish to leave all this behind. Let me tell you about it."

Lockhart, Texas

The big house was empty. Rambling aimlessly from room to room, up and down the stairs, following dust motes dancing in mellow afternoon sunlight, he moped. A house like this one, stolid and rough-hewn like its bare oaken floors, shouldn't be empty. It should be a switching station for domestic traffic, full of people, busy and bustling. There should be kids barreling around in minimal clothing, barefoot and oblivious to the chili pepper heat that kept them from playing outside. There should be dogs chasing them or at least watching through tolerant eyes from some shadowy corner.

If he thought about it—and he often did—the house had history, and he believed history of all sorts was valuable—and often entertaining—only if it was contemplated and reviewed every once in a while. If you were willing to do that, a house like this one spoke volumes in every creak and groan of its old timber skeleton. It was so much more than simple shelter.

On a little catch-all table at the foot of the stairs, there was a letter from the Texas State Historical Association claiming that back in 1860 or so Texas Governor Sam Houston had given one of his fiery anti-secession speeches to a crowd gathered in the shade of the two live oaks that still stretched long serpentine limbs over the front yard. The house hadn't been built then. Those were the days when Comanches watered their ponies in the creek that still ran along one side of the house. There were chipped flint arrowheads to be found on the banks of that creek, and he contemplated digging a bit in the black mud. Who would he show them to if he found an artifact or two down there?

He lost interest and wandered onto the screened back porch where he could see the surrounding land and a solid slice of the little town that had grown like Topsy in the years before and after the house was built around 1915. Perched like an old sentry on the edge of that town, the house occupied a strategic site that overlooked a stretch of the old Chisholm Trail where Longhorn cattle and other market beeves were driven from Hill Country ranches toward stockyards or railheads. The surrounding lawns this time of year were carpeted with bluebonnets, and their fragrance carried through the back-porch screens on the same little breeze that brought the aroma of hickory fires from the barbecue joint up the street. It would be suppertime before long, but he wasn't hungry. He was lonely.

He could see a stand of Indian paint brushes pushing through a patch of backyard weeds that needed his attention. He contemplated rolling out the riding mower and making a quick pass before sundown, but it didn't seem…well, it just didn't seem right. Joy in that chore came from watching his big dog barking and running in circles as if the mower was a giant cat or some kind of motorized squirrel sent to torment him. Bear, the Golden Pyrenees who now claimed all sectors of the house and surrounding lands, was on temporary duty helping out as a comfort animal at a children's hospital in Austin. Mr. Bear was doing time in an impromptu petting zoo where kids with cancer could visit and play with pets who provided unconditional love. Bear was the kind of big, lovable teddy bear that could sense when someone needed a morale boost. It was tough to loan him out, but Bear was in good hands and would revel in the attention lavished on him for a couple of weeks.

A stiffening wind advertised beef brisket smoked to Texas perfection, and he glanced at the clock on the mantle over the fireplace. It was a bit early for a snort but—what the hell—when you're alone, Happy Hour is when you say it is.

In the kitchen, he glanced through the front windows to see if the family of white-tailed deer that lived in the woods below the house were thirsty enough to brave a drink from his bait ponds before full dark. Still too hot for thirsty deer, he decided, but he was a little more royal than they were in the animal kingdom. He splashed TX bourbon into a semi-clean glass fetched from a sink cluttered with too many dirty dishes and reached for the pitcher of branch water he kept on the windowsill. There was just a splash left in the pitcher. He'd have to make a trip before long down to the little dam he'd made in the creek to collect a bourbon mix tastier than what flowed from faucets in the house.

His wife was always worried that he'd ruin his health with his evening drinks. She didn't mind whiskey as much as she worried about parasites or ugly bugs in the creek water. He didn't really think so, but maybe she was right. She was about a lot of other things. Anyway, he had another month of whiskey and water drinking to find out, and he was feeling a bit Nietzschean about that. *Whisky that does not kill me makes me strong,* he thought with a grin, and drained off half the first snort of an evening that loomed lonely and uninspiring. His wife might find a bloated corpse when she returned from her three-month sabbatical at National Chengchi University in Taipei, but he doubted that would happen. He'd swallowed an ocean or two of whisky in his years in uniform during which it was part of mandatory fun, and his liver was still managing to cope.

He carried a freshened drink toward the dining room where there were two dusty boxes piled on his wife's prized table, a stodgy, stained, and stocky old platform that had likely been used to butcher hogs at some point in its colorful history. Before she left, his wife had compiled a short list of long-ignored chores that she thought would keep him semi-sober and focused while she was away. The boxes represented part of that. They were filled with old photos and papers from his side of the family, and she wanted him to sort them, then take her on a little trip through his ancestry when she got home.

Shake sighed, shook his head and went back to the kitchen for the whisky bottle. He squinted at the level and then reached into a cabinet for his back-up. A mind-trip back to Southeast Missouri with whistle stops to visit a cloud of dimly remembered country kinfolks was at least a two-jug exercise. There were ghosts and discomfiting haunts back in those bayous.

∆ ∆ ∆

Most of what he found as he pawed through the first box was stuff he hadn't seen, and certainly hadn't thought about, for years. It was baby Shake mementos, so far removed that it seemed irrelevant, just dim cues that failed to spark any conscious sense of a younger version of the man he was now. And how could they? When does effective memory really begin?

In a shabby little album made of brittle craft paper with a molding cardboard cover, he found the telegram informing his father, then serving on a warship somewhere in the Pacific, that a male offspring had entered the national census. Mother and son doing fine, the telegram said. And they probably were about that time in the waning years of World War II. There was work for anyone able, and family farms were thriving in an effort to keep the country nourished while forces on the other side of the globe struggled to tear each other apart. Who would imagine in those war-weary days that the scowling and birth-wrinkled little prune in a collection of fading newborn photos would grow into a scarred veteran of other wars down a line that America was even then drawing in the sands of time?

It didn't appear that he'd suffered any deprivations as an infant. Elsewhere in the box he found a couple of wartime ration stamp booklets filled out in his name—Sheldon Davis. It would be a decade or two later when he became known as Shake and the Sheldon of his birth certificate faded except as it appeared on official civil or military documents. There were ration stamps remaining in the booklets that authorized purchase of milk and formula. So it appeared he'd gotten fed, watered, and clothed in those early years without undue sacrifice. No middle name on any of the documents from his childhood, not even on the kitschy little certificate proclaiming him runner-up in a local Most Beautiful Baby Contest. Shake remembered asking about that, but couldn't recall getting any kind of definitive answer. His paternal grandmother, a pioneer woman who was Minerva Woody before she married grandfather Everett Davis, once told him that a little boy so special didn't need more than two names. There was a full-size portrait of her in the box showing a slightly frumpy woman with rimless specs perched on a strong nose. Grandma had the look of a determined survivor in that photo. She certainly was that, a farm-bred woman, reared in hardship, who knew how to raise a family and get things done as and when they needed doing.

Shake poured more whisky in his glass and grinned at the woman who had been most influential in his early boyhood years after his parents split over booze and bad-tempered disagreements concerning the direction of their post-war lives. There was a story he loved about his grandparents, really the only familial legend that he could recall. Grandad had been elected Sheriff of Scott County, the only Republican to hold that office in a yellow-dog Democrat region of bootheel Missouri that considered itself a traditional stronghold of the Civil War south in spite of mid-western geography. On a day when Grandad was down with the flu, a gaggle of prisoners he'd locked up for bootlegging moonshine hooch attempted a jailbreak. The story goes that Shake's father, then a pre-teen Boy Scout, had rushed home to inform Grandpa that his prisoners were about to fly the county coop. As Grandpa was too ill to do much about it, Grandma Minerva stormed down to the lock-up with a loaded double-barrel 12-gauge and put an end to the disorder. The first time she'd told him that story, Grandma had proudly showed Shake the shotgun that she still kept handy in a kitchen broom closet.

Among the formal portraits, each lovingly retouched to blur any real-life blemishes, there was one that he thought he ought to frame one of these days—maybe next to a current photo of himself, just for a startling contrast. It showed a chubby, laughing baby, sitting fat and sassy in a light blue jumper, an image that conveyed innocence and pure joy at just being alive. Someone had paid to have that photo taken. It was hand tinted by the photographer who added twinkle to his blue eyes and a rosy blush to his fat little baby cheeks.

He pulled a faded ribbon from a batch of odd-shaped photographs, different cameras and different drug-store formats. Someone—likely his mother—had collected the photos in chronological order with dates and ages scribbled on the reverse. Baby Sheldon was posed with his Mom in a miniature man suit with a crop of straw-colored hair carefully parted and lacquered. His mother looked down on him lovingly, mirroring the smile he showed for the camera. Her teeth were present and pearlescent. Her son was missing a few. And there was a shot of the Davis family on the front porch of a rented four-family shotgun house. It was dated a year after the war ended, but Shake could see the stain of dark memories clouding his Dad's face.

There was a lot more, but Shake had cracked his back-up bottle and decided to move on to the second box. That contained more mysteries than memories. Some of the photos and the odd certificate or two concerned his matriculation at Missouri Military Academy for his high school years. No clouds over that. It was what started him on a long, bumpy road to a career in the U.S. Marine Corps. Someone had even saved the three rejection letters he got after failing to score well enough on his academic exams when he was trying to bull his way into the Naval Academy. He pondered dumping those in the trash but put them back. Couldn't hurt to remind himself of why he started his military career as a buck private at Parris Island rather than a Midshipman at Annapolis.

Three photos caught his attention and he laid them out on the table where he could examine them in the soft, early evening light streaming in from west-side windows. Someone had juxtaposed them in a little plastic accordion arrangement. There was a shot of him on the deck of a bull-nose tugboat, looking cotton-topped, skinny, and deeply tanned. It was from one of the best summers he could remember of his teenage years, the summer he spent as a deckhand on a Mississippi River tug pushing or pulling barges from St. Louis south to New Orleans and back. The next one was of the SS Admiral, an old art-deco paddle-wheeler homeported in St. Louis that offered excursion cruises on the river when he was a boy. Shake remembered running all over that ship with his friends and cousins, watching in awe as the big side-mounted wheels churned muddy water and the adults sat be-lowdecks drinking cheap Budweiser. The final photo of the three showed an older gent who looked remarkably like photos of Mark Twain when the great author was Samuel Clemens piloting steam-powered paddle-wheelers up and down the Mississippi. The subject was posed in a naval-style frock coat with brass but-tons and wearing a pillbox hat featuring an embroidered name. The hat was Navy blue but the frock coat was a lighter color, not white, likely some shade of grey.

Shake got a magnifying glass for a closer look and determined that the man in the photo was a crewman—more likely the cap-tain given his brass buttons—of a ship called the *Natchez*. It was one of those posed shots—subject standing stiff and still, with one hand tucked away in his coat—reminiscent of photos he'd seen from the Civil War era. A penciled date on the back con-firmed that the shot was taken some time in 1862. A scrawl below that date caused him to grin and reach for his glass. "Pewter fol-lows Uncle Fielding down the river." Pewter he knew. It was a nickname his grandparents had started to call him when his un-ruly hair began to take on a lighter cast, an exasperating phenom-enon that led to the premature advent of white hair at around age 23. But who the hell was Fielding? If he was a great uncle, Shake could not remember ever hearing the name mentioned. He couldn't detect any familial similarities behind the shaggy eyebrows and walrus mustache.

He was about to head for the computer in the den to do some research when another photo on top of a nearby stack caught his eye. This one showed a World War I soldier in uniform complete with doughboy high collar, pie-plate helmet and wrapped leggings. The uniform was mud-spattered, but the 1903 Springfield rifle the man held by his side was clean and looked well-maintained. Closer examination with the glass revealed that the man was a Marine. The emblem on the front of his helmet was an early version of the eagle, globe, and anchor minus the fouled ropes, and Shake could just make out part of the Indian Head patch on the man's left shoulder. It was dated 1918 and taken of someone called "Uncle Tanner" at *Bois de Belleau*. That didn't need clarification for Shake or any other Marine. The man was a veteran of the epic WWI Battle of Belleau Wood in France, the epic struggle in which the German enemy had reportedly branded the U.S. Marines, then serving as an element of the Army's 2nd Infantry Division, with the *Teufel Hunden* sobriquet which later morphed into Devil Dogs.

But whose uncle was he? If Shake had a relative who fought with the Marines in World War I, he damned sure wanted to know the details. Across all the years he'd listened to war stories from the males in the family, he'd never heard of another Marine. The Davis clan, by birth or marriage, all seemed to have fought in the nation's wars as either soldiers or sailors.

He reclosed the boxes, dusting them and stacking both in a corner. He snapped a fingernail on the two most interesting photos and carried them to the den where they kept a powerful computer his wife used in her academic work. With a second puzzled look at the WWI photo, he set it under a desk lamp and made a mental note to call a buddy in the Marine Corps History Division at Quantico early the next morning. There was a guy, a retired Marine working there, who owed him a favor or two. In fact, he thought as he fired up the computer, that very guy—Chief Warrant Officer Charlie Rowe—was a dedicated World War I buff who knew just about all anyone could know about Marines in what some short-sighted optimist back in 1918 had called The War to End All Wars. With a little coaxing, Charlie would probably be able to provide some help identifying the old Marine in the photo or at least give Shake a place to start a search. If he was an uncle, Davis was probably the family name. And how many guys would be on the muster roles with a first name like Tanner? He snapped on the lamp and shot a cell phone photo of the picture. He'd upload that and send it along in an email to Charlie before he called.

Google was full of stuff on Mississippi river boats of the paddle-wheel era. He scrolled past all the Mark Twain material and found an interesting treatise on some of the more well-known river steamers. There was a *Natchez* listed. In fact, there were seven boats by that name ranging through the "golden age of steamboats" on the Big Muddy from about 1830 to 1880. Given the date on the photo, the second to last of the steamers named Natchez was most likely to be the one he wanted. The text said *Natchez VI* was a Cincinnati-built boat that measured 273 feet stem to stern. It was primarily a cotton hauler from southern to northern ports along the Mississippi and could carry about 5,000 bales.

What made Shake think this particular boat might be the one in the photo of someone's uncle Fielding was the stuff about its role in the Civil War. The *Natchez* had reportedly carried Jefferson Davis from his river plantation home at least part way to Richmond, Virginia after he was elected president of the rebel alliance. The paddle-wheel steamer was also used to transport Confederate troops to Memphis, Tennessee and other riverside battle sites during the war. After Union forces captured Memphis, the *Natchez* reportedly escaped to a hideout on the Yazoo River where it was burned to keep it from falling into enemy hands.

Shake leaned back in his chair and contemplated the computer screen. The longer he stared at old, soft-focus photos of the river boats, the more intrigued he became. He rose and fetched the photo of himself working on the Mississippi tug and brought it into the room where he put it down beside the others. He remembered the muggy days working on the boat, doing the dirty work that older, more experienced hands wouldn't do, listening at night to the stories they told about adventures at ports up and down the big spill of water where their muscular tug pushed or pulled a balky string of overloaded barges.

And they had some terrific tales, told with profane glee. Stories familiar to them from overtelling and embellishment but fascinating to a teenage boy. Stories about roaring times on the water and in every waterway transportation hub from St. Paul down through the Mississippi Delta to New Orleans. It was like one long, lurid adventure tale out of American history, and Shake had been mesmerized. He spent much of his off-duty time tossing in a hot rack belowdecks imagining himself as one of those river rats, a swaggering hard-ass, up for anything and everything, a sailor on the great artery that split the continent and fueled the commerce of America in the days before airplanes, trucks, and interstate highways. He sat there in his Texas Hill Country house, separated by many miles and years from that place and those days, sensing intriguing shadows of teenage dreams.

Maybe intrigued wasn't the right word. His heart was beating a little faster than should be expected after a couple of stiff drinks, and he felt a tension in his facial muscles. Glancing up at a mirror hung on the wall to his left, he noted that he was grinning. Or what passed for a grin. It was more like an evil grimace, if he was honest about it. But it was familiar. He slugged at his whiskey again, closed his eyes and contemplated the tingle in his belly that crawled up from bowels to chest and then steamrolled right into his brain. He knew the feeling intimately. It was a form of curiosity, he guessed, that sense that he needed to know what happens next, what was on the other side of that hill between imagination and reality. He'd felt the tingle many times in his past, not so much lately, and found he missed it. Sometimes, particularly in a combat zone or when he was immersed in some dicey mission for an alphabet soup federal agency, he felt that same tingle. A clawing, irresistible curiosity. What's next? What momentous, potentially deadly thing is about to happen…and can I survive it? The answer, the only way to scratch that persistent itch, was to just go, get into it, do the dance, pull the trigger.

Maybe just sleep on it, he decided. He took a last look at the photos and shut down the computer. Images danced in his mind as he climbed the stairs. Nothing coherent, just a flickering collage of steamboat skippers and WWI doughboys who seemed to be winking at him, smiling, beckoning him to join them. He lay still in his bed watching the images float across the ceiling, listening to the cicadas in the trees outside the house and the bass croak of bullfrogs in the creek. It might be interesting, he decided then, to see if maybe Thomas Wolfe was wrong, and you can go home again.

Δ Δ Δ

He had no real plan as he sat in the kitchen sipping coffee. The itch and tingle were still there. A fitful few hours of sleep hadn't done a thing to damp them. The photos sat propped up beside a bottle of hot sauce that he'd used to fire the eggs he'd fried for breakfast. The kid posed on the bow of the river tug looked loony and clueless, so he turned that photo over and pushed it aside. The *Natchez* skipper—Fielding?—and the doughboy—Tanner?—peered back at him with a certain similarity in their expressions. It wasn't hard to imagine they were related, and possibly somehow related to him. Both men, separated by 50 years or so when the pictures were taken, had the same squint to their eyes, as if they'd seen some wild times and it took a squint to be sure there was no threat out there on the other side of the camera. And their faces, one clean shaven and the other bristly around a walrus mustache, were alike beyond familial, lips forming something between wizened grin and grimace. If they appeared in panels from a comic book there would be dialog boxes that said: We've seen some shit, young agent. Come on over and we'll tell you about it.

He grabbed his phone and swiped until he found the photo he'd shot last night of the doughboy picture. When he found Charlie Rowe's email address, he sent the photo with a promise to call in the next few minutes. Sipping a second cup of coffee, he idled around until the phone pinged to let him know the photo was delivered. Then he checked his watch and called. Retired Chief Warrant Officer Charlie Rowe, a creature of long-ingrained habit, would be in the office at Quantico even if it was too early for the nine-to-fivers at the Marine Corps History Division.

"Shake Davis! How the hell are you, man?"

Charlie had caller ID on his phone and no inclination to bother with the standard greeting required of other cubicle-dwelling government employees. When they were both relatively young Staff NCOs serving with the 6th Marines at Camp Lejeune, they'd made a pilgrimage together to Belleau Wood in France. It was a wild time that ate up nearly all of their two weeks' leave, but it was worth it. Even in those days, Charlie was becoming a recognized expert on Marine participation in World War I.

"I'm good, Charlie. Just cooling my overheated heels down here in Texas."

"At least it ain't a government grey cubicle, Shake. I thought you'd be eyeball deep in some sneaky-pete stuff. What happened? Bayer die or get fired again?"

As a close friend for a lot of years, Charlie Rowe was one of a few who knew about Shake's off the official record activities for various agencies, mostly at the behest of a shady character they both knew simply as the man who calls himself Bayer.

"He's still poking around in dark corners, Charlie, but I'm trying to retire for real. Last couple of times I tried, couldn't make it stick."

"Do you some good to relax, man. You keep running around like we used to back in the day and the meter might quit ticking before its time. Know what I mean? You need to keep your ass planted down in Texas with your child bride and that horse you call a dog."

"It's all good, Charlie. Did you get the photo I sent?"

"Yeah, I've got it up right here on my screen. You said it was taken in 1918?"

"That was written on the back of the photo. I suspect by my grandmother. I think the guy's name is probably Tanner Davis…or maybe Tanner Woody. He might be a relative and if so, he'd be the only other Jarhead in the family."

"Well, I can see part of the Indian Head patch on his shoulder and the background sure looks like France, so I'm guessing he was a member of the Marine Brigade. Which means he'd have to be 5th Marines or 6th Marines, or maybe one of the machinegun outfits that were attached to the brigade."

"Can you dig around on it for me, Charlie?"

"Records from that time are fairly spotty, Shake, but I'll give it a shot. You still got the same numbers?"

"Yeah, but if you don't get a response right away, call my cell. I'm gonna be on the road for a week—maybe two." Until that moment, Shake had intended to do nothing more than investigate the photos. Now he found himself planning a road trip, back to Southeast Missouri, back to a time and place that seemed as remote to him right then as outer space.

He ended the call and laughed quietly into his coffee cup. *What the hell am I doing?* He dug around in his old files and found the address of a cousin who still lived back there. Sarah was a first cousin, daughter of his Dad's sister, and she fashioned herself the keeper of family history. She'd written him a time or two over the years with questions he couldn't answer. Sarah was into all kinds of genealogy. She might have a lead or two that would help him identify Fielding and Tanner and how they were related to him or to the Davis family in general.

When he called the Caldwell County government offices, Shake's friend the county sheriff promised to keep an eye on the house. Shake left him a cell number and an approximate date when he'd be back in Texas. It was only a guess, but it served to put some starch into a flimsy plan. All he knew for sure was that he was headed north, and the tingle was intensifying. He plugged Sikeston, MO into Google Maps and went to pack what he'd need for a long road trip.

When that was done, he'd figure the time differential between Texas and Taiwan and give Chan a call. And tell her what? That he was off on a…he didn't even know what to call what he had in mind. A quest seemed to fit better than anything else.

She'd understand…maybe.

Taipei

Her phone buzzed, dancing across the nightstand as Chan Dwyer Davis rushed around her dorm room picking up the papers and purse contents that she'd need for another day on the platform at Chengchi University. It was her personal phone rather than the one she'd been issued by her faculty advisor for use in Taiwan. The ID told her it was Shake calling, but he usually checked in with her on the weekend, and today was Wednesday. She grabbed the phone and accepted the call hoping there was nothing wrong with her husband or with Bear.

There was no problem at home, not with the house or with their beloved dog, Shake quickly assured her, but Chan detected an uneasiness in his tone. There was something he wanted to say, something that he thought might be mitigated by banter about her welfare and inquiries about her teaching chores.

"I've got a few pages of notes about Chinese food, lousy plumbing, and language frustrations for you, Shake. Stuff I was saving for your weekend call. We can go over it now, if you want, but I think there's something on your mind other than a standard sitrep."

"Well, yeah, Chan. You know those boxes of photos and stuff that you wanted me to sort through?"

"I hope you're doing it. You've been promising that trip down memory lane ever since we moved to Texas. I'm expecting a full exploration of the Davis family tree when I get home."

"Yeah, I'm doing it. And that's the thing. I found some stuff that really made me curious, stuff I didn't even know existed. Some ancestors I've apparently got who I really want to know more about. You know?"

"Did you call that cousin of yours? Can't remember her name but you told me she's the resident Davis family historian."

"I was gonna do that, Chan, but—I don't know—I kind of decided it might be better, or at least more interesting, to just head back there and do a little exploring. You know? I mean Bear is fine for another week or two. I think maybe I'll do a little road trip. Get some details and have a good story or two about the family tree when you get back. Is that nuts?"

"I don't know if it's nuts, but it files as unexpected in my book, Shake. I can't get you to talk about your family or childhood beyond sketchy mumbles, and now you want to go back to Missouri and stroll down memory lane. What's up with that?"

He spent the next ten minutes trying to explain himself. Chan heard about the unknown Civil War steamboat captain and the mysterious World War I Marine. Those were military connections that would understandably pique her warrior husband's interest, but she sensed there was something more behind the road trip he outlined. And that outline was vague and impromptu from a man who prided himself on preparation, a guy who firmly believed and often reminded her that proper prior planning prevents piss-poor performance. He seemed to be asking for her blessing or approval, and there was an element of fear to that. At times his tone reminded her of a little boy standing on the edge of a dock, wanting adult reassurance that it was OK to just jump off into the water.

She listened until he ran out of explanations and then told him she thought it was a good idea. He should just do it, she said, just have some fun and do some exploring. She'd be anxious to get periodic reports. It was what he wanted to hear. And Chan knew her husband well enough to realize the trip back through his childhood haunts was about much more than a couple of mysterious ancestors, regardless of what he said in the phone call.

She was curious about his background and childhood experiences, always had been since the day she realized she was in love with Shake Davis. So much of what he told her came as a result of overdosing on whiskey or incessant wheedling. And not much of that was in sufficient detail to answer the questions she had beyond the chronological timeline of events that he generally related. What she really wanted to understand was what made her husband the man he was, the man she loved and respected for his character and kindness as much as for his varied and often lurid experiences around the world. Somewhere in Shake's past there were things, personal, emotional, and psychological experiences that he was reluctant to relate—even to her—and he'd often said that she was closer to him than anyone he'd ever known.

In the years after they were married, Chan had learned some personal things about Shake from his best friend Mike Stokey, the man Shake considered his blood kin despite no familial relation between the two. Some of that was helpful, some of it answered nagging questions about Shake's character or habits that were directly related to his wartime and paramilitary experiences. Mike had told stories that helped explain superficial things like his reluctance to sit with his back to doors, why he amassed various weapons and practiced so diligently in their use. It gave her an understanding of why he would appear naked in public rather than leave the house without a razor-sharp pocketknife, and why he was so meticulous about his clothing and always folded his underwear. War stories revealed why he made some of his often jarring but insightful comments about world news or some bloviating politician on TV. Yet there was much more that she wanted to know beyond the obvious, so much that Shake either claimed he couldn't—or wouldn't—remember. He had a knack for dissimilation or obfuscating when she probed too deeply. That only made her more curious. What was he like before the Marine Corps? What things made him want to serve most of a lifetime in uniform doing dangerous things? What was it that made his heart so big and strong? How could a man who had witnessed such cruelty and brutality, a man whose working life was steeped in extreme violence, emerge on the other side of it all with any degree of tolerance, any empathy for weakness in others, or the kind of gentleness that he often displayed?

It could be he didn't know. Or if he did, it could be that he didn't consider those early influences relevant or important. And now he did? Maybe Shake was at a time in life, a stage in his perspective on the things he'd done in that life, that he was willing to look back to where it all started. Shake often told her that age was just a number. You only get old if you let yourself go down that road. How many times had she seen him sitting on the edge of their bed early in the morning, his wounds and scars glistening with sweat while he stretched and grunted his body into motion? "Another day above ground," he always said with a tight smile. "The Old Man is knocking but I ain't gonna let him in." So maybe the Old Man had a toe or two stuck through a crack in Shake's door.

Walking across the university campus toward her first lecture period, Chan found a vacant bench and watched the chatty student mobs milling around between buildings. She had time to review her notes on the laptop, but couldn't bring herself to it. She thought momentarily that she wanted to be with Shake on his journey into the past. No, that wouldn't be right or fair to him. She'd feel like an eavesdropper, an interloper or a spy. And he would likely be reluctant to delve deeply while she watched and judged. Best let Shake work it out on his own and get comfortable with her questions later.

On the Road

He was north of Waco, fighting white-line fever and sweeping his eyes from flat patches of cactus and scrub that stretched to a distant horizon back to the GPS program on his phone. There wasn't much of interest in either direction. At this point, the most attractive feature of north Texas was the state's celebrated wide-open spaces. Somewhere out there to the west was the *Llano Estacado*, the Staked Plains that rambled over much of west Texas and most of eastern New Mexico. It was a place Shake had wanted to visit ever since he heard country artist Gary P. Nunn include it in the lyrics of a song that outlined what the singer loved about Texas. A buddy in Lockhart told him every true Texan had to visit the *Llano*, but he'd missed it so far. He was tempted to make a side-trip, but he needed to keep some semblance of focus on this improvised journey. And Google Maps simply advised him the short route was run 35 North to Oklahoma City, then cut right to 44 East which would take him to St. Louis. That was the first leg.

As far as his vague plan went at this point, he thought to stop for maybe a day or so in St. Louis, maybe find the old SS *Admiral* stern-wheeler and take a riverboat ride. After that, straight south down 55 to Cape Girardeau. And then what? As the miles rolled on and he took the ring route to skirt Dallas traffic, Shake found himself in the middle of a mental argument between logic, which told him he could do all the required family research with a couple of phone calls, and an irresistible whimsy that pushed him to investigate in the environment of the relatives in question. If they were relatives and not just random family acquaintances or friends.

Who knew? Who cared? Well, I do. Shake laughed and cranked up the radio to hear Willy Nelson hammering Trigger through his signature song. *On the road again, just can't wait to get on the road again.* He had the same feeling of limitless freedom that he experienced on his 16th birthday when he got his first driver's license. And here he was on the road again, heading for the part of the country that he'd fled so long ago for fear he might have to spend the rest of his life there. A jagged, unreasonable fear that he might be doomed to live and die in Southeast Missouri as so many of his friends and relatives had. The damn place seemed to be sucking at him like quicksand. Irony. Can't wait to leave and then can't wait to get back and see if what you left still reflected the reasons you left.

Truth be told, he said to the driver of a silver BMW that blew by his pick-up with a wave from the Stetson-wearing driver, those mystery photos are only part of this quest. Some of what I'm really after, he admitted to a semi trucker who passed as Shake eased back onto 35N on the other side of Dallas, is some kind of confirmation that I made the right decision. Was I right or simply rebellious so long ago when I flew away from home against the advice of a family that thought I was just being downright uppity, looking for a life above my raising? Headed out to see what was on the other side of worldwide hills with no thought of return to what everyone else in his circle considered an expected and acceptable way of life.

Shake shut down the A/C and lowered his window. There was a sweet smell to the humid air that swept through the cab of his truck. Oke City and then hang a right with a bead on the

Gateway Arch. Nothing to it but to do it, keep the hammer down and just roll through the country he loved, noting both warts and wonders.

MV Petrel

arco Sanpere flicked his smoke over the rail of the merchant ship that was wallowing in some fairly big waves. He watched the moon bob up and down as the deck rose, twisted, and plunged under his feet. They were about a day and a half from the rendezvous off New Orleans at which point he would enjoy kicking a few black asses. He was more than a little tired of pretending to be a solicitous escort and babysitter for that gaggle of *kafirs* down below decks.

His buddy Samuel Imshana, an old pal from their days with the 13th Demi-Brigade, said it was necessary to play it cool and keep the Africans healthy and clueless. He was probably right. The money was good. More than that. The money was unbelievable for a guy whose only skill was humping heavy loads, busting heads as required, and putting rounds downrange on whatever target was designated. *That is the Legion for you*, Marco thought as he turned his back to the wind and lit another smoke. *La Legion Etrangere* was a good outfit. Chow was wholesome and regular. Pay was reasonable, especially when you served most of your enlistment in a shithole like Djibouti where there was nothing to spend it on, but Marco had run through most of his savings on a wild time in Brussels shortly after discharge. That wild time involved a knife fight that left a fellow Belgian bleeding to death outside a bar and set the cops on Marco's trail. The only way he knew to avoid arrest and cover his tracks was to run back to the horn of Africa where some other ex-Legionnaires would guard his back until the heat died down a bit.

He was flat broke after two weeks in Djibouti and out of people willing to lend him any more money. He thought about reenlisting right there in Djibouti and let the Legion hide him when the cops came looking, but that wouldn't work. These days even the Legion wouldn't cover for a man wanted for murder. Marco leaned on the rail, feeling salt spray on his face and remembered the day his luck finally changed. It was in that downtown joint—*La Parisienne*—where his old *Caporal Chef* from the 3ʳᵈ Company at *Quarier General Monclar*, tended bar. And out of the blue, Samuel Imshana showed up with an offer that seemed too good to be true.

"Finally found you," Samuel said as he walked up to the table where Marco sat nursing the beer which had cost him his last three francs. His old friend was carrying two fresh beers. He slid one across the table as he straddled the chair opposite Marco. "I tried that address you gave me in Brussels."

"Wasn't there long," Marco said as they clinked beer bottles in a toast.

"Long enough to get your tits in a wringer, *mon ami*. Cops had the place under surveillance. They're looking for you."

"I know that, Samuel. And that's why I'm back in this cesspool."

"I figured you might run back here." Samuel Imshana reached into a pocket and came up with a silver case containing the small cigars he preferred. When he leaned across the table to offer one, Marco glanced at the ornate amulet hanging from a gold chain around his old section leader's neck.

"What's that?" Marco gestured at the necklace with the little cigar he'd just lit. "You look like some kind of fucking fag."

Samuel held the amulet up to the light and Marco got a better look at the rampant lion scribed in relief inside a large brass circle. It was surrounded by a gaudy ring of gemstones.

"It's tribal," he said, dropping the amulet and hitting on his beer. "Leadership symbol, from the Ibo tribe of Nigeria. Before the Legion, those were my people."

"I remember you told me you were from Nigeria, back when we were *Engage Volontaires* at Aubagne and I was trying to teach you to speak French. You didn't tell me you were some kind of *kafir* royalty."

"It's a family thing, Marco. I picked it up from my father. He died shortly after I went back to Lagos."

"I didn't think you'd reenlist." Marco toyed with his beer and looked at his old friend carefully, squinting through a cloud of pungent cigar smoke. Whatever Samuel Imshana was doing in his post-Legion life, it was paying well. He wore an expensive silk shirt with cufflinks showing milky jade set in gold frames and the sunglasses he'd folded onto the table when he sat down bore a Gucci signature. They looked like something that cost more than a Legionnaire made in a year.

"Looks like you're fairly flush. I could use a little loan if you could spare something."

Samuel Imshana dug in a trouser pocket and tossed some bills on the table. "I can do better than that, Marco. I'm here to offer you a job. I need a man who can handle himself, someone I can trust."

Marco slid the bills to his side of the table. It was a lot of money, too much for even an old Legion friend to offer without some strings attached. He removed the top two bills and slid the rest back across the table.

"I'll have to owe you for this much," he said and pointed at the remaining cash. "I can't get involved in anything worth that with cops looking for me."

"Cops will eventually find you here. You know that, Marco. You need to get out of Djibouti. What I'm offering will take you to Lagos with me where we get you some new papers, passport and all that—and then to the U.S. I'm talking about big money and minimal risk."

"What's the job?"

"We're going to pick up some people in Nigeria, take them to America, and just keep them safe for a while. If it all works out, we repeat the process."

"How much?"

"Your cut is ten thousand…U.S. dollars."

"For half that you could get any man in Africa. Why me?"

"Because I trust you, Marco." Samuel Imshana shoved the stack of bills back across the table. "And because a job like this requires trust—and teamwork—the same things we learned in *La Legion Etrangere, n'cest pas?* I require a man who can handle himself and watch my back. Is that you?"

"When do we leave?" Marco Sanpere reached for the money and stuffed it into his jeans.

Cape Girardeau

Deeter Manson was doing his best. He'd bluffed, promised, whined, and offered a sweet deal, but the fat man who owned Pedro's Roadhouse out on 55 south of the city wasn't having any of it.

"You got a buck thirty on the fuckin' bar-tab, asshole. Last week you was gonna pay this week. Now you're in here cryin' the poor-ass? I ain't buyin' it, Deeter." The fat man plonked a dinged and dented baseball bat on the bar next to Deeter's beer and pointed at it. "I told you what was gonna happen if you showed up without no cash for me."

"Jesus Christ, man. You know I'm good for it. Couple of frat rats is havin' a big party on the weekend. I'm supplyin' their weed. That's three bills on Saturday. I'll give you two of it before closin' time on Saturday night. I swear it, man."

"I heard that shit from you before. You was gonna get a draw on your salary at the fire-brick plant. Remember that?"

"I got laid off, man…"

"You got fuckin' fired, Deeter. You think I don't know about shit happens around here? That's how come you ain't got no severance pay."

"I got on over at Honker's, dude. Payday with that asshole is Friday. It won't cover the nut but I'll give you whatever he pays me…no shit…promise."

The fat man whacked the bar top with his bat and Deeter shoved back on his barstool. "I ain't had lunch yet, so I'm gonna delay spreadin' your fucking brains all over the joint for a while.

You got until we close at two tomorrow mornin'. Either show up with the cash or I come lookin'."

Deeter Manson glared at the fat man as the bar owner disappeared into the back of the joint slapping the bat into an open palm. He fought off the temptation to heave his mug at the fat bastard's head. The dude had goons on his payroll all over the place, and Deeter had enough trouble for now. What he needed to do was pick up a load of primo weed and find a place on the Southeast Missouri State campus where he could hawk it in a hurry.

He wheeled his Toyota Land Cruiser into the driveway of his widowed father's house sending a spray of gravel rattling off the sheriff's foreclosure notice. *Fuckin' old man dies with no insurance and a big-ass mortgage on this shithole,* Deeter thought, as he charged into the house and snatched his last beer from the fridge. *I can't catch a fuckin' break.* His deal with his two shit-heel cousins was for delivery of a kilo of weed on Friday, but that schedule would have to be advanced. He needed the stuff right now.

He was pacing the ramshackle front porch arguing on the phone about an early delivery on consignment when a black Lincoln Navigator wheeled into the driveway. It looked like a cop ride, but the dude sitting shotgun with all the ink on his arms was no cop. Hard motherfucker like the black dude behind the wheel, but Deeter knew enough about cops to believe his visitors wouldn't be flashing law creds. Guns maybe but no badges. He told his cousin he'd call back and slid the phone into the pocket of his jeans.

"Your name Deeter Manson?" The black guy rested a foot on the porch steps and looked around while his tattooed buddy stood back a way and looked in the other direction like he was on guard or something. The guy doing the talking had some kind of funky accent. He wasn't local and likely not even a fucking American.

"Depends on who's askin'. Who the fuck are you?"

"Names don't matter if you're the man we're looking for. Could be we've got a job for you and the way I hear it, you could use a little income."

"You guys work for Pedro?"

"Never heard of him…and who we work for ain't important right now. We're here to offer you a little work. You interested or not?"

"How'd you get my name?"

"You made some friends in the county lock-up, Deeter." The black man reached into his trouser pocket and came up with a roll of bills. Deeter noticed the top one was a c-note. "Didn't take much of this to get your contact information."

"What kind of job you got in mind?"

"You got a driver's license? You drive a truck?"

"I ain't got no chauffer's license."

"Talking about a box truck, Deeter. Standard license covers it."

"When's this job start?"

"Undetermined right now. Probably early next month."

"Don't do me no good, man. I got bills to pay. Shit like that."

The black man stepped up on the porch and his buddy moved closer. "Suppose you're the kind of man who does what he's told and don't ask a lot of stupid questions, could be we'd put you on a kind of retainer." The black man unrolled his cash and fanned some bills. It looked like they were all hundreds.

"What's that mean?"

"You stupid or something?" The tattooed man stepped up beside his buddy. He looked like he had much less patience. "We're trying to make a deal, right? We pay you some money and you stand by with your mouth shut until we give you follow-on orders. That simple enough for you?"

"And it's just about drivin' a fuckin' truck?"

"It's about keeping your mouth shut, doing what we tell you and driving a truck when and where we tell you."

Deeter eyed his visitors. They were obviously a couple of things that he recognized: Bad-asses and backed by serious money. Likely they were talking about a drug run. It wouldn't be his first. Anyway, if it wasn't about killing somebody or some kind of bullshit deal that would get him busted for a long stretch inside, he was in.

"How much we talkin' about here?"

The black man snapped off a few bills and waved them in front of Deeter. "Deal is five hundred right now. Another five if we don't call you to work in two weeks. Job starts when we say it does. We drive you to Louisiana. You drive the truck back here to Missouri. All that works out, you make a grand on this end. That simple."

"So it's five…maybe double that just for waiting around?"

"Waiting around, staying low-profile and out of trouble. You get in a tangle with the law and we never heard of you."

"I'm in…" Deeter held out his hand to shake. His visitors ignored that and put five 100-dollar bills in his outstretched hand.

"Gimme your phone," The tattooed man said. When he had the instrument, he pulled his own out of a pocket and punched in Deeter's number. "Don't go no fuckin' place without this," the man said handing Deeter back his phone. "We'll be in touch."

They walked to the vehicle, fired it up, and wheeled down the driveway. Deeter stood looking at the cash in his hand. It would get the fat man off his back which was a good and very healthy thing. He could wait on the dope delivery and add that cash when he shifted it onto the fraternity party animals. He'd cool his heels working for that asshole at Honker's, play it chilly and maybe score enough to get the fuck out of this town. St. Louis was good. It had non-stop action for a dude looking to score. And Deeter Manson was back on the hustle.

New Orleans

tanding on the deck of the old ship that had carried him and nine others across the sea from Nigeria, Jambon felt something was wrong. It was nothing specific as yet, but his instincts told him to be cautious. There were some unexpected changes, and he didn't trust the explanations despite reassurances from Samuel Imshana. They could see the lights of America in the distance, and everyone was anxious to stand on American soil, seeing first-hand the wonders underneath those lights. But the ship had stopped before docking, and they were told that they must transfer to a smaller boat which would take them ashore. Mr. Imshana and the other man in charge of their little group, the one called Marco with many tattoos up and down his arms, explained this was necessary because they did not have regular passports. They had to land at another place where American officials would recognize the papers each man carried. And then they would meet their new employers and proceed to the hospital for training.

Each man in the party had the papers they'd filled out during the voyage in hand with their small luggage bundles. It all seemed forthright according to what they'd been told, but Jambon still felt leery. They'd had no dinner, and Marco had begun shoving people around rudely over the last few days. He was acting nervous, a change in attitude as if he was afraid of something. If anyone should be feeling fearful, it was Jambon and his Ibo brothers, about to start a new life in a strange land, working at jobs they knew nothing about. It was explained that they must be free of the HIV virus, and that seemed normal and correct for people slated to work in a hospital, even if they were simply cleaners and laborers, but it all seemed hurried and haphazard as Jambon and the others carefully climbed from the deck of the larger ship to a smaller one with barely enough room for them and their baggage.

The smaller boat carried them on a long, bumpy ride, moving steadily away from the lights of New Orleans. And then the boat made a landing deep in a swamp. They were ordered ashore where they were immediately swarmed by mosquitos. Two men were waiting for them. They did not look anything like a friendly welcoming party, and none asked to see their papers. When Jambon and some others began to complain, demanding reasons for this treatment, guns were revealed. Samuel Imshana and Marco pointed pistols and told them to sit quietly. They would remain in the swamp overnight. Anyone who complained or tried to escape would be shot.

As the leader, Jambon stood demanding answers. He got none. Marco shoved him down among the others. There was nowhere to run. The swamp surrounding them looked evil and dangerous. Jambon and the others sat quietly in a circle on the damp ground and prayed. It was all they could do for now. Jambon Imbasa knew then that they'd been tricked. What he didn't know was what might happen to them next here in America—where they were promised the chance to live free, work hard and prosper.

Joplin

He paid five bucks at a toll booth on the northeast side of Tulsa which gave him access to the Will Rogers Turnpike and less traffic to fight over the 88 miles to the Missouri state line. He checked a few of the mileage markers and saw Joplin was the first familiar place he'd encounter after leaving Oklahoma. Meanwhile, there was little to do except keep it between the ditches and muse about how the plains looked like big bird feeders with pumpjacks bobbing up and down like famished storks all across the Okie plains. Where would Oklahoma be without its sprawling subterranean oil pools—and Sooner football, of course. Big oil and big football, the blood that flowed through so many and fueled so much around here. If you just don't get it, if you're some sort of Yankee wimp, drop by any bar or café from Oklahoma City to Austin in October when the Red River Shootout at the Cotton Bowl is imminent. They may be rioting in Africa, they may be starving in Spain, maybe they've got hurricanes in Florida—but let's talk football, man.

A toothy jackass on a state border sign welcomed him to Missouri. His own ass was aching from the steady rumble that ran from the road through the truck's suspension, and he was hungry. Shake spotted an off-ramp for Joplin and took it. He'd get something to eat and find a place to sleep before the long run across Missouri, through the Ozarks, and on to the Big Muddy.

The Top Hat Bar & Grill was co-located with old-timey cabins that looked comfortable enough on the eastern edges of Joplin. He didn't expect a gourmet dining experience or deluxe accommodations. They weren't affordable in this area of the country, not needed and not expected by travelers, most of whom were hunters or fishermen heading for the Ozarks. He parked the pick-up, handed over a credit card at the desk, and got a key to one of the cabins plus a stack of clean towels. The kid at the desk recommended the burgers at the Top Hat and told Shake he'd get a discount if he showed the barkeep—Ol' Billy Ray—his cabin key. Shake noticed the name on a tag pinned to the kid's chambray shirt.

"Sessler," he said. "I used to know a guy in high school named Sessler. You got family around Joplin?"

"Far as I know, we got Sessler's all over this area. You got a first name?"

"He was Guy Sessler. I think his Dad ran a taxi service in Joplin."

"Gotta be my Uncle Guy, then. He went to Missouri Military Academy. That where you went?"

"Yep. It's gotta be the same guy. You got a number for him."

"I got a number, but you won't reach Uncle Guy. He died last year. Heart just give out one day. I could hook you up with Aunt Alice. She still lives in town." The kid scribbled a number on a pad and handed it to Shake along with his credit card.

"Y'all ort to give Aunt Alice a call. Might be she'd remember you."

"Maybe I will," Shake said and headed for his cabin. But he wouldn't call. Last thing he needed on a family quest was a downer and a grieving widow. There was probably going to be something like that waiting for him on the other side of the state. Remembering the dear departed ought to be a joy, but it rarely was.

Ol' Billy Ray eyed his cabin key, raised a bushy eyebrow, and shouted to someone in the Top Hat's kitchen to fry one up medium rare. There were no other customers in the joint, and Shake made some comment about slow business. Ol' Billy Ray shrugged, said it was still early and "mah reg'lars be in directly they finish work." He drew Shake a tall glass of Bud Lite, slid it over, and went back to his copy of the Bass Pro Shop catalog. He was reading it on an iPad which Shake found mildly amusing. Apparently, the days of saving mail-order catalogs for use as toilet paper in the outhouse were long gone in Joplin and environs. Shake recalled that the main outlet, the mothership of the Bass Pro Shop fleet, was just east of here in Springfield. Another side trip he wanted to make but wouldn't on this trip.

Over a really good burger with fresh onions and a toasted bun, Shake thought about the Sesslers of Joplin. Specifically, Guy Sessler, the short, blocky, and crew-cut member of that clan who had been the Cadet Battalion Commander at MMA the year before Shake graduated. Guy had joined the Marine Corps some time before Shake did, and they'd met once on a pistol range at Camp Pendleton. Guy finished his enlistment, got out, and returned to Joplin. Another example of that celebrated hometown suck that Shake avoided like the plague. Over the years, Guy had found him on occasion and called. He wasn't very busy and the taxi service he inherited from his Dad didn't take much more than occasional attention.

During those random calls, Guy Sessler never wanted anything much more than a chance to reminisce, to relive for a few minutes what must have been the high point of his life, the days when he was in command of the cadet corps at MMA. It was as if he needed validation that it was as cool as he remembered, to relive scraps of his halcyon days with someone who was there to witness them. Apparently, there hadn't been much to recall after his time at MMA that meant much to Guy Sessler. When Shake tried to steer the conversation around to current events, Sessler answered in mumbles and always found a way to get them back to those high-school years.

Shake shared a fondness for the time he spent at MMA but for different reasons. For him, the time away from home living at a military school was the first big step he'd taken to launch himself out of what he'd come to realize was a standard, dead-end lifecycle for so many of his boyhood friends and peers. Those high-school days were memorable and valuable. Four years of tough, no-nonsense classic education with high demands on body and brain. When it was over for Sessler, and just one year remaining for Shake during which he was tapped to serve as Cadet Battalion Adjutant, they planned a road trip.

It was supposed to be a long, loose careen across the Ozarks bound for Joplin in Sessler's new Chevy Corvair, a graduation present, an avantgarde rear-engine vehicle, and the epitome of cool among car-crazy teenagers of the early 60s. Shake had two weeks before he was to report aboard the river tug where he'd been hired as a deckhand for the remainder of that summer. They barreled through the Ozarks, did some fishing at Bull Shoals, ate a lot of catfish and caught some good-size largemouth bass. They had such good luck fishing top-water lures that a local restaurant bought their entire catch for two straight days and paid for the fish with three cases of beer that neither Shake nor Sessler was old enough to legally purchase. And that led to a spectacular end of their sojourn shortly after they roared into Joplin, low on gas and high on beer.

They finished what was left of the beer after the trip from Lake of the Ozarks while parked along a downtown side-street. There was some vague plan about crashing a Joplin High School summer dance being discussed, and it seemed like a good idea to resupply. Sessler said he knew a place across the line in Oklahoma where they could get a case or two, cash on the barrelhead, no ID required, and no questions asked. Thoroughly baked on Budweiser, they headed for the state line, which they found by hitting one of the stone markers head-on doing about forty. Sessler's Corvair was a convertible which allowed the impact to launch Shake, in those pre-seatbelt days, right over the windshield and about 20 feet into a freshly plowed farm field. The Corvair was technically in Missouri. Shake was planted painfully in Oklahoma. No harm done to his flexible and well-conditioned teenage body, but the wreck took the steam out of their spree. Staggering back across the state line, Shake was reminded of something his grandad always said. God just seems to protect drunks and idiots.

Guy's father sent one of his cabs and a tow-truck to solve their immediate problem, but Shake had no desire to hang around Joplin and suffer shrapnel from the flak Sessler was about to take over the incident. He caught a Greyhound headed east and suffered through a horrible hangover before he finally reported aboard the *Angelina*, a bull-nose tug waiting for crew and cargo at St. Louis. Papers and certified qualifications not required in those days. If a kid was not a demonstrable dipshit, had the necessary muscle and motivation, he could find summer work on the river tugs.

ΔΔΔ

He was headed north to skirt the Lake of the Ozarks, admiring the lush hills on one side of the highway and the azure blue of the lake on the other, when his phone buzzed. It was Charlie Rowe calling from Quantico. He pulled over on a gravel road that led to one of the area's many fishing camps.

"Hey, Shake…you get my email?"

"Haven't checked, Charlie. I'm on the road."

"Where?"

"Right now, I'm parked near Lake of the Ozarks."

"Why?"

"Chasing ghosts, I guess. I'm eventually headed for some family contacts. See what I can find out about that Marine…and some other stuff…you know."

"Well, I can maybe help you with one of the ghosts. I found a monograph from some officer who was with 6th Marines, wounded in mid-June 1918. He was interviewed in a French hospital. He mentions an NCO named Davis who got a DSC. That narrowed it down some, so I looked into the Army files from the time—the Army handed out all the gongs back in those days—and found a citation for Corporal Tanner M. Davis, 73rd Company of the 6th Machinegun Battalion, 4th Marine Brigade. Gives his place of enlistment as Missouri. That's gotta be your guy, right? I guess that hero stuffs runs in the family. Anyway, I sent you a full run-down in the email. You ought to check that shit once in a while."

"I'll do it as soon as I can find some wi-fi, Charlie. I really appreciate the effort."

"I ain't through yet, Shake. Guess where your guy got his DSC? Fucking Belleau Wood, right? This guy was one of the original Devil Dogs. And guess who was his First Sergeant."

"Now how the hell would I know that?"

"Because I told you about it back when we went to Belleau Wood. Remember?"

"It was a long time ago, Charlie. I'm lucky if I remember any of what you told me on that trip."

"Jesus, Shake, you got a full-on computer in your head when it comes to weapons and tactics, but you can't remember what happened yesterday. The First Sergeant of the 73rd Machinegun Company, attached to 3/6 at Belleau Wood, was Dan Dailey."

"He of the two Medals of Honor—one for China during the Boxer Rebellion and the other for fighting Cacos in Haiti."

"That's the one, Shake. Your relative, or whatever he turns out to be, was one of Dan Dailey's Marines. Probably got his ass chewed by a certified hero. Now I'm really interested, man. Keep me advised on anything you discover."

"Copy all, Charlie. I'm gonna get off now and find some place to read your email. I'll get back to you if and when I've got anything to report." Shake heard an uncharacteristic sigh on the other end of the call.

"You know what I'd really like to do, Shake? I'd like to get the fuck out from behind this desk and take another trip over there to France, walk them old battlefields, like we did that time on leave, remember?"

"I remember, Charlie. Think you'd be able to stay out of trouble this time?"

"Wouldn't matter if you were there with me like last time, Shake. I gotta go. Read your fucking email."

A fishing camp ten miles up the winding road that surrounded Lake of the Ozarks advertised cabins, cold beer, a fully equipped bait shop, and free wi-fi. It was mid-afternoon, but

Shake decided he could afford a day's delay and a night's rest. He still hadn't hammered any hard checkpoints into his itinerary, so what difference did a day make?

He checked in to the Knotty Pine Lodge, bought six cold beers at the bait shop, and got the password for the wi-fi connection. There was a breezy porch attached to his cabin complete with rocking chair. Shake settled in, popped a beer and dove into his email. Charlie Rowe had been thorough as usual. There was a lot of stuff that wasn't useful, but he did find out that Corporal Tanner M. Davis listed an address in Sikeston, Missouri as his home of record. That was helpful as Shake's relatives were clustered around Cape Girardeau, Sikeston, and the Scott County seat at Benton. It was beginning to look like Marine Corporal Davis was definitely a relative. Charlie's research indicated Cpl. Davis had been "invalided out" of service in January 1919, but there was no information on the type of wound or injury that made him an invalid.

There was a copy of the man's Distinguished Service Cross, a very high decoration for a Marine in those days. It cited Davis for heroic conduct during the fighting on 11 June 1918 near the area of Lucy-Bouresches. Shake knew what that meant. Those were two little villages that faced Belleau Wood on the south side. If a Marine or soldier was fighting in that area, he was facing a metric shit-pot full of Germans dug in deep and solid in the infamous forest.

The citation lauded Cpl. Davis for rallying survivors and leading a bayonet charge into those woods after his machinegun ran out of ammunition. Apparently, Tanner Davis was a take-charge kind of guy when the defecation struck the oscillation. That made Shake smile and reach for another beer. He'd probably have liked this guy, relative or not. He tipped the beer toward the darkening sky and toasted Corporal Tanner M. Davis. Then he closed his eyes and tried to paint a mental picture of the man in the bloody cauldron at Belleau Wood in June 1918. It wasn't hard. Shake had been there, very likely on the same spot at some point long before he knew anything about Cpl. Tanner Davis of the 6th Machinegun Battalion.

Aisne-Marne American Cemetery, France—1976

After 14 hours sandwiched into the cheap seats of an Air France flight and a couple more aboard a bus from Paris to Belleau, they were happy to stretch their legs among the grave markers of the American Cemetery. There were more than 2,000 of them here, including a couple-hundred marked simply "known but to God."

Gunnery Sergeant Shake Davis walked reverently among them, his hiking boots barely making a dent in the plush, pristine grass, and noted most of the dead were from the 4th Martine Brigade, Allied Expeditionary Force or AEF. And most of them bought it right there at Belleau Wood, he knew, glancing north at a dark-green forest on the other side of the cemetery. One of the most pivotal and bloodiest battles of World War I was fought here with U.S. Marines in the vanguard. Every Marine knew about Belleau Wood. It was an iconic touchstone of Marine Corps history, taught and celebrated right up there with Iwo Jima and the Chosin Reservoir in Korea. And these days—Shake smiled at the thought—even the battle for Hue City in Vietnam, a bloody fight where he'd shed a fair amount of his own blood.

Still, not many Marines could visit remote places like Iwo Jima, and none of them could get into North Korea on a battlefield tour without getting arrested or shot on sight. If you wanted to do a pilgrimage and wander through a big slice of Marine Corps history, you went to France and visited Belleau Wood. And if you wanted to do that kind of thing on a budget and a tight schedule of just two weeks annual leave, you went with a subject-matter expert like Gunnery Sergeant Charlie Rowe who was at the moment scrambling around the gravestones with a notebook jotting down names and dates.

Charlie was a good friend from Camp Lejeune where they both served with the 6th Marines, modern members of one of the two Marine regiments that fought at Belleau Wood back in 1918. Charlie was always the CO's choice to teach the mandatory Marine Corps History classes. The man was a serious amateur historian with a special interest in Marine battles of World War I. There might be a few pros who knew more about the Battle of Belleau Wood, but they'd be few and far between. If you wanted the gritty details beyond the big picture—and most Marines did—you went directly to Gunny Rowe. You should come prepared to stay a while and take copious notes.

Every year when he had the time and money, Charlie Rowe flew to France and visited Belleau Wood. This year, he asked Shake to come along, hoping to inoculate his buddy with the same passion he had for the history, the feel, the essence of what Charlie Rowe considered sacred ground. *It does have a certain mystique,* Shake thought, looking out over the symmetrical spread of grave markers. They were placed so precisely, aligned so perfectly, that it wasn't hard to imagine them as a unit of Marines, all standing at attention in ordered ranks waiting for an inspection by some hard ass like Black Jack Pershing or Old Gimlet Eye Smedley Butler. The place fairly reeked of gravitas and Marine Corps mojo.

"C'mon, Shake. Let's go see the wheat field." Charlie spoke in whispers, reflecting his reverence, nodded to the south and started walking. Shake tagged along, taking in the sights and listening to his friend recount the essence of the battle. He'd heard a lot of it before, either in one of Charlie's history classes or over beers at the Staff NCO Club. Walking the actual ground and looking where Charlie pointed as he talked, Shake was getting a much clearer mental picture. And Charlie talked like a Marine rather than a historian, which made it all so much more interesting and understandable.

"It was an ass-kicker all around, Shake. They lost more KIA in this one fight than we'd lost in the 143 years of Marine Corps history up to that point in June 1918. The Brigade in those days was about ninety-five hundred dudes on the muster rolls. They lost a thousand KIA right here with about four thousand wounded, which figures to about a fifty-five percent casualty rate. Lots of the Marines were gassed. When the Germans got desperate, they started lobbing in mustard gas. You think tear gas is a bitch? Imagine trying to advance through thick yellow clouds of that shit. It could blind you or melt your lungs before you even had time to mask up."

"I didn't know they used gas during the battle." Like every other Marine, Shake had been trained in the use of a Field Protective Mask in various gas chamber exercise where troops were introduced to the effects of CS, or tear gas. He'd even experienced it for real in the fighting at Hue during the Tet Offensive of 1968. But Mustard Gas, phosgene and chlorine of the type used in WWI, was a whole different animal. That shit didn't just cause choking and watery eyes. It could kill you or screw you up so badly that you wished you were dead.

"Yeah, there's not much mention of it in the history books." Charlie shrugged and pointed over his shoulder at the backpack which contained his notebooks and other research material. "But you gotta know that by the second week of June, a lot of the fighting around here was being done by guys in leaky gasmasks."

They stopped at a little crossroads village that a sign identified as *Lucy-le-bocage*. "You can get a good view of the layout from here," Charlie said, pointing to the dark patch of woods to their right front. "That's Belleau Wood itself. It's runs about a mile north-south and about half that east-west. The Germans are holed up in there tight as ticks, Shake. They've got about two thousand guys inside the woods with about thirty machineguns."

Charlie pointed down a road on their right. "Down there about half a klick is the village of Bouresches, where the Krauts have another hundred troops and six machineguns." He pointed at a field of knee-high foliage waving in a light breeze. Wild wheat. In another month or so, it would turn to a golden carpet covering what looked to be 800 meters or so of wide-open ground. "From Bouresches, the Germans can pour enfilading fire on anybody that tries to cross that wheat field and get into Belleau Wood."

"I'm betting it was right out there in the middle of all that waving wheat that Gunny Dan Dailey made history, right?"

"Dan Dailey was already a big part of Marine Corps history." Charlie shrugged and shook his head. "He got the Big One in China and another in Haiti. At the time of the Belleau Wood fight, he was First Sergeant of 73rd Company, 6th Machinegun Battalion, attached to 3/6. They considered giving him a third Medal of Honor, but that seemed like a bit much even for Dan Dailey, so they gave him a DSC which was later converted to a Navy Cross." Charlie took off striding to the east. "Let's go get a look at the woods from out in the middle of that field. The guys who came at the woods from that side ran into a meat-grinder."

They crossed the road leading from Lucy to Bouresches and walked into the tall green wheat. The village that held the enfilading Germans and their Maxim machineguns was off to the right. As they walked into the wheat field, Shake could see the roofs of small buildings on the eastern horizon. They were definitely in range of rifles and Maxim machineguns out here from that direction and also from defenders in the wood itself. Crossfire.

They walked silently for a while, eyeing the wood line to their left until Charlie stopped and looked around, seeming to measure distances in his mind. He pulled Shake down to a knee so they could look at the wood from the assholes and elbows perspective that the Marines must have had during their assault in 1918.

"It was probably right about here, if it happened at all."

"If what happened?"

"If Dan Dailey actually said *C'mon, you sons of bitches. Do you want to live forever?*"

"You mean there's some question about that?"

"I have my doubts, Shake. It don't line up with the facts. See, that line is quoted by Floyd Gibbons who was a war correspondent for the Chicago Tribune at the time. He didn't ID the guy who supposedly said it. He just attributed it to a Marine Sergeant. Gibbons was with 3/5 at the time over on the west side of the wood." Charlie pointed off to the west which would be on the other side of Belleau Wood. "Now, Dailey is on this side with 3/6, so how could he be the guy Gibbons quoted?"

"Beats me. How come it always gets credited to Dailey?"

"Marine Corps magic, Shake. After the war, the CO of 3/5 claims it was one of his Staff NCOs which would eliminate Dan Dailey from consideration as the inspirational leader, but here you got a double Medal of Honor man in the fight, and it seems like something a guy like that would say, right? So, Mother Marine Corps decides it was Dailey and fuck a bunch of facts. Dailey never formally denied it. He was probably yelling all kinds of crazy shit himself over on this side while trying to get his Marines up and moving through an artillery barrage and a wall of machinegun fire. He could have said something similar, probably did, but if Gibbons wasn't just blowing smoke up his readers' butts, it wasn't Dan Dailey he heard yelling that line that we all know and love."

"You ever mention this to the boys up at Headquarters Marine Corps?"

Charlie laughed and charged off toward the wood line. You shittin' me, Shake? You don't tug on Superman's cape, and you don't piss into the wind. I ain't gonna be the guy who claims Dan Dailey never said what Mother Corps says he said."

The ground between the wheat field and the edge of Belleau Wood was overgrown with tall grass, but it undulated underfoot in spots. Shake recognized the pattern of depressions. Shell holes. This area must have been blanketed with a rolling artillery barrage designed to build a wall of deadly steel all across the final approaches to the actual woods. He knew about arty barrages firsthand and had intimate knowledge of the pucker-factor produced by close rounds. He stood looking back at the wheat field where there was no cover at all and damn little concealment. The staggering casualty rates at Belleau Wood made sense. He'd lived through some serious combat actions in other places at other times but conceded the odds would be against him if he'd been an NCO with the 6th Marines in June of 1918.

"So, this is the wood itself," Charlie said, looking into the shadows with a kind of quiet reverence. He turned and pointed at a road that ran north-south on the west side of Belleau Wood. "By mid-June you got the whole brigade, 5th Marines to the west and 6th Marines to the south, all trying to get in here. They're taking a licking, but they keep on ticking. An outfit from 6th Marines finally clears Bouresches in some serious MOUT action, house-to-house, and 5th Marines have secured the high ground to the west which anchors the allied line. They been at it, bleeding like slaughter-house hogs, for almost two weeks. Most of the junior officers and NCOs KIA. Now it's time to get into the woods proper and dig the remaining Krauts out of their holes."

"When was that, Charlie?"

"Started around 11 June. And that's when the mustard gas shells started to drop."

They walked into the gloom, noting holes in the ground that were overgrown but still discernible between stands of oak, larch and elm trees. It would have been tight in here, trying to winkle out an entrenched enemy with nothing more than grenades, rifles and bayonets. In a fight like that, you weren't battling muzzle flash or fleeting shadows. You were looking right into an enemy's beady-ass eyeballs and the clashes must have been horrendous, right down at the basic human level where only the fittest, fastest and most furious survived.

"You don't live through something like this using your basic four hours of bootcamp hand-to-hand combat instruction, do you?"

Charlie looked at him in irritation and leaned back against a tall oak. He swept his arm across the shadowy interior of the wood. "It was the ultimate test, Shake. The one none of us ever wants to face. You know? No fucking holds barred, and anything goes if it kills the other guy. It started with rifles and machineguns, then it was down to bayonets, and then entrenching tools, rocks and sticks. And finally, there were guys in here tearing at each other with their fucking fingernails and teeth. The words close quarters battle don't half cover what went on here. It was the ultimate test of human endurance, basic survival…rage…cruelty…savage stuff. I think that's what attracts me to it, you know. I just keep trying to imagine that—and can't."

Shake knew precisely what his friend meant, but it was getting a little heavy, a little deep, and they were supposed to be on leave, having a good time. They needed to lighten up.

"So where's the Devil Dog Fountain? We'll get a drink of water there. And then get a bunch of stronger drinks somewhere else. How's that for a plan?"

Charlie smiled and led off heading for the northern reaches of Belleau Wood. They walked a mile or so before they emerged from the woods facing a road and a low stone fence. "Somewhere around here it came to an end," Charlie said. "26 June 1918, and Major Maurice Shearer, CO of 5th Marines sent a message up the chain: "Belleau Wood now U.S. Marine Corps entirely.""

"And thanks to the Germans whose ass they just kicked, the U.S. Marines became *Teufel Hunden*…Devil Dogs."

"Uh…maybe not."

"What?"

"Truth of the matter is that term was used in a Marine Corps magazine for the first time in April 1918, two months before the fight at Belleau Wood started. And it was used incorrectly, by the way. A native German speaker would have said *Hunde* not *Hunden*. And he would have said *Teufels* not *Teufel*. Likely some clown in the PR department made up the term."

"Holy shit, Charlie! You're blowing holes in all kinds of sacred Marine Corps cows."

"Don't matter where it came from, Shake. It became the stuff of legend." He swept an arm across the forest at their backs. "And Belleau Wood became *Bois de la Brigade de Marine* forever more. Winners write the history, my man."

"I need a drink."

"And you're gonna get one—a very special drink. Follow me."

ΔΔΔ

They climbed the stone fence and walked up a paved road for a while, then made a right to enter the village of Belleau. It was like stepping back in time, strolling into the pages of a European history book. Shake could easily imagine doughboys mingling with locals up and down the cobblestone street that meandered around the center of Belleau and the fountain where local residents once drew water for cooking and other chores. It was the residential heart of the Count of Belleau's estate. At one point in its existence, the village was the entry point for the Count's 200-acre hunting preserve. For modern locals, it was a great spot to picnic or wander through the nearby woods. For foreign visitors—and most of them were Marines—it was the home of the Devil Dog Fountain.

"Most people don't think about it," Charlie said, "but that's why the village and the woods are called Belleau. It's French, right? *Belle*, good…and *eau*, water."

The fountain nestled in a small clearing in the middle of the ancient village. It was composed of rough-hewn local fieldstone, moss covered with patches of scale and overgrown with ivy. It featured a small semi-circular pool that caught the spill from the actual fountainhead. And that fountainhead which spit water into the little pool was the source of great Marine mysticism. According to lore and legend of the Corps, a Marine who drank from the Devil Dog Fountain at Belleau somehow ingested the spirit of the men who fought at the great battle in June 1918. A sip or two was supposed to give the drinker special strength and protection in battles to come.

Shake stood scrutinizing the fountainhead. He'd always been a dog lover and kept any number of breeds when he was growing up. He'd even rescued a few canine waifs at various overseas locations and kept them around as clandestine pets. But this thing staring back at him—the Devil Dog of Marine Corps legend—was…well, different. Water poured in a steady stream from the mouth of some stone sculptor's idea of a fierce canine in attack mode. The pooch slobbering well water from his jaws was a Bull Mastiff. According to Charlie, it was a representation of the mastiff hounds that were used for hunting years ago in pre-PC days when locals needed meat and there was no ASPCA around to bitch about it. The dog's ears were cocked forward, a gaping maw showed some serious fangs. The Devil Dog fountainhead had an aggressive jut to its jaws, framed by clumps of moss that made it look like the animal had been grazing on local greenery. There was a feral look to its black marble eyes as if it was ready to rip heads off shoulders. And Shake was closing to a distance where that would be entirely possible if he was facing flesh and fur rather than black marble.

"So the drill is," Charlie said as they stood looking at the fountain, "you stick your mouth right there where the water comes out of his jaws and suck up a big slug of the magic elixir."

Shake bent over and eyed the dog carefully. "And then I'm good to go forever more, right? Bulletproof? No more Purple Hearts?"

"It's magic, Shake. You just gotta believe."

Shake peeled off his Marine Corps baseball cap with an embroidered emblem on the front and clapped it on the dog's head. It looked about right, so he saluted and bent to sip the well water. He was thinking about nasty bacteria and potential diarrhea, only planning to take a sedate sip of the metallic-tasting water, but Charlie had other ideas.

"Don't be such a pussy," he said and shoved Shake's entire head under the water. "The more you get, the better it works."

Held firmly under the cascade, Shake was forced to suck up about a quart of the Devil Dog water before Charlie finally released him. He shook his head and sputtered for a while and then pointed at the pool. "Your turn, asshole."

"To complete the magic, we gotta go over there and say a prayer in the chapel." Charlie pointed to a nearby stone structure featuring stained glass depictions of WWI doughboys. Shake turned to look and by the time he turned back, Charlie had ducked for his sip and was standing there smiling. "It's called a tactical deception, my man."

Shake considered wrestling Charlie and tossing him ass-first into the pool, but that seemed like sour grapes, and he'd never been a sore loser. No sense starting now. "Mark it down, Charlie. I owe you one."

Charlie reached in his pocket and flashed a fistful of French francs. It was quite a wad.

"How about I buy us lunch and a belly full of French beer and we call it even. I drew most of my shipping over money for this trip and I'm feeling like a big spender."

ΔΔΔ

They hiked east down a narrow, paved road straddled by thick bocage toward Bouresches where they'd obtained a room at a small inn before their visit to the cemetery and Belleau Wood. Just down the little village main drag was a joint called Café De La Place. The sign said café, but Charlie and Shake knew a bar when they saw one.

"I'm not exactly fluent in French, my man." Charlie pointed at a rustic sign overhanging the sidewalk. "But I'm guessing any joint that calls itself of the place, must be the place."

They strolled inside and found a table near bay windows that looked out onto what had to be the Bouresches main drag. Every other road seemed to be some kind of alley between a sparse collection of old buildings. There wasn't much going on inside or out, just a few cars that whizzed by on an irregular basis, no pedestrians in sight. The only other customers were two burly dudes hugging the bar and sucking up draft Kronenbourg. They looked like local farm hands or maybe construction workers. Both of those guys badly needed a shower. A rickety ceiling fan blew fecund clouds of body odor that mingled with the smell of stale beer, cigarettes, and rancid grease.

When Shake walked up to the bar to order a couple of beers and a menu in a halting mix of French and English, they gave him the fabled *you ain't from around here* stink-eye. He ignored it and carried the beers back to their table. Charlie had spread his notebooks and research material. He was busy jotting down impressions from their visit. They drank their beers, pretty good stuff by American standards, and planned the next step of their trip. Charlie wanted to head for Chateau Thierry the next day where he could do a little more touring at the site of another major World War I battle. Shake was loose and indifferent about it. He mainly wanted to relax, forget about some pending personnel problems that were awaiting his attention back at the outfit. These relatively remote regions of France seemed like as good a place as any to do that. His plan was to just follow Charlie around, maybe learn a little military history and simply soak up some atmosphere that wasn't Marine Corps green.

A couple of crude ham and cheese sandwiches arrived borne by a ruddy-faced woman who was apparently delighted to get out of what passed for a kitchen at the Café De La Place. She was hippy and buxom, packed into a printed sun dress that was covered by a grease-stained apron. A bubbly, chatty sort, she seemed anxious to watch them eat while trying out her version of English conversation.

"*Brigade de la Marines,*" she said smiling and pointing at Shake's hat. "*Tres bien.* Very good. We like come to visit here."

"Well, we like come to visit here, too," Shake said around a bite of his baguette. The ham and cheese were on the thin and tasteless side, but the bread was delicious. "Lots of…what's the word…*histoire ici.*" The woman clapped her hands and patted Shake's shoulder, amused at his attempt to insert a little French into the conversation.

"*Oui, mon dieu. Une grande bataille ici,*" She waved a chubby hand in the general direction of the windows. "*Le grande bataille en la bois de Belleau.* Long time past. *N'cest pas?*"

The sandwiches and beer were mostly gone, but their hostess made no move to collect plates or return to her kitchen. The two hard cases at the bar made some snide comment. You didn't need to be fluent in French to recognize these guys thought she ought to shut up and get back in the kitchen where she belonged. The woman shot them a withering glance and then went back to her conversation with Shake. His country twang which generally butchered pronunciation of what few French words he knew seemed to delight her.

Charlie got bored with the little flirtation, grabbed their empty beer glasses and went to the bar for refills. That's where he made a rookie mistake. When he went to pay the tab, he hauled that big wad of colorful bills out of his jeans. The redolent pair at the bar took it all in and cut a glance at each other. Charlie didn't seem to notice but Shake did. He continued flirting with the cook who had by this time pulled up a chair but kept an eye on the guys at the bar. They had a couple more beers, then tossed some coins at the barkeep and disappeared into the shadows at the back of the place. Shake was trying to describe what part of America they were from, using a napkin and pen to draw a crude outline of the North American continent, when Charlie interrupted.

"*Pardon, mademoiselle, ou sent les toilettes?*"

She barely looked up, just waved a hand toward the back of the joint. Charlie stood grinning as he maneuvered out from behind the table. "Careful, Shake. This chick's got the hots for you. Somebody might gonna get laid tonight."

Shake waved him away and went back to his drawing which was hardly accurate or to scale. The state of Missouri as depicted took up about half of the American land mass and North Carolina covered most of the rest. They were just discussing the proper French pronunciation of Camp Lejeune when Charlie disappeared into a dark alcove at the back of the bar. At that point the situation got complicated.

"Hey, fuck you, assholes!"

Shake looked up and heard a loud thud coming from the direction Charlie had taken. The woman stood and rushed to investigate but Shake blew by her, hearing what he recognized from experience as the sound of a fight in progress. He ducked inside a foul-smelling toilet area and saw Charlie pinned up against a wall over a galvanized trough that served as the urinal. Charlie was tossing some ineffective punches, but he was bent over backward and off balance. Shake rushed to grab the guy choking Charlie when the second of the pair stepped into his path. The guy had one of those long, wickedly curved, and lethal *Opinel* pocket-knives pointed directly at his throat.

Shake took a step backward and looked around for a weapon. There wasn't much at hand in this little toilet and not much room to maneuver. At his back, the woman was screaming something. Shake recognized the word *gendarmes* but it didn't look like a situation that would just simmer until local cops arrived. The man behind the guy with the knife had bloodied Charlie's nose and was digging around for the wad of money. Charlie was kicking hard but losing the struggle to a much larger and determined assailant.

That's when the blade man made his move. He took a long horizontal swipe at Shake with the knife. He was no close-in fighter. The swipe was so vicious that he wound up half turned around and off balance. Shake took the opportunity to kick him hard on the outside of his knee and the guy lost his footing momentarily. Then he came up, charging and slashing at the air between them. Shake stumbled backward to avoid the blade and bumped into a towel dispenser mounted on the wall. The big heavy box unhinged on one side and drooped at an angle. It wasn't much of a weapon, but it would have to do.

Shake reached back and jerked the dispenser the rest of the way off the wall. When the knife man made his next lunge, Shake sidestepped and brought the towel dispenser down as hard as he could on the back of the man's head. That did it. The guy dropped the knife and collapsed bleeding from an ugly gash in his scalp. Shake kicked the knife away from easy reach, gave the downed man an insurance kick to the ear and then charged for the man who was beating on Charlie. The man spun to meet Shake's charge which gave Charlie time to recover. Shake swung a roundhouse at the guy's nose while Charlie shot a hard right-left combination into his kidneys. Shoving past his assailants, bleeding from a broken nose, the second man bolted for the door.

"Did he get your money?"

Charlie wiped at his own bloody nose and shook his head. "Just a couple of bills he could reach." He jerked up his trouser leg and showed a bulging sock. "The rest is right here." Charlie must have seen the lay of the land when he went to the bar and stashed most of his cash in a sock. Typical Marine thing. Most carried their cigarettes or other bulky items in a sock to avoid unmilitary bulges in uniform pockets.

"*Nous avons appele la police!*" The cook was standing alongside the bartender, both of them staring at the unconscious man on the floor of the toilet. The barkeep had a few profane comments that Shake didn't catch but Charlie interpreted to mean the goon bleeding on the deck was a local troublemaker who deserved what he got.

Shake was checking to be sure he hadn't killed the man when two local cops arrived. One of them escorted Shake and Charlie outside while the other one stood with a notebook listening to the cook and the barman tell the story of what happened. The cop watching them with his hand resting on the flap of his holster could hear most of the interview inside as it was being conducted at high decibel levels. He shook his head and smiled a couple of times.

After about ten minutes, the chatter subsided, and an ambulance arrived. The cop had a few words with the EMTs, and they walked inside carrying a med kit and a stretcher. They looked bored as if this kind of thing happened all the time in quaint little Bouresches. The inside cop emerged, snapping his notebook closed and carrying the knife in a plastic baggie. He spoke passable English as he asked to see their passports. They handed them over and the cop took a cursory look before handing them back.

"Where do you stay?"

Charlie pointed up the street and named the little B&B they'd selected for an overnight in the village. The EMTs came out of the bar carrying the goon on a stretcher. He was still out but his head had been bandaged. There was an exchange of words with the cops before the ambulance crew loaded up their patient and took off headed up the main drag.

"That guy gonna be OK?" Shake didn't want to be hung up in a long investigation or wind up facing a homicide charge.

"He will live," the cop said. "It is not the first time we have business with this man."

"You need anything from us?"

"The staff here has described what happened. I have no doubt it's the truth. As I said, we have had encounters with this man before. We will now search for his friend."

"That's it? We free to go?"

"*Oui*…and I hope you enjoy your time in France."

They did that for another eight days before they had to catch a flight home. Charlie had some significant additions to his historical research. Shake had a great sea story that he gleefully told at the Camp Lejeune Staff NCO Club two weeks later.

ΔΔΔ

The last beer was gone, and the sun was setting into the waters of the lake when Shake checked out of his memory banks and looked at his watch. If he had the time differential figured right, his wife would be off work about now. He grabbed his phone, checked the country code prefix, and punched in the numbers. She answered on the second ring.

He let her know where he was, described the blissful view of the lake, and complained that he didn't really have time to do some fishing. He'd always had such good luck luring lunker bass out of the shoreside weed patches that he thought it was a shame not to give it another go.

"Don't see why you don't," she said. "You got your little Zebco in the truck, right?"

"Yeah, and it's tempting, but I'd probably get lucky and wind up with a stringer of fish that would go to waste. I'll pass and let someone else get the fat ones this time. Anyway, I need to hit the road."

"So you're anxious to get rolling? Back to the old home place? I'm remarkably surprised, Shake."

"I guess I'm feeling the old hoodoo, Chan. Feeling that big suck that draws some people back to the place they went overboard trying to escape. The irony is not lost on me. I was thinking about it on the drive up here."

"I get it. Just consider yourself lucky I don't embark on that kind of nostalgia trip. My Dad from North Carolina and my Mom from some village outside Bangkok? We'd go broke on plane tickets."

"I wouldn't mind another little sojourn to Thailand. Remember I got a pal over there."

"Yeah, I remember—and he runs a bar in hooker heaven. Not gonna happen, Shake."

They talked domestic issues for a while. Shake listened quietly to news about what she was doing and tried to keep the conversation light. He missed her, missed the intimate, comfortable feel of just having her around most of the time, whether he was in the mood for affection or not. He came to realize as she chatted about one of her Chinese students, a guy she said was a closet communist, that Chan was such a huge, reliable part of his life. She deserved to know all she wanted to know about him. And if this trip involved as many personal revelations as he thought it might, he vowed to share them with her. If that was painful or embarrassing, so be it. She deserved nothing less for just putting up with him and his roving nature. "At least you aren't off on some half-assed mission that's likely to get you killed," she said. "What's the next stop?"

"Just gonna blow on out of here in the morning and head for St. Louis, I guess."

"That's near MMA, isn't it? Where you went to high school?"

"Yeah, couple hours northwest."

"You gonna stop by the old alma mater?"

"Hadn't considered it. I been kind of focused on Mark Twain country and a bunch of country cousins that I probably won't remember."

"You ought to swing by and take a look at MMA."

"Think so? How come?"

"As long as I've known you, Shake, you always talk about the teachers you had there and how important that school was to you. Seems to me if it's that important to the life and times of Shake Davis, you ought to pay a little visit. You're that close, why not?"

"Maybe I will. Just a couple hours to look around, you know. Then I'm gonna shake the family tree a little bit and head home to pick up Bear."

"Love to both of you. I'm gonna get some sleep."

He fiddled with the phone and set a new destination on Google Maps. Missouri Military Academy in Mexico, MO. Other than the Marine Corps, it was the one element that most shaped what he was to become later in life. That was worth exploring as part of this quest. *What he hell*, he thought as he stripped and collapsed on the bed. *If you're gonna conjure up ghosts from the past, might as well visit them all.*

Mexico, Missouri

The program running on his phone guided him through the mountains and down onto the flat land that stretched eastward across Missouri toward the Mississippi River. This was family farm country, or it used to be many years ago when pioneer families, either by choice or chance, halted here and sank roots into the fertile black loam, raising lush crops and kids to help with the back-breaking labor required to survive. From the looks of things as Shake blew past fields of corn, sorghum, and soybeans, Big Agriculture had displaced most of those small and fiercely independent families. He saw huge combines painted John Deere green roaring across the fields, most of them bearing the logo of some national agricultural conglomerate. The farmers in bib overalls that he remembered from rural burgs like Auxvasse, Centralia, and Wellsville were nowhere in sight.

As he turned north onto Highway 54, he passed a huge automated baler churning out rolls of hay that would dry under the sun to become cattle feed. He felt a familiar twinge in his lower back. Maybe he was just road weary, but Shake recognized that pain. It was familiar from long hours he'd spent as a teenager bucking hay bales onto flatbed trucks for farmers that grudgingly paid local kids 50 cents an hour in harvest season. It was a rite of passage for boys back then, a way to make a little spending money and develop the kind of bulging biceps that made you a chick magnet.

Now Big Ag copied the European model. Why bale hay when you could just form it into convenient rolls? *Just as well,* he thought, glancing at a roadside sign that told him he was just three miles from the Mexico city limits. Local farmers—if there were any left—probably didn't need kids to help these days. Plenty of immigrant or migrant labor available coming up and down the Mississippi looking for work.

He made a right turn at the city limit sign and passed a strip mall that was new, at least to him. The K-Mart parking lot was nearly full. Business was apparently booming with hefty females pushing strollers or shopping carts full of groceries. None of them were really fat, but they were all plus-size with ample curves stuffed into tank-tops and yoga pants. He didn't imagine the local K-Mart did big business in skinny jeans. When he was a cadet at MMA, shopping was a simple matter of going to the square in the middle of town that hosted a few long-established and locally owned stores. You did business with people you knew, people who knew you and your needs. Usually notions, lotions, a poodle skirt, a new pair of jeans, or bib overalls.

The square in the middle of Mexico was still there, still a perfectly rectangular slice of rural America with a courthouse or municipal building at the center, but the Civil War cannon was gone, and all the perimeter shops were different. The Walgreens with an old dial-up phone booth in the back of the store was gone. In pre-cellphone days, he'd haunted that booth, hiding behind the accordion privacy door and feeding dimes to make clandestine calls to local girls. Nobody old enough to own a phone—and that seemed like just about everyone he saw walking around the square—had need for phone booth privacy. They could simply walk away from eavesdroppers with their phone glued to an ear. None of them would know what to do with a rotary dial anyway.

Replacing the corner Walgreens was a cellular service outlet where you could sign up for unlimited minutes and they'd toss in a free phone, according to a sign that was plastered across a big display window that used to feature a colorfully decorated tree circled incessantly by a model train at Christmas time. Cadets wrapped in their winter uniform overcoats used to stand by that window, waiting to meet townie girlfriends, elbowing each other every time the model train whistled or puffed little gouts of fake smoke. No need for kitschy touches like that anymore. If you wanted to see trains, there was an app for that.

At a stoplight he rolled down the truck window to check his bearings with a rawboned mailman in shorts and heavily inked calves who was collecting from a corner box. The guy was friendly enough and walked over to rest his elbows on the truck.

"I seen them Texas plates," he said. "You lost?"

"I guess maybe. I used to go to school here, but lots has changed."

"MMA or MHS?" Mailman grinned and wiggled his fingers to show off a graduation ring from Mexico High School. There had always been a bitter rivalry between the local high school boys and the MMA cadets, mostly over available females who could choose from an abundance of panting suitors and often played on both sides of that fence

"MMA…long time ago. Just gonna take a look while I'm passing through."

"Easy to find MMA in a burg this size." The mailman pointed up the block. "Just go around the square one more time and make a right at East Jackson. That dead-ends at MMA."

"Appreciate the help."

"Ain't no thang, Texas. Y'all have a nice day."

The mailman ambled over to his truck leaving a cloud of English Leather in his wake. Shake shivered at the scent. Right there at the old Walgreens he bought about a gallon of that stuff and used it liberally long before he actually needed to do much regular shaving. It was a favorite of the girl he'd been madly in love with during his last two years at MMA. He followed the directions that led him down a broad avenue lined with old oaks and stately whitewashed houses. He was trying to remember where his old girlfriend lived, somewhere around here. Becky—something—was her name, he remembered as the MMA campus came into view.

Not quite ready to commit, he drove a loop around the area, flooded by incoherent images of his past, looking for his favorite A&W root beer stand out where Highway 54 intersected town streets. Cadets loved to buy that stuff in big waxed cones, just slightly smaller than what urban repair crews use to mark off work areas. It was gone. In its place was an outlet for some Stop & Rob chain peddling cheap gas, stale pastries, and 40 kinds of beef jerky. Shake turned back toward the campus and idled in his truck, facing MMA, trying to decide if this side trip was worth the effort. He was caught somewhere between anxiety and dread. What if nothing was the same? What if he was sorely disappointed by what he found? What if the good times he recalled turned out to be just fabrications, fading memories?

Through his bug splattered windshield, he stared at a ruler-straight driveway that was bisected by a strip of grass and an old fountain. That was Senior Walk. It was a little patch of green facing the main Admin Building that was restricted to only senior cadets. In his day, access to Senior Walk was a much cherished and jealously guarded piece of Academy ground. It was deserted now, and he saw only a few cadets in their ROTC uniforms wandering among the campus buildings. *Probably still in classes*, he thought, glancing at his watch, or studying for final academic exams. In a week or two after that, the campus would be deserted for summer vacation.

He parked the truck along Grand Avenue, which fronted one side of the campus perimeter and got out to stretch his back. Walking toward the campus, he punched the key fob to lock the truck. *No need for that*, he thought as he walked back onto Missouri Military Academy for the first time in decades. Mexico these days doubtless had its share of teenage rebels, delinquents and thieves, but those douchebags would steer clear of the regimented and austere environment of MMA. Better pickings over at the K-Mart parking lot.

There had been some significant physical changes to MMA in the years he'd been absent, but he still spotted familiar landmarks. The little body of water called Teardrop Lake was still there. Cadets skated on it when the lake froze over in hard winters, but Shake never got the hang of it. He still had an aversion to cold weather and most things connected with it including skis and ice skates. At the bottom of Teardrop there was likely enough cadet uniforms items to outfit an army, all tossed into the drink by graduating cadets who swore they'd never return. Some meant it. Most did not.

He noted a couple of newish-looking buildings that he couldn't identify as he walked up the drive turning his head this way and that, catching glimpses of ghosts in a few familiar haunts. Even the vaunted main admin building with its white stone steps and Doric columns had been refurbished. Inside were staff offices for the Commandant of Cadets, the Academic Principal, and staffers who kept the Academy running on a tight, regimented schedule. There used to be a library or reception area inside that housed trophies and honors won by the school or individual cadets. Shake had contributed to a few trophies won by Academy baseball and football teams.

He stopped abruptly at the base of the steps, remembering a rule that said cadets could enter the building only by the back doors. The pristine steps were reserved for visiting dignitaries or campus staff—or the bugler who posed on those steps to sound daily reveille, taps, and other calls throughout an Academy day. Violators of that regulation and a dizzying array of others were faced with extra study hours that cut into sparse free time, or "tours," involving various punishments of a military nature such as policing the area or cleaning weapons in the armory.

Piss on it. Shake grinned and marched up the forbidden steps. He reached for a pair of polished brass handles and swung open the Admin Building doors. The musty smell was the same, and maybe he detected the scent of fear and sweat from generations of cadets who were called to the Commandant's office to face the martial music for serious transgressions from AWOL to breaking barracks after Taps on a clandestine midnight run to that root beer stand that no longer existed.

A petite woman with reading glasses perched on her nose stopped with an arm full of papers and asked if she could help. Shake gave his name and class date, saying he was just looking around. She badly wanted to call someone who could take him on a tour of the campus, but he talked her out of it. He wouldn't be here long, he said, and asked if the big door off to their right still led to the library.

"Well, it's not much of a library anymore," she said pulling open the door for him. "We mainly use it for conferences and to store all the awards these days." And was he sure she couldn't get someone to show him around? He was sure. "Don't have a lot of time. But thanks for your trouble."

Shake was looking at his class yearbook that he found in a collection of leather-bound volumes along one wall of the library when one of the nearby trophies caught his eye. A sign beneath the tarnished, old-fashioned loving cup said it was the Wallace M. Fry Trophy for Excellence in Public Speaking. Shake had never discovered who the vaunted Wallace M. Fry really was beyond the fact that he was an MMA Cadet, Class of 1903, a noted young speaker who was later somehow connected to the Future Farmers of America.

He picked it up from the shelf and rubbed on the brass plate that contained a list of names. The speech contest was one of the major events marking the end of an MMA academic year. Shake had won it in his senior year with some amateurish bleating about the Cold War and nuclear escalation, topics that he knew virtually nothing about beyond the research he did in preparing his speech. His presentation had been an exercise in acting more than anything else, full of schmaltzy, over-rehearsed hand flourishes and vocal intonations. Still he won. His name was right there engraved on the trophy.

"Long time ago—but I remember that night."

Shake nearly dropped the trophy as he spun to see a short, smiling man in an Army green uniform with major's oak leaves on the epaulets and ROTC brass on the collars. The Indian dark hair had gone grey on the fringes, but the toothy grin and hook nose could only belong to Paul Baum, his roommate in A Company for one of the four years Shake spent at MMA.

"Paul Baum! Pablo? What the hell are you doing here?" Shake took the outstretched hand and shook his head. "It's been…what…twenty years?"

"A little more than that, I guess, but who's counting. The secretary called me. She remembered that I was a classmate, same year as you."

"Yeah, but what the hell are you doing here? At MMA? I thought you went back to Oklahoma City, to go to school or something."

"Started OU about the same time you joined the Marine Corps, Shel…"

"Hold on, Pablo." Shake held up hand to interrupt. "Sheldon was your roommate a couple of centuries ago. The Marine Corps tagged me as Shake and that's what I go by these days—regardless of what it says in the yearbook."

"OK. Guess you had to do something to keep people from calling you Shelly. I seem to remember a few fistfights over that."

"That's it. But it doesn't answer my question. What are you doing here at MMA?"

"Teaching, Shake. Mostly American History and Spanish. I graduated from OU with teachers' credentials, bummed around Puerto Rico and Central America for a few years. Then I got married and had to earn a real living, so I applied here and got hired. Been here nearly fifteen years now."

"Damn, it's good to see you, Pablo."

"Great to see you again, man! Let me show you around a little bit. There's a bunch of new stuff you won't believe around here."

ΔΔΔ

There was indeed a bunch of new stuff. Shake marveled at most of it, gawking like a hayseed on a first big city visit. MMA had spent a lot of money on facilities over the years since Shake knew the campus intimately. Paul said some of the money came from successful alumni, but most of it was from wealthy parents of the foreign families that sent their young kids to MMA for a solid, disciplined college-prep curriculum. And a great many of the school's cadets were foreign born, some Asians and a lot of Latinos.

New buildings included an extensive gym with an Olympic standard pool on one level. Paul called it The Gymnatorium. It was huge compared to the rickety old structure where the basketball Colonels of MMA played home games with surrounding high schools. And it certainly smelled better than the old musty jocks and sweat-sock miasma that Shake remembered from his time as a young athlete. The gym had spaces dedicated to boxing and wrestling which were certainly better than the jury-rigged canvas square Shake remembered from his days as an Academy welterweight. He'd been more of a brawler than a boxer in those days, a flat-footed, left-handed jackhammer who took punishment and waited—usually too long—for an opponent to give him an opening. He usually lost to fancier boxers, guys who studied the techniques of the sweet science.

Paul walked him past an array of high-tech workout machinery, but Shake kept looking at the boxing ring, remembering an intramural fight with a cadet from California—Spurgeon or something like that—who was a dancer in the ring with quick hands and a roundhouse right that landed like a sledge. Shake lost the fight in the third round when that right hand caught him on his left ear, and he dropped like a bad habit. He staggered for days after that until the fluid of his inner ear finally settled.

Roaming the back side of the campus, areas that were well away from the carefully groomed facades designed to impress visitors, MMA felt more familiar. He recognized the little outbuilding where Sessler and generations of other Cadet Battalion Commanders and cadet staff officers lived, a little perk which reinforced the ages-old military concept of RHIP. Rank Has Its Privileges, and if you are good enough to obtain exalted rank, there's no need for you to live in any of the barracks where lesser beings were subject to constant inspections and regular harassment. Shake had lived there in his senior year when he was appointed a Cadet First Lieutenant and Battalion Adjutant.

Turning along the back-campus road that led to MMA's main athletic field, Paul pointed to a structure on the left causing Shake to freeze in place. He knew this building, inside and out. It was basically two stories of concrete, an upper classroom area and a lower basement area that housed the weapons armory and small-bore rifle range. "You spent a hell of a lot of time down there in the armory as I recall." Paul swept his hand upward toward the classroom where MMA's music department held classes and rehearsals. "And I spent most of my time up there with a trumpet glued to my face."

"Yeah, I remember you were a hell of a musician. And you were the Drum Major of the marching band senior year, right?" Shake remembered that Cadet Paul Baum had been a musical savant. He played all sorts of brass instruments in all sorts of Academy bands. "You still screw around with your trumpet?"

"Well, I still play it," Paul chuckled. "Mostly when one of the cadet groups needs a horn to sit in for some performance or other." He started down the road toward the athletic fieldhouse, but Shake was glued in position trying to see through the windows of the armory.

"Damn, Pablo. I'm having some serious flashbacks here." The armory, home to the active duty officers and NCOs who served as instructors in MMA's Military Sciences department, housed a variety of weapons on which cadets were trained, everything infantry from .50 caliber machineguns to rocket launchers, all used in mandatory ROTC classes that were part of every cadet's life. If he was being honest about it, Shake thought that the MMA armory and all the fascinating weapons it housed was a big part of why he eventually chose the military career path. He knew about rifles and shotguns before MMA. He came from a family that hunted regularly for deer, squirrels, rabbits, and birds. Anything they could kill, Grandma cooked. But time spent in the MMA armory, around the real and darkly fascinating weapons of war, the stuff right out of Sgt. Rock comic books, turned Shake into a genuine gun geek. It was certainly the beginning of the long love affair he had with the M-1 Garand rifle.

Every cadet in those days was issued a weapon for which he was totally responsible. Cadets in the ranks drilled with the M-1, while Cadet NCOs carried the M-1 carbine slung over a shoulder at parades and during other military training events. When he became a cadet officer, Shake had to give up the shoulder weapon he loved and attend drill and ceremonies carrying an M1902 Army officers saber. There was prestige in that, but Shake missed the heft and smell of the M-1 resting on his shoulder. He often went to the armory to study that rifle or just play with one during off hours. He was encouraged by a couple of really good Army NCOs, including a leather-tough bulldog named Staff Sergeant Walter Wheeler, who had fought through Korea with the 8th Army before he wound up at MMA as an ROTC instructor.

"Remember Wheeler?" He turned to look at Paul. "He used to be the instructor and drill-master for the Fusileers."

"I remember that dude. Hard ass, but he seemed to like you. You were on the drill team when they took State honors, right?"

"Yeah, and that was all Wheeler's doing. Worked our asses off."

"Did you know him in Vietnam?"

"No. He was with some outfit down in the Delta and I was up north on the DMZ. I didn't hear he'd gotten killed until a couple of years after the war. Hit me kind of hard."

"Always seemed odd to me," Paul shrugged. "Here's a dude lived through Korea and then he gives up cushy duty at a military school and volunteers to go back to combat. How come a guy does that?"

"You had to know Wheeler. He was a soldier, in the truest sense of that word. I think he felt like he had to go, you know, be where the action is. He was probably thinking he'd save some of us from going if he volunteered—something like that, I guess."

"I guess. Anyway, we don't have guys like that anymore."

"There aren't many men like Wheeler, Pablo."

"I mean we don't have active-duty types at MMA anymore. Haven't had any for a long time now."

"What's that mean?"

"Just what it sounds like, Shake. Back in the seventies when the whole country was wrapped up in anti-war sentiment, the Army stopped assigning active duty soldiers to Junior ROTC at military schools. Needed them elsewhere, I guess. Anyway, now it's just a few retired guys. A lot of the *military* in Missouri Military Academy these days is just smoke and mirrors, fancy uniforms and drill, but the edge has gone. There's no more field exercises, and the emphasis is mostly on academics. It's more like a regimented boys-only college-prep school."

Shake pressed his forehead on an armory window. "Did they get rid of all the weapons?"

"All gone, my friend. All the drill and parades are done with dummy rifles."

"Jesus." Shake could see the rifle racks inside the armory that used to house long, oiled, and lethal lines of beautiful M-1s. Those Garands had been replaced by toys, little lightweight models of something that looked like old Springfield bolt-actions.

"C'mon, Shake." Paul grabbed at his elbow. "Let's get a look at the football field. We stay here any longer and you'll be in tears."

They stood in an upper tier of the bleachers overlooking the athletic field where Shake had played as a starting pass receiver on the MMA Colonels for a couple of years. Paul told him that football was just coming back at the academy. It had been canceled, replaced by soccer for a couple of years when doting parents got worried about injuries and the student body was flooded with rich kids from South and Central American families who knew that game much better than they did American football.

"A couple of big donors, mostly alumni that played football here, ponied up some money for equipment and we brought Colonels football back a year ago."

"How they doing?" Shake breathed in the verdant smell of well-manicured grass rising from the field below them.

"Not as well as when you were playing. We're trying to re-learn the game." Shake just nodded. He was remembering a crucial contest played against Kemper Military Academy, a traditional rival, during which he'd made two touchdowns, one on an end-around running play and the other on a long Hail Mary he caught in a scrum near the endzone and carried over for the winning score.

"You guys won the gold football your senior year. right?"

"Yeah. Kemper got caught flat-footed when we ran out that Lonesome End stuff. Coach Bailey had been watching West Point all year and decided to give it a try. He picked me to float out there because I was tall, and our quarterback would just loft the ball downfield expecting me to find a way to jump up and catch it."

"You know Kemper closed, right? And Wentworth is gone too. We're just about all that's left of military schools in the Midwest."

"Jesus. Let's go get a drink."

"I've got a last class in about a half hour." Paul pulled up a sleeve and consulted his watch. "That's about fifty minutes, and then I'll run home and change. We can meet up at a little pub I like. Remember much about downtown?"

"I remember the Liberty Theater down there. It was the make-out palace where we used to take town girls on movie dates. That still there?"

"Yeah. Kind of artsy-fartsy these days. The old section of Mexico is trying to reinvent itself without much luck." Paul pulled his phone from a uniform pocket. "Just Google Brickcity Bistro. We can get a few beers and something to eat, say…about six?"

ΔΔΔ

Shake swung by a motel on the outskirts of Mexico and got a room. He insisted on it despite Paul's invitation to stay overnight at his place. Shake was trying hard not to be depressed by the changes at MMA. He had an indistinct fuzzy-blue feeling mixed with an edge of anger. It had nothing to do with physical changes at the school. All he'd seen of that looked like improvements. But he was feeling like MMA, the place that played such a large, significant and mostly happy role in his young life, had been gutted, emasculated, turned into some sort of effete finishing school. He wanted a private room to try and digest all that, to decide how he felt about what his old roommate was telling him. He wasn't at all sure what he'd find on the other end of this trip, but the little visit to MMA had him mostly convinced that old Tom Wolfe had it right all along. Maybe you can't go home again. Or if you do, you won't much like what you find.

He parked on a side street, near what used to be the throbbing heart of downtown Mexico when he was a cadet at MMA. It was rundown and seamy along most stretches of Liberty Street, one of the major downtown thoroughfares. In some places the Chamber of Commerce was trying to preserve the art deco feel, but most of the brownstones and brick buildings seemed to sag under the weight of long neglect. Gainfully employed residents once lived here and worked nearby, but those solid citizens moved, probably following commerce as it expanded into the suburbs or bigger cities. They left the homeless, shiftless, or hopeless types Shake could see hanging around the abandoned railroad station or in darkened alleys sitting, staring, occasionally sucking from jugs wrapped in plastic bags. The old Liberty

Theater was still there, a perky gingerbread anachronism amid a short block of drab structures that straddled it. A renovated marquee advertised a double feature. Shake had never heard of either film.

Likely MMA cadets no longer brought their dates down here. So where did they go to make out, to assuage the raging hormones for a little while? He was fairly certain that important aspect of teenage life had not changed. Probably a simple matter of finding some place secluded or out of the weather and firing up the laptop, he decided, as he turned into Washington Street. Just ahead, about halfway down the block, a local entrepreneur had scrubbed one of the original brick facades and gussied it up to look like an old-timey, speak-easy joint called the Brickcity Bistro. Shake walked to it and pushed through the entry, letting his eyes adjust to the gloom, expecting to see a barkeep with waxed mustaches and sleeve garters.

The interior was your bog-standard sports watering hole featuring big-screen TVs mounted over the bar where four or five couples in preppy chic were glued to college sports broadcasts. Mizzou's Tigers were battling the Nebraska Cornhuskers in a baseball game that was tied in the top of the sixth inning. He could hear the ping of an aluminum bat as the hitter at the plate connected for a fly ball to left. There were a few other couples munching on bar snacks at mushroom tables across from the bar. Shake maneuvered around them and saw Paul waving from a booth near the rear of the joint. As Shake slid in opposite his friend, Paul shoved a mug of beer across the table. "Figured you might need this," he said. "You gotta be suffering from culture shock."

"I'd say that's fairly accurate, Pablo." Shake wiped sweat from the frosted mug and held it up to the light. Neon signs around the place proclaimed that the Brickcity Bistro proudly served Anheuser Busch products. As a Missouri native Shake had always been a little snobbish about the beer that a couple of German brewers launched on the world back in the 1850s from St. Louis. He was expecting the familiar bite of an ice-cold Bud. When he tipped the mug his nose bumped into a large slice of fresh orange. He plucked it from the foam and looked at Paul.

"What the hell is this?"

"Blue Moon," Paul laughed and held up his own mug. "You never had one before?"

"I lean toward good bourbon when I'm in a drinking mood. When I drink beer, I kind of stay loyal to Bud or Michelob, you know? Gotta be one of the best things that ever came out of St. Louis…other than the Cardinals."

"Around here these days, Bud is kind of the working man's beer, you know. Younger people like to experiment. There's all kind of IPA and local craft beers that they like. What was good enough for Dad isn't good enough for them. Things change…"

"I hope to shit in your mess kit." Shake plopped the orange wedge back in his beer and drained half of it. It wasn't bad but it wasn't the taste of Missouri beer either.

"I can get you a Bud. They've got it on tap."

"Nah, this is fine. I'll get used to it." They drank in silence for a moment, looking at each other, searching for a way to start a conversation that would cover a couple of decades since they were both cadets at MMA.

"This is weird, isn't it? I mean running into each other again after so long out of touch. Where do we start?"

"The beginning usually works best." Shake waved at the bar and held up two fingers. When fresh beers arrived, he launched into his story. He told Paul about his time in the Marine Corps, some of the places he'd served, some of the combat he'd seen in Southeast Asia and the Middle East. Paul knew about some of that, particularly some of the actions Shake was involved in during the war in Vietnam. MMA faculty made a big deal of it at the time when the war was very unpopular most other places in the country. Shake's name and graduating class were listed on a Memorial Wall of Honor at the Academy.

Shake glossed over most of the missions he'd undertaken for intelligence agencies around the world after retiring from active duty and included his first failed marriage. He spoke of his current marriage, his move to Texas, and talked for a while about his daughter. "Tracey's really something, Pablo. Big time oceanographer, doing research at Woods Hole. Commission in the Navy Reserve. Beautiful woman, smart and ambitious. I screwed up a lot of things over the years, but Tracey ain't one of them."

They ordered Reuben sandwiches and more beer. Shake started eating and tossed the conversation ball across the table. Paul filled him in on his college days, his teaching jobs all over Latin America, facilitated by fluency in Spanish, a subject that Paul excelled in at MMA and elsewhere during his education. Paul's wife was a lovely Latina that he'd met in Puerto Rico. They had one boy, but Paul had steered the kid away from MMA. He was an OU graduate, a medical doctor working free clinics in Central America. He finished with a shrug and a brief description of what he did in MMA classrooms. Paul admitted it was weird for a while. He'd hated most of his instructors at MMA, then suddenly he was one of them.

"So what do you do when you aren't teaching, Pablo? Play golf? Hang out in joints like this? What?"

"I'm really into Civil War history, Shake. I run a group of Civil War reenactors. You know? We've got all the uniforms and gear. Maybe it's a little weird like we're a bunch of Walter Mitty's or something, but I get a kick out of it."

"How come Civil War?"

"I'm an American History teacher, right? And I've always been fascinated by the Civil War. Missouri is a great place to study that."

"It is? Maybe I'm a little vague on state history but wasn't Missouri one of those neutrals, what did they call it…border state?"

"You really want me to get into this, Shake?"

"Sure. Why not?" Shake signaled a passing waiter for refills. He was thinking about one of the pictures in his pocket, the one showing a Civil War era riverboat captain. "I could use the education."

"OK, so the first thing to know about it is that Missouri was a slave state ever since it became a state back in 1821. As things heated up over the slavery issue, leading inevitably toward war, the state became increasingly important." Paul leaned back in the booth and spread his arms. He was in full classroom lecture mode. "Now Missouri was important because of the geography, right? It's in the center of the country and marks the edge of the western frontier in those days. Northern free-staters and southern slave-staters had Missouri chopped up into factions, pissing and moaning at each other right up to the start of the Civil War. When war is declared in 1861, Missouri is right in the middle of everything, and both sides know that control of the Mississippi

River, especially the economic hub at St. Louis, is crucial. So Missouri at that point becomes a strategic territory, what the Federals called the Trans-Mississippi Theater."

"Damn, I didn't realize the state was that big of a deal."

"It was huge deal. It was like the state was divided, you know, and both sides wanted control of it. By the end of the war, they figure about a hundred-thousand Missouri residents fought with the Union Army and about thirty thousand fought for the Confederacy."

"So the local Yankees had the edge."

"For the most part, but that didn't sit well with slave-owners and Southern sympathizers, mostly in the southern and western parts of Missouri. And that gave rise to some really bloody guerilla actions."

"Like Quantrill's Raiders. I studied a bit about that. For a while there, the Marine Corps was very interested in guerilla warfare."

"Yeah, guerilla leaders like Quantrill and Bloody Bill Anderson were the big names. The stuff they did was brutal. They led a ragtag bunch known as *bushwhackers*. Hence, the term to be bushwhacked."

"Did regular formations fight here? You know, infantry and cavalry regiments and like that?"

"Oh, yeah. Both sides wanted complete control of the Mississippi, and that meant they had to secure bases of operation up and down the state. There was large-unit fighting all over the area, from the Iowa and Illinois borders in the northeast to the Arkansas border in the southeast. Hell, most people don't know that the first major battle of the war west of the Mississippi took place in

August 1861 at Wilson's Creek. That's just a little southwest of Springfield."

"How'd that fight come out?"

"South won it. Union lost their first general in combat, a guy by the name of Nathaniel Lyon. It was a hell of a fight."

"Damn...I drove right by there on the way up from Texas."

"Should have stopped, Shake. It's a great place to get a feel for things military back in those days. Sometimes I take a group of cadets down there to study Missouri's role in the Civil War. Get this. If you count minor actions and skirmishes, Missouri was the site of more than twelve hundred distinct engagements between Reb and Yank outfits. Think about that, Shake. Only Virginia and Tennessee saw more action than Missouri during the Civil War."

"So does the Navy get involved? I mean, there's the Mississippi and that's a big stretch of water plus all the nearby rivers and tributaries. Seems like there'd be some naval action involved."

"Lots of it—all up and down the river with the hub of the action centered on St. Louis. The Federal forces decide they need a brown-water navy to take and keep control of the waterway that runs from Minnesota down to New Orleans, so they hire a guy named James Buchanan Eads..."

"Like in the Eads Bridge? The one that connects St. Louis with East St. Louis, Illinois?"

"The same. And Eads is a river-salvage expert, an engineer who knows every twist and turn of the river. He gets a contract to build a flotilla of ironclads for the Union, heavily armed and shallow draft so they can operate up and down the river, steam right up all the other rivers and tributaries that flow into the Big Muddy."

"So what are the Rebs doing to counter that? I know they had a Navy of some kind."

"Yeah, but not much of one compared to the Union, which has got a lot of industrial might supporting their shipbuilding efforts. By mid-war, most of the bigger Confederate ships were down south or off the southeastern shore trying to run the Union blockades. The Rebs understood they likely couldn't mount a naval force to match what the Union had on the Mississippi, so they mostly relied on building big forts up and down the river where they could try to stop the Union naval forces from pushing south. Grant and a couple of other Union generals realized the advantage gained by combining navy and army forces to gain mobility."

"Smart move. The Marine Corps is still doing stuff like that."

"And it worked a treat, Shake. By the time Vicksburg fell in summer of 1863, the Union had almost complete control of the Mississippi and that effectively split the Confederacy in half. The South's static defense on the rivers couldn't handle the Union's mobile offense which combined army and navy elements. Bottom line in a military and economic sense, losing control of the inland waterways all but dismembered the Confederacy."

Shake reached into a shirt pocket and retrieved the envelope containing the two pictures that sent him on his trip. He selected the one of the riverboat captain and pushed it across the table. "What's that look like to you, Pablo?"

Paul studied the photo for a while and then tapped it with a fingernail. "Riverboat captain or some kind of officer on a riverboat, I'd say. From the uniform, I'd expect it was sometime during the Civil War period, give or take a few years."

"Bingo. Turn it over."

Paul flipped the photo and dug out of pair of reading glasses. "Yeah, thought so. 1862. And the uniform is definitely Confederate States Navy. Who is this guy? And who is Pewter?"

Shake grinned and ran a hand through his thatch of white hair. "Pewter would be me. It's a nickname my grandparents gave me when this mop started to turn at an early age. You can forget that part—and please do—but someone thought I might wind up working on the river, I guess. I did a summer there working on tugs between my junior and senior years."

"And you've got an uncle named Fielding?"

"Not that I know of. I don't know whose uncle Fielding is. That picture was among some old family stuff and it intrigued me. That's one of the reasons I'm making this trip back here. I'd kind of like to find out about that guy and some other family stuff. Seemed to me while we were talking about the Civil War, you might be able to shed some light."

Paul adjusted his glasses and held the photo under the light hanging over their table. "The embroidery on his hat says Natchez…"

"Yeah, I looked it up. Something like seven or eight paddle-wheelers named that. Boat number six seems to fit with the date. Supposedly, it was a cotton hauler, but with the uniform and all, I was thinking maybe it was in Confederate service or something."

"You thought right, Shake. I know about this boat. Before and during the war it hauled more than just cotton from the south. The Natchez of that era was also big in the slave trade. The owners used it to transport slaves from New Orleans' markets upriver to farmers who needed labor. There were big estate owners up and down the river who bought and used slaves."

"Well, that's depressing, and entirely typical of my family, I guess. We might have been geographically Midwesterners, but down in SEMO, most folks considered themselves hard-core southerners."

"I can do some research on it, but right off the top of my head, I can tell you that the *Natchez* was involved in a famous confrontation at Tower Rock Island."

"Where's that?"

Paul fiddled with his phone and called up a Missouri Map. He enlarged and area and showed it to Shake. "Closest thing you might know would be Perryville." The map showed a little patch of green in the middle of a long blue line representing the river as it ran along Southeast Missouri toward the state's bootheel.

"I know Perryville," Shake said. "I think we played Little League baseball with them when I was a kid. This island thing looks like it's offshore between Saint Genevieve and Cape Girardeau."

"That's it. Not much there anymore, but it's a big sliver of rock that gives an excellent view up and down the stretch of river around the area."

"I'm from right around there, but I never heard of it. How is the Natchez involved?"

"Early in the war—sometime in 1862—I forget the exact date...the *Natchez* was carrying a load of recently purchased slaves from the markets down around Vicksburg upriver to some cotton plantation owner at Cape Girardeau. The story goes that the Natchez had to duck and weave a lot to avoid Union gunboats and mostly traveled at night. But one night just about the time they'd got Cape in sight, the *Natchez* was attacked by Union gunboats. The captain steered around the opposite side of Tower

Rock Island for some cover from the incoming fire. He was getting shot up pretty bad, and in the confusion, a bunch of the slaves escaped. They took shelter on the rock until the *Natchez* retreated downriver. The union sent some boats to rescue the slaves, and the story goes that a bunch of them volunteered right then to fight for the Union."

Shake stared at the picture wondering if this Uncle Fielding might have been the captain involved in that fight at Tower Rock Island. No way to know for sure, but he had some talking points for Cousin Sarah, and she might be able to connect the dots. "Pablo, this is really good stuff. I appreciate it. You know, it gives me a place to start."

"I'll do some nosing around in my reference material, Shake." He pointed at the photo. "I mean, we might be looking at the guy who skippered the *Natchez* during the fight at Tower Rock Island. Would he be Fielding Davis?"

"Beats me. But there can't be many people named Fielding, can there? If you run across that name, give me a call."

Their conversation turned to slightly more contemporary matters. Paul, the history teacher, wanted to know about Shake's experiences fighting in Hue during the communist Tet Offensive of 1968. Shake had just enough beer aboard to mess with his barriers against detailed descriptions of the one battle of his long experience in Vietnam that still bothered him, so he went through it day by day, describing his actions on the south side of the city and up to his wounding on the north side in the attack on the Citadel at Hue. He finished the tale with a shrug and a wave at a waitress for another round.

"Well, that explains a few things," Paul said reaching for an envelope on the seat next to him.

"Like what?"

"Like these…" Paul pulled two pages from the envelope and laid them on the table. They were copies of clippings from the Mexico Ledger and the MMA Eagle newspapers dated March 1968. "I did some quick searches before I came down here." He pointed at the papers. Both read the same; both had a picture of Shake lying in a hospital bed with a Silver Star and Purple Heart pinned to the sheets stretched across his chest. The headlines were slightly different but the nut of it was that a local boy, an MMA grad, was a certified hero wounded in action.

"That made a big splash in a small burg like this, Shake. You probably weren't aware of it, but relatively few of the guys in our class at MMA or graduates from around that time ever ended up serving in Vietnam. I mean, I never went, college deferment and all that. But you'd think guys from a military school would wind up in Vietnam around that time, right?"

"Probably too smart for it. Maybe the experience at MMA taught them how to stay out of fights like that."

"Still it seems weird. I've always wondered about it." Paul put the papers back in the envelope and handed it to Shake. "Take these with you. More grist for the Sheldon Davis family mill." He stood up and offered his hand. "I hate to do it, but I've gotta go, Shake. Classes in the morning." Paul picked up his phone and punched in Shake's contact information and then reached for his wallet. Shake waved him off.

"On me, Pablo. I really enjoyed seeing you again. I'm leaving in the morning, but you've got my number. Call me once in a while. I'll do the same."

He finished the beer on the table and waved off refills. When a waitress came for his credit card, he glanced up at the televisions over the bar. Mizzou had lost to Nebraska five to four in 11 innings. There was a great wave of pissing and moaning among the bar patrons as he signed the check and walked out the door. Warm air mixed with a gentle breeze cleared his head a bit as he wandered around and found his truck. It had been a hell of a day—and an interesting night—he decided as he wheeled onto Highway 54 and headed for his motel. The beer was a good idea. Took the edge off what he was feeling about MMA. That was something he could chew on during the trip down to St. Louis in the morning.

At the motel, he pulled his old Marine Corps ALICE pack out of the back of the truck and fumbled for his room key. It was stamped with Number 114, but Shake had no idea where that might be among the long row of doors leading left and right of his parking slot, so he shouldered the pack and started wandering. There was a bright pink neon beer sign flashing at one edge of the motel structure, sort of a corner bar among the guest rooms. He stared through the window and saw a row of drinkers at the bar plus a few splayed around some nearby tables. The barkeep was pouring whiskey or something besides beer into a customer's glass.

What the hell, he thought as he headed for the entrance. It was only a little after nine. Plenty of time for sleep if he was bound to get any tonight. There was a lot on his mind, a lot to contemplate and digest. A little bourbon couldn't hurt, might keep him down and out after his head hit the pillow. He walked in, nodded at a waitress hanging around the near side of the bar. Her forehead wrinkled in a frown and she stood staring at him with a weird smirk. He turned toward the dark interior and checked his fly just in case he'd forgotten to zip. Nope. He was zipped up tight.

Maybe it was the military pack or his scruffy old UT Longhorns hat. Didn't matter.

He found a table and dumped his pack. Then he stretched and scoped the array of bottles behind the bar. Looked like all the standard bar brands, but he wanted something a cut above Jack or Jim tonight. He wandered up to the bar and got a closer look. The waitress, a buxom woman with thick glasses and at least 20 pounds overload for the skirt she was wearing, put her hands on her hips and glared at him. *What the hell is her problem*, he wondered, as he looked over the liquor selection. On the top shelf he spotted Woodford Reserve and Maker's Mark flanking a bottle of his favorite when he wasn't in Texas or couldn't get TX bourbon. He caught the bartender's attention and ordered a double Bulleit on the rocks with a splash of soda water and pointed at the table where he'd left his pack.

The hefty waitress delivered his drink a few minutes later, spreading a paper napkin and then plopping the glass down hard enough to rattle the ice cubes.

"Hello, Shelly." She was staring down at him with a penciled eyebrow arched over the frames of her glasses. This had to be someone he knew from his pre-Shake days, but he couldn't remember anyone who looked like her.

"Hey, listen…I'm sorry but do I know you?"

"You remember these?" She waved a hand across her chest as if presenting her breasts for inspection. "You used to know them pretty well."

He looked at her again, squinting in the dim light. He was smiling, trying to be polite. She was not. It had to be someone who knew him from MMA…and there was only one girl, one girl he'd dated with a memorable set of…

"Becky?"

"That's me. I might have changed some, Shelly, but I recognized you the minute you walked through that door."

"Well, damn. It's great to see you." But it wasn't. The years had not been kind to his old steady girlfriend, the one he took to all the dances and formal balls at MMA, the one who loved to make out but maintained an immutable restriction that precluded much more than open and regular access to those boobs peeking over the top of her peasant blouse. He wondered how she managed to see through the thick lenses affixed to little pixie frames. They made her soft brown eyes look like magnified pinpoints, like a couple of piss-holes in a snowbank. Becky had always been short. Now she was short and stocky verging on fat, with scruffy hair cut into a bob and a bad set of teeth that screamed for dental attention.

"I always expected you to come back, Shelly. I just thought it would be a long time before this."

He gulped at his drink, trying to decide how to handle this unexpected confrontation. He remembered writing her some fairly intense mash notes after he graduated, telling her he'd come back one day, and they could get married. The Marine Corps put paid to that and he eventually stopped writing. She didn't. He got letters from her, perfumed with little hearts as punctuation marks, right up until the time he went to Vietnam.

"Jesus, Becky. I'm sorry. I guess we just sort of fell out of touch."

"You fell out of touch, Shelly. I didn't."

"Well, it was Vietnam, you know…war and all that."

"Uh-huh. I know about that. I followed it in the papers. You married someone else, didn't you?" Her eyes were watering, and she mopped at the edges with a bar towel she pulled from her skirt pocket. "I waited for you, Shelly—a lot of years."

"Jesus, Becky. We were just kids then. You know how that goes…young love, first love and all that."

She put a clammy hand on his shoulder and squeezed. "I know I never stopped thinking about you. I never stopped missing you. And now you're back."

"Just a quick visit, Becky. I went out to MMA today and looked around. Leaving in the morning."

She leaned over giving him a good look at her breasts. He could smell the White Shoulders scent that he remembered from make-out dates at the Liberty Theater. "I get off at eleven. What's your room number?"

He polished off his drink. "Becky, that's not gonna happen. I'm married, and we're both way too old for that sneaky stuff."

She did a little dance step and stomped her foot. Then she reached for his empty glass and showered him with wet ice cubes. "That drink's on me, Sheldon Davis! It's been a long time coming but I'm here to tell you you're an asshole."

She stormed off and began yelling at the bartender. Everyone else in the place was staring, most grinning at the in-house entertainment they'd just witnessed. Shake picked up his pack, nodded at the crowd and left. When he finally found Room 114, he walked in and double-locked the door. If he got lucky, if Becky got the pent-up poison and frustration out of her system, he wouldn't spend the night in Mexico ignoring a jilted, long-ago lover pounding on the door. He showered quickly and collapsed on the bed. But he didn't sleep much.

They had been kept in a place that looked and smelled like a hospital—but probably was not—for nearly two weeks. Samuel Imshana and Marco guarded their room constantly. They carried little devices that caused painful shocks and herded them everywhere they went, mostly to meals in a stuffy little cafeteria and to the baths where they were ordered to scrub thoroughly twice each day.

No one believed they were waiting for anything like what they'd been promised anymore. Most believed they were in some type of American jail or prison. Maybe waiting for trial or punishment for entering America without the proper clearances. None of them knew what lay ahead as they did menial work around the building at odd times of the day, but they agreed it was not something good. You didn't need to keep men prisoner if you did not intend them some sort of harm. Two of their number, younger men who had been woodcutters and were very strong, tried to escape by running from the cafeteria toward a door at the end of a dark corridor. They were quickly caught. Both men were put in chains but not beaten or otherwise harmed except for the shocks that forced them to submit. Neither of them had been seen since. And that's when they began to get the little blue pills.

The medicine administered twice each day made Jambon Imbasa groggy, but there was no way to avoid the dosing. Each man was lined up in the corridor, the medicine was dispensed, and either the man or the woman who dressed like doctors checked their mouths with a flashlight to ensure they swallowed.

Samuel Imshana or Marco stood nearby with bottled water and one of the shock-producing devices in case anyone failed to co-operate or comply.

After the morning meal, Jambon and Desmond Amara were taken from the sleeping quarters to work in another room that was adjacent to the corridor. It was a place they had never seen before, full of machinery. The centerpiece of the room was a table beneath a brace of lights. It didn't take much imagination to real-ize it was a medical operating theater. No talking was permitted but in whispers as they passed each other, mopping the floor with a strong disinfectant, Jambon and Desmond speculated that per-haps they were being held here for some sort of medical experi-ments. Maybe that's what happened to the two men who had tried to escape.

Marco stood just outside the room they were cleaning. He was talking to another man who had brought cups of coffee. This man was older than the other two they saw regularly. He wore the same loose green hospital garb as the others, but there was some-thing different about him. He seemed confident, chatty, and ab-sorbed in some story he was relating to Marco. What little of their conversation Jambon could hear seemed to be about money. He swept his mop closer and heard an exchange during which the older man pinched Marco's tattooed forearm skin. "Just this much," the man said, "maybe half a teaspoon of ground skin and you've got five hundred dollars." The man in the medical clothing spoke English with a strange accent Jim could not immediately identify. It seemed to have an Afrikaans lilt.

"Maybe more," Marco laughed, "given all the pretty pic-tures."

Jambon's bladder was full, and he needed to empty it, but the toilet they always used was back in the sleeping quarters. He propped his mop against a wall and moved to the doorway where Marco and the other man were standing. He asked to use the toilet.

Marco merely nodded and pointed at a door on the other side of the room. "You got three minutes to piss and get back here," he said. "And leave the door open."

Jambon opened the door and found the toilet. Near the wash basin was a small window that let him look into another room much like the one they were cleaning. What he saw shocked him so badly that his urine stream stopped abruptly. On a pair of tables in that room were the two men who had been taken away after trying to escape. They appeared to be dead. They didn't look to be breathing and no man could live with the ugly gashes he saw in their chests and stomach areas. One man's leg had been laid open from hip to knee but there was no bone visible. And on the other man's body, raw, bloody muscle was visible where patches of skin had been removed from his stomach and thighs. Jambon gasped, remembering the conversation he'd overheard.

This was not some sort of medical experiment. And it was not something you did to punish a man for trying to escape. This was something else. And Jambon Imbasa had a frightening idea of what that might be.

St. Louis

There was a note pinned to his motel room door the next morning. Becky regretted "acting like an ass" last night. She was sorry. And she was still using little hearts for punctuation. At least she'd let him sleep the night in peace. It wouldn't be hard on him to see Mexico and all the associated memories in his rearview mirror. He ate a quick breakfast, gassed the truck, and swung southeast headed for St. Louis.

His plan—at least something that might pass cursory muster as a plan—was still way too vague even after all the time and miles since he'd left Texas. The experience in Mexico and at MMA had demonstrated that simply winging it involved too many emotional boobytraps. And, come to think of it, who the hell was he to impose on people, to force them back down memory lane? People had lives. That led him to thinking about his cousin Sarah. All wrapped up in the World War I mystery and his call to Charlie Rowe, he'd forgotten to give Sarah a call. She was the daughter of his Uncle Gene and Aunt Vivian. Aunt Vivian was the only female of the three Davis kids and the second born. There was an older brother. Shake's dad was the youngest of the three.

Sarah was a couple of years older than Shake. He remembered her driving him places before he was old enough for a license. And he recalled that Sarah, who had always fancied herself the official family historian, was married to a farm-equipment salesman who retired to become a professional fishing guide. They spent a good deal of time each year in Florida. Might be they were down there now. If so, he was about to hit a dead end.

He pulled into a truck stop near Warrenton, got coffee, and fired up his phone. Sarah's home number in Sikeston was in the contact list. Beyond an email address, it was the only number he had. If she was off fishing with her husband, things would get complicated. He wasn't about to spin around and head for Florida. He should have thought this all out and called before he left home. It would have been smarter and more efficient to send her the photos in an email—but that might have precluded this trip. And Shake had to admit he was having a semi-enjoyable time. The call dropped to Sarah's answering machine and he sat smiling, listening to her soft southern drawl as she chatted a message about leaving a name and number and promised to call back soonest.

"Hi, Sarah. This is a bolt from the blue I know, but it's your cousin Shake…or Sheldon, I guess. I'm near St. Louis and hoping I can come by Sikeston to see you. Got a couple of family questions, and I thought maybe you'd have the answers. Please give me a call back when you get this."

He gave his mobile number and went back to his coffee, hoping for a quick return call and idly staring around the little restaurant area of the truck stop. There were lots of customers, truckers in greasy hats and cowboy shirts, families rumpled from the road who were neck-reining rowdy kids. There were wire pinwheel displays of Missouri Mule fridge magnets, St. Louis Cardinal keychains, and other tourist tchotchkes. Nearby was a round table full of locals who looked like they gathered here regularly. Some were in casual business attire, others in bib overalls or weathered Levi's. Waitresses hovering around with aluminum coffee pots called some of the men by name. Jovial, familiar atmosphere, maybe a local Chamber of Commerce or Kiwanis Club meeting, he guessed. A burble of conversation floated over the group. It was easy to pick out the regionalisms. These guys weren't St. Louis city dudes. They had the country twang and speech cadence he remembered. It was a hillbilly mash, slightly nasal, a tendency to chew words, extending or shortening syllables.

"Sheee-it fahr," he heard a man in bibs and Purina Feeds hat say to his neighbor at the table. "Cards ain't got but a coupla gahs that maht be able to hit a bull in the ass with a bass fiddle." Lots of multi-tonal laughter at that. It was country but not Texas country or any other country, except maybe down deep in the Ozarks. Shake had grown up speaking just like that. Harassment at MMA and later in the Marine Corps embarrassed him into working on a change in the way he spoke, the words he used, the way he sounded. Over the years he'd excised most of the hillbilly, but he still occasionally slipped. He still said *git* instead of *get*. And he never knew where to place the emphasis on theater. Was is Thee-*ate*-er? Or Thee-iter?

He was halfway to his truck carrying a go-cup when his phone buzzed. It was Sarah, and she was nearly breathless with excitement over his call. It had been so long, she said. She'd been wondering about him down there in Texas. She was sorry to hear he didn't have his wife with him as they'd never met. Sarah was home and digging out all her family reference material right now. Did he have the address in Sikeston? And when did he expect to come by?

Shake had the address in Sikeston, the old place on West Gladys, and he'd likely arrive either tomorrow late or early the next day as he wanted to stop by St. Louis for a little bit. It was all OK with Sarah. Her husband was fishing in Florida, but she was home with nothing but time on her hands.

ΔΔΔ

Google The Great, Navigator to Lost Wanderers, pointed him toward downtown as he fought his way through traffic on Highway 64 past Forest Park headed due east. He could see the famous St. Louis Gateway Arch in the distance, thinking maybe he'd explore that a little bit once he…well, he wasn't sure why he wanted to make this stop on the way south following the river. Maybe it was just getting down to the water, sponging up Mississippi River atmosphere. His research notes jotted down while he was in range of free wi-fi at the Warrenton truck stop indicated the oldest part of St. Louis was around Laclede's Landing. Wikipedia said it was named for French fur trader Pierre Laclede who landed there back in 1764. It was the start of St. Louis' reputation as the commerce hub of the middle Mississippi region.

All very interesting, but what was he really after here in this city? Likely not boyhood nostalgia. He didn't remember much about St. Louis beyond a few trips north from Scott County to ride the old SS *Admiral* and a few visits while he was working tugs on the river. The stop was hard to justify from a logical perspective. The answers he was after were probably with Cousin Sarah 100 miles south.

He found a parking lot near the corner of 4th and Market, pulled into an open slot, and sat looking through the windshield at the Gateway Arch, standing just a block or two away and gleaming in mid-morning sun. Shake pulled the picture of somebody's Uncle Fielding out of a pocket and stared at it. *Well, you old Rebel Sailor, did you steer the* Natchez *into port here in St. Louis a time or two? Did you offload cotton or slaves right here?* Asking made him feel a little better about this nebulous stop on his family quest. He locked the truck and followed signs toward the riverside park and the base of the arch. Maybe he was rationalizing, but he began to feel like this might be part of another battlefield exploration. That was one of his favorite activities and he'd done it all over the world, from Western Europe to the most remote WWII battlefields of the Pacific. He was starting to obsess over the story about a river battle at Tower Rock Island.

Or maybe the attraction was something else, he admitted. Maybe he was coming to realize that things he ran away from when he left Missouri so long ago, things he really never took time to study or understand, were some kind of missing link. Like it or not, he was by birth a child of places in America that were more important than he'd ever realized. Maybe places like St. Louis and points south on the river now coming into sight had magnetism of a kind. Huckleberry Finn thought so. Tom Sawyer thought so—or at least Mark Twain thought they thought so.

Strolling through manicured grounds, weaving his way through throngs of tourists, he reached a broad esplanade. Entrance to the arch was to his left. To his right was a dock where tourists in shorts and straw hats, herding excited kids, lined up near a dock, waiting to board one of two excursion boats. The sign advertised historic Mississippi River cruises for a nominal fee. As they idled dockside absorbing the flood of paying passengers, two pristine vessels bobbed like bathtub toys in the current. One was named Tom Sawyer and the other Becky Thatcher. Nice touch. Samuel Clemens would be proud.

They looked nothing like the old SS *Admiral*, the art deco aluminum behemoth of his memory. These much smaller boats were built, trimmed, and painted to look like sets from a local production of *Showboat*. At least the music he heard from ship-board speakers wasn't from the musical. No Cap'n Andy and Queenie references here, no darkies sweating under cotton bales. PC Nazis would lawyer up and sue the city into ruin if they made that connection today. Lots of black families waiting in line for the riverboat rides. Did they have a clue about the old cotton trade and the slave supported commerce on the river? Probably not. And probably just as well. Shake decided to pass on riding the river with Tom or Becky this trip.

He got in line and paid 14 dollars for a tram ride to the top of the arch. Seemed like something he ought to do. The damn thing was completed in 1965, about the time he was headed for his first tour in Vietnam as a Lance Corporal, but he'd never actually seen it. As the line snaked slowly toward the little pods that carried passengers 630 feet up over the river and then, hopefully, back down again, he absorbed some of the data streaming on queue videos that lined the route. The arch was designed as a monu-ment to Thomas Jefferson and his ideas for American expansion in the early 1800s after the Louisiana Purchase. That sparked the flood of early pioneers and settlers who began to cross the Mis-sissippi headed west. Famed Finnish architect Eero Saarinen de-signed the Gateway Arch, and the city ponied up $13 million to get it built. Now it was a very big Missouri deal, right up there with other cash cows like Budweiser, Cardinals baseball, and Blues hockey.

The tram to the top involved riding in little pods that seated five people, all facing center with their knees touching. Shake snuggled in and smiled at a Mom, two kids, and a tattooed teen-ager whose t-shirt said he was *Bad to the Bone*. The ride up was a little jerky, the pod lurched a bit as mechanisms kept it level when ascending the curve of the arch. Through the pod door, Shake could see stairs that seemed to zig-zag upward along the route. That would be a climb of 63 stories leading to a massive heart attack for most of the tourists he'd seen waiting in line for the ride.

The view from the top was spectacular. He could see the vast urban sprawl of the city on one side and the long velvet ribbon of the Mississippi on the other. Aircraft and trucks, maybe even a few remaining railroads, now carried the bulk of American interstate commerce, but the mighty Mississippi was still busy. He could see the sort of tugs that he once helped crew maneuvering north and south for maybe 30 or 40 miles in either direction from his perspective at the top of the arch. Most of the squared bow, shallow-draft tugs looked just as he remembered them, fitted with "knees" or big plates mounted forward for pushing barges, sometimes as many as three or four, loaded with commercial cargo of all types. He spotted one tug churning behind three barges loaded with new cars heading south to showrooms in cities somewhere along the river. It had surprised him at first and later amused him that most people thought of tugs towing barges. In reality they most often pushed rather than pulled.

Tower Rock Island was somewhere down below to the south, he thought as the little pod began its descent. He looked but couldn't spot it, probably too far south or hidden behind one of the serpentine loops the river made as it curved its way down toward the delta and New Orleans. He wanted to see that little rock. He wanted to stand on it, looking around with eyes half closed - as he did on Mt. Suribachi, Iwo Jima, Bloody Nose Ridge, Peleliu, at the La Fiere Bridge in Normandy, and at Bastogne in Belgium—imagining himself in the brutal fighting at those places. Drawing on his own combat experiences, visits like that gave him a feel for what must have really happened beyond the descriptions in war novels or history tomes. He'd never been able to make a family connection to any of those places before, and he wished he'd known about Corporal Tanner Davis when he'd visited Belleau Wood years ago. Now maybe he'd get a shot at something like that right near where he grew up, right here on the Mighty Mississippi.

He gobbled a couple of hotdogs slathered in sauerkraut and mustard at a curbside stand and washed them down with a Dr. Pepper. On his way back to the lot where he left the truck, he spotted a little joint appropriately called the Tiny Bar. He ducked inside out of the noon sun and straddled a barstool. A young guy with clanking bracelets on both wrists and a tightly bound man bun took his order for a glass of draft Michelob. It was served in a tall frosted pilsner and as Shake tipped the glass, he spotted an old fly-specked black and white photo on the wall behind the bar. It showed the SS *Admiral,* looking like a big overturned aluminum bathtub, churning along the river with crowds of boaters on the lido deck waving at the camera.

"She's long gone now."

The comment came from an older gent in faded khakis and a chambray shirt two stools down from him. He was deeply tanned and wrinkled, smiling at Shake and pointing at the picture. "Name's Carl Botts," he said extending a work-roughened hand. "Long time ago, I worked on the old *Admiral.*"

Shake shook hands, gave his name and mentioned that he rode the boat as a big treat when he was a kid up to St. Louis with relatives south of Cape. "We never took her that far south," Carl said. "Mostly we just loaded up here at St. Louis (he pronounced it Sant Loose) and cruised down to Columbia, Illinois (pronounced Ill-a-noise) and then spun her around and come back upriver."

"I guess the last time I saw the *Admiral* must have been about 1957 or so. What happened to her?"

"Lots since then." Carl slid over and polished off his beer. Shake bought them both a refill. "Not makin' enough money, I guess. Anyways, they turned her into an amusement center kind of thing back in eighty-seven. That's when I got canned. No need for deckhands. Then they turned her into a casino in early nineteen-ninety. They shut that down after the gangs and all them criminal assholes begun running around down here. Them church folks was all up in arms about it, you know. Sold the damn thing for scrap in two thousand eleven."

"Well, I saw where they've still got cruises going…the Tom Sawyer and the Becky Thatcher."

Carl Botts snorted into his beer glass. "Mark Twain be rollin' over in his grave if he seen that shit."

They had another beer and Shake left. He paid for parking and then steered a course to intercept Highway 55, heading south for Sikeston. He smiled as the CD kicked in with his favorite Paul Simon collection. *I am following the river, down the highway, through the cradle of the Civil War…I'm going to Graceland…*

Not quite, Mr. Simon…but close.

Belize City

D r. Ephraim Warner, DVM, PhD, was bored with the veterinary medicine conference after the first day. He was now four days into it, finished with his presentation and gladly missing most of what his distinguished colleagues from around the world had to say. Not that he wasn't enjoying the exotic locale and the luxury hotel accommodations, but he had lots of other things on his mind. He signaled the bar boy for another pina colada and squinted into the bright sunlight glinting off the hotel's infinity pool. If he had just half of the money a messy divorce was costing him, he could buy a place right here in Belize and maybe put in one of those pools.

He was more than a little ready for that. His valuable working time these days was way too frenetic and difficult for a man who was a department head at a major midwestern university. In fact, it was potentially ruinous. He'd even had to engage in a little illegal side hustle taking care of neighborhood pets for money under the table. And money was getting increasingly tight as he paid exorbitant legal fees to a slew of voracious attorneys fighting another slew of voracious attorneys his wife had hired in St. Louis to rip off every dime he had. And if those lawyers turned up evidence on a couple of extramarital affairs he'd had with students, he was at an inglorious end to his academic career. It looked a lot like his dream of retiring to Belize or someplace like it was on a semi-permanent hold if not blown completely to bits. And that was just the long-range element of the jeopardy he was facing.

When he got back to Cape Girardeau, there was the pressing problem of the new veterinary medicine complex. The damn place was his idea, and it was running behind schedule and way over budget. The bureaucrats and bean-counters at SEMO were hounding him constantly. They'd have flatly rejected his request to attend this conference on the school's dime if it wasn't such a feather in their academic cap. And if he was forced to declare bankruptcy as his lawyers were recommending, he'd likely be fired and replaced in a heartbeat. Dr. Ephraim Warner was in a bad bind. He signed the tab for his fresh drink, tossed the spread of fruity garnish onto the pool deck, and took a long gulp.

Maybe he was just digging himself into a deeper hole, adding complications to an already complex situation, but the offer from the man who approached him shortly after he checked into the hotel was interesting. More than that, it was almost irresistible, a lifeline that might rescue him from looming disaster. The guy knew all about him when he made initial contact in the hotel bar. He was effusive in his praise for Warner's academic credentials and interested in the new veterinary medicine annex at SEMO. The meeting was certainly out of the blue, no previous inkling. The contact man said he represented Aegis Enterprises Worldwide. Dr. Warner knew something about that outfit. The university had done some business with medical research labs owned and operated by the conglomerate. At first, over a friendly drink, Dr. Warner thought perhaps he was onto a lucrative potential investor, an outfit that might help him with funding the new operation at Wittenberg. It turned out to be much more than that during a conference call with Arthur Solano, the multi-billionaire who headed the investment empire. If Dr. Warner was interested and could be trusted, there was a huge payday on offer, the kind of money that might satisfy his wife's lawyers and keep them at bay. Solano was cautious in his pitch, details to be spelled out in a later call if Dr. Ephraim Warner was interested and ready to make a deal.

After the call, Dr. Warner did some diligent research, sweating over his laptop in his hotel room, wondering if he was pondering professional suicide or looking at a deal that just might put his life and his plans back on track. The pitch was shady even absent specific detail, but Arthur Solano was the real deal, a respected investment maven who wouldn't make this kind of proposal unless he felt it was safe, at least for him. Still, there wasn't much available in public sources about the man himself which made Dr. Warner a bit leery. It was hard to believe Solano would personally condone much less fund a thing like this. On the other hand, if the money on the table was real, it might be worth the risk, and Warner was senior enough to mitigate most of that if he played it right.

Dr. Warner finished his drink and reached for his phone. The Aegis rep said the number he provided was Mr. Solano's private line. It was secure and would be answered anytime day or night.

Sikeston

S hake passed the place Marine Corps documents listed as his official home of record. It wasn't really. Cape Girardeau was merely the place he originally enlisted. He'd spent most of the early years in Sikeston or Benton which were both farther south toward the Missouri bootheel. Still, he'd decided to backtrack a bit before heading home and give Cape a quick look. Shake's Dad had been a standout football player at Southeast Missouri State University in Cape back in the days when it was just a teacher's college. That was worth a stop, he guessed. And once he scratched the itch that was driving him, he could just spin around heading for Arkansas, major highways and high speeds all the way back to Texas.

Sikeston had grown a good deal since he'd last seen it. Rolling into town he passed a few small truck-patches tumbling over with big watermelons. Huge things, nearly ready for picking at this time of year. Sikeston was known in Missouri far and wide for its crop of giant watermelons. There was even a summer festival with free iced slices of juicy, sweet melon for local kids. When Shake stayed with his Aunt and Uncle in Sikeston, his cousins showed him how to get an early start on the harvest by raiding a patch or two and running off with melons that they didn't have to share with other kids. The plunder was delicious, but the kick was in evading the local growers who usually spotted their raids and chased them off with salt-loaded shotgun rounds.

Getting showered with rock salt from some farmer's double-barrel 12-gauge stung, but it was all part of the action, the adventure. You developed a suspicious red rash that was hard to explain at bath time, but it was all wink and nod. Every kid in and around Sikeston stole watermelons in the summer. No harm done.

Shake followed directions for Sarah's house, remembering a time in Southeast Asia. He was a boot Corporal aboard a landing ship off the coast of Vietnam. They were getting ready to make an amphibious raid on what someone said was a VC staging area south of Danang. A Gunnery Sergeant was giving them a pre-landing pep talk.

"For most of you," he said, "this will be the first time you ever get shot at…" Not me, Shake smiled. I've been shot at lots of times running out of watermelon patches. But he didn't bother the Gunny with that information.

West Gladys Street was just as he remembered it. A tree-lined, lazy street bordered by sturdy frame houses, mostly painted white with contrasting wooden shutters and cared for by long-time residents. Most of the homes were relatively ancient by modern standards with a distinct antebellum architecture featuring big gabled front porches, usually complete with a couple of rockers or a porch-swing. When he spotted Sarah's house, the one she inherited from her Mom and Dad, it looked a lot smaller than he remembered. *Or maybe I'm just a lot bigger*, he thought, as he shut down the engine and waved at his Cousin Sarah.

She was waiting on the front porch, looking disturbingly like her mom, Shake's Aunt Vivian. She had the same bright eyes behind rimless specs and the same little laugh lines at the corner of her mouth. Sarah was taller than her mom, but everyone was as Shake remembered it. Aunt Vivian had been a little package of southern-fried dynamite, often getting right up in the grille of her two bigger brothers, Shake's dad and his Uncle Kenny, for their frequent missteps. Shake's dad was the youngest of the three kids and one of her favorite targets, given his tendency to run off behavioral rails at frequent intervals.

"Lordy, you're a sight," Sarah said giving him a muscular hug. "It's been so long…" She backed off a bit and looked him up and down. "You look just like your Dad, Sheldon."

"Sarah, I realize it's probably hopeless at this point, but could you call me Shake? I haven't gone by Sheldon for years."

"I can try," she said, opening the screen door leading into the house. "But you'll always be little Shelly to me. Let's go inside. I've got some sun tea brewing just like Mama used to make. And you can tell me all about yourself—starting with how little Sheldon Davis became Shake—whatever that means."

They walked through the cool interior of a house that Shake noticed hadn't changed much since the last time he'd seen it as a teenager. Some different furniture and appointments, but he knew the way. They were heading for a sunny breakfast nook just off the kitchen. It was Aunt Vivian's favorite spot, and there was a big sweating jug of tea on the table where the sun beat on it and turned it into the sweet tea that seemed to be a staple of the south. While Sarah busied herself with ice, glasses, and lemons, Shake gave a brief version of how he acquired the nickname

"Started in the Marine Corps, I guess. It's tough on a Sheldon in that macho environment, you know? I made rank fairly fast and that led to some of the guys calling me a "shake and bake" corporal, you know, just pop him in the oven and he comes out with stripes on his arms. Eventually that morphed into Shake, and I just stuck with it."

"Good a story as any, I guess." Sarah sat across the little kitchen table from her cousin and smiled. She cocked her head from side to side, examining him. Looking for the little kid she remembers, he guessed. He felt slightly intimidated, the same way he used to feel when he was facing her mom for some often-required disciplinary discussions. "We have a history of odd names in this family," she said topping off his iced tea.

"Yeah, Sarah, that's one of the things I wanted to talk to you about."

"Well, there's plenty of time for that. I've got a big pile of scrapbooks and research material in the living room. But I want to hear about what's happening with you. I know a good deal of the Marine Corps stuff. We got right regular updates. But how about after you retired?"

He wasn't about to get into some of the clandestine intelligence missions he'd run, so he talked about his marriage, divorce, about his daughter, and his subsequent remarriage. She made a few notes on a little scratch pad, wanting to know the family names and dates in everything he recounted. He did his best, showing her a few pictures of Tracey and Chan on his phone. She took the phone and expertly tapped into his photo files. "If it's OK, I'm gonna email some of these pictures to myself. We really need to update your branch of the family tree."

"Sure, Sarah. Have at it. I don't mean to dominate the conversation here. How's your family?"

"All good." She smiled and handed his phone back. "Jim's down in Florida taking some high-rollers out fishing. Be back next week, he says. My two kids are all grown now. The boy is over in Kansas City running a bank. He's married to a great little gal from Cape, and they've given us a couple of grandkids. My girl is in graduate school at MU, studying sociology. Lord knows what she plans to do with that."

"All still in Missouri, huh? Pretty close to the old homestead."

"Not all of us got bitten by the wander-bug, Shelly...or Shake, sorry."

"Yeah, I know. Even the ones who wandered off to the military or go to school somewhere else always seem to wind up back here, don't they? Why do you think that is, Sarah?"

"Could be lots of reasons, I guess. Sometimes they take a look at the other side of the hill and decide by comparison that this side is better. People are more comfortable with what they know, what they grew up knowing, it seems to me. All those other places where people talk differently and think differently...that can be a little scary when you're young."

"It can be scary when you're old too, Sarah." Shake chuckled and looked out a nearby window. There was a huge oak still standing out there. He'd shot his first fox squirrel out of that tree with a little .22 rifle when he was ten. "I just never felt that pull to come back here."

"Well, unlike some of us, you had a really tough time here...your Dad and all."

"Yeah, I guess." Shake frowned at a painful memory and picked up his tea glass, anxious to get off that topic.

"I'm sorry," Sarah said reaching across to touch his hand. "I didn't mean to bring up a painful subject."

"It's OK, Sarah. I've come to grips with that." But he hadn't—ever—and Shake realized he'd have to deal with it all once again now that he was so close to where it happened. "Can we take a look at some of the albums. I want to ask you about a couple of guys..." He pulled out the pictures. "I don't know them, but that's Grandma's writing on the back of the pictures, so I'm thinking maybe they're relatives."

Sarah led him into the living room where piles of photo albums and documents were laid out on a coffee table. Next to the table was an easel bearing a genealogy chart in the shape of a tree with all sorts of branches and dotted lines connecting little boxes inscribed with names and dates. She sat and examined front and back of both photos with a magnifying glass.

"Where did you get these photos?" Sarah picked up her own phone, put the pictures under a desk lamp. "I'm gonna make copies if you don't mind."

"Sure, go ahead. They were in a couple of boxes somebody sent to me after my Mom died. Most of the stuff was just childhood papers and snapshots, but those two photos puzzled me, so I wanted to do a little research, you know?" He pointed at the doughboy pictures. "For instance, I found out that this guy was Tanner Davis, but I don't know how—or if—we're related."

"You are surely related," Sarah said, carrying the picture to the easel and pointing at one of the boxes connected to his grandparents. "This is Tanner Milton Davis, and he's your great uncle, Grandpa Everett's brother. I've got some other photos of him in here." She opened one of the old albums and paged through it. He looked at a couple of shots depicting a younger version of Grandpa Everett standing next to a stooped man in a straw hat and dark glasses. Grandpa looked hale and hearty. The other guy looked stooped, frail, and damaged as he leaned heavily on a cane. "That's Tanner and our Grandad around 1920 or 21."

"He was a Marine, fought in World War I at a really famous battle," Shake said. "A buddy of mine found a citation for heroism at Belleau Wood in France. You know what happened to him?"

"Oh, yes. Granddad didn't like to talk about it much, but his brother Tanner was gassed during the war—mustard gas or something, I think. He was nearly blinded, and his lungs were just all torn up from it. He came home sometime in 1919, right back here to SEMO, but the doctors couldn't do much for him."

Sarah hesitated, chewing a lip and looking from the photo to Shake. "He just couldn't abide it, I guess. He killed himself in 1923." She pointed at a photo and obituary from a local newspaper.

"Well…" Shake mumbled. "Looks like that's another thing that runs in the family."

"I'm so sorry, Shelly. Maybe we should get some lunch and come back to this later. I've got some ground venison thawed, and I was going to make hamburgers." She headed for the kitchen before he could protest.

Deer-meat hamburgers were a treat that he hadn't enjoyed for a lot of years. They had a pleasant lunch at the kitchen table, laughing at mutual memories. Sarah had a mind for detail and regaled him with unfamiliar family stories while paging through one of her scrapbooks. When she cleared the dishes, poured more tea, and brought out big slabs of key lime pie, Shake pointed at one of the scrapbook photos that showed their grandparents posed on a porch with their three kids, circa sometime in the 1930s.

"Is the Benton house still there?"

"Still there," Sarah nodded. "In fact, it's vacant these days. The previous owners moved out and put it on the market."

"Might drop by there on the way up to Cape."

"You sure about that? Won't do you any good to pick at scabs, Shelly."

"Seems to me," he shrugged. "If you're rolling down memory lane, you should make all the pertinent stops. I spent a lot of time in that house."

"You know best, I guess." Sarah stood to clear the dessert dishes. "Let's go take a look at that second photo. I've seen it before or one like it anyway. I believe I can tell you some things about that one."

Sarah went back to her charts and documents, shuffling and searching until she found what she wanted. "I'm fairly certain this is Fielding Woody," she said pointing at the picture of the riverboat captain. "He would be from Grandma's side of the family. She was a Woody before she married Grandpa, you know, and they were all died-in-the-wool Southerners. He was from Cape and worked on riverboats from the time he was a boy. When the Civil War started, he went south, and they put him in command of the *Natchez*, I guess because he knew the river so well. So, Fielding Woody would be…let's see…a great, great uncle—two or three greats. I'd have to check to be sure, but he's related to us through Grandma's line."

"A buddy of mine told me a story about the *Natchez* and a fight down around Tower Rock Island."

"Oh, yes. That's true according to tales they told, anyway. Did you hear about the slave mutiny?"

"Well, what I heard is that he got in a fight with some Union gunboats and some slaves he was carrying escaped."

She picked up a couple of pages stapled together and handed it to him. "When the fighting started and all the Confederate sailors were busy trying to save the ship, a couple of the slaves got loose and took control. It's all in there. That's part of an oral history I found in the archives at SEMO. The university's got an extensive Civil War collection."

Shake read quietly for a while. The eyewitness was a crewman on the *Natchez* who was aboard during the Tower Rock Island fight in 1862. Shake pointed at a paragraph on the third page. "It says here that the slaves obtained some muskets and pistols and demanded the release of their companions held belowdecks. Two crewmen who tried to prevent the escape were killed."

"That's what it says," Sarah confirmed. "And it also says that Captain Fielding Woody put the slaves ashore on the island to prevent further bloodshed."

"Maybe it's just the old warhorse in me, Sarah, but I'd really like to go out there and see that island."

"Well, I've never been, but there can't be much there. It's just a big pile of rocks in the middle of the Mississippi."

"But it's right around Cape, and I'm headed in that direction anyway. Maybe I can get somebody up there to take me out to Tower Rock."

"Why don't you just take Jim's bass boat and go yourself? It's parked on the trailer out in the garage. Jim always keeps it tuned and full of gas. You can take the boat, launch it at Cape, and run out to Tower Rock. If you're headed home after you visit Cape, you'll have to come back by here anyway, and you can just drop off the boat then."

"You sure Jim wouldn't mind?"

"Lord no, Shelly. He's always complaining that the boat and motor need exercise. Have you got a trailer hitch on your truck?"

Jambon Imbasa did not mention what he discovered about the two dead men. As a leader, it was his responsibility to reassure his friends and what he now knew would merely sow panic. And panic would be no help in their situation. They needed a plan of escape, something that stood a chance for success. He knew it was merely a matter of time before the same ugly fate befell the rest of them. He had the germ of an idea and Jambon began to develop it at night, thinking hard as he lay on the rough cot.

On the second day after his discovery during a cleaning detail, Jim decided to confide in Desmond Amara, who was a level-headed man, an athlete who was a very swift runner. Desmond found it hard to believe at first, but Jim assured him it was true and described in detail what he'd seen from the toilet. They vowed to keep it a secret between them for now and worked on the scheme Jambon had decided to try.

All the work they had been given so far involved washing up or cleaning in one place or another, always under the watchful eye of an armed guard. None of them had been outside yet, and Jim needed to get them out of the building. He asked to speak to Samuel Imshana in private.

"Some of my people are getting sick," Jambon told him, knowing that lie would spark interest. For what was being planned, their captors would want healthy men. "Others are becoming very weak. As you know, Mr. Imshana, we are used to exercise and sunshine. We get none of that here and it is very unhealthy for us."

"There is a doctor," Samuel Imshana said. "He will examine anyone who falls sick."

"Of course, but would it not be better for everyone if we could just get outdoors for a bit each day…to walk around or do some sort of exercise?"

Two days later, the captives were taken outside for the first time. They were allowed to walk around for one hour, under guard, and confined to a small clearing. From the edges of that clearing Jambon and Desmond got an idea of the basic layout. The entire area was surrounded by a metal fence. There was a small herd of cows cropping grass near a dense thicket of woods at the rear of the building. Dogs were kept in a pen on another side. Toward the front of the building, two cars were parked. That direction seemed to be the only one that was not blocked by fencing. It was less than 50 meters from the clearing to the parking area. A fast man could cover that ground quickly.

Jambon and Desmond developed more detail at night, siting by themselves in a corner of the sleeping area. They decided to stop taking the pills and worked out a way to hide them behind the teeth at the back of their mouths. The people who gave them the medicine and checked their mouths seemed mainly concerned that none of them stuck the pills under their tongues. The ruse worked. Jambon and Desmond flushed their pills down the toilet for the next two days.

They began to set up their escape scheme. Desmond, the athlete, organized everyone into teams during the exercise period and began to teach basic calisthenics. The rest of the men, aching for distraction and physical action beyond mopping and cleaning, joined in enthusiastically. Marco and Samuel Imshana were amused by it all at first. Then they quickly became bored with watching the Nigerians heaving, leaping, and jumping around in the clearing.

In another day or two, Jambon told Desmond, it would be time to make their move.

Benton

Shake swung north to pick up Highway 55 which would lead him to Benton and then on to Cape Girardeau. He was careful making turns and kept his speed down until he got used to hauling a trailer behind the truck. Jim's bass boat was a beauty, sleek and well-appointed with a big Evinrude mounted on the stern, a sun awning, and a pair of padded fishing chairs. There were even two extra cans of pre-mixed fuel. It was the kind of boat a serious fisherman would be proud to own, and Shake didn't want to return it damaged in any way.

The town limit sign reminded visitors that Benton was the seat of Scott County and claimed a population of about 600. If that was true, the majority of Benton citizens likely lived on outlying farms or old homesteads. The center of commerce, such as it was, seemed cramped and jammed around a little downtown crossroads. Andy Legrand's bar, the shabby sweatbox of a poolroom that used to be right around that crossroad was gone now; the space was occupied by a little diner that advertised fried catfish all day. Shake had made dozens of trips from the house to Andy Legrand's when he was a kid sent to fetch his Dad home for supper. The feed store where Grandad used to play Eucher with his cronies in a back room, puffing steadily on unfiltered Old Gold cigarettes, was still there and still selling Purina animal feed of all kinds.

Just up the main drag, across from the County Courthouse, sitting in an expanse of overgrown lawn, was the Davis family homestead. He parked the truck and sat staring at the house. It looked lonely and forlorn with a for-sale sign pegged to the front porch and a realtor's lock on the front door. It was two stories but seemed rather cramped, smaller than Shake remembered. He got out of the truck but hesitated to go any closer. Shake's father had lived a lot of his younger years in that house. After the divorce, he'd returned here to live with his parents while Shake's Mom went to St. Louis for work. Shake was passed around from one bunch of relatives to another, usually back and forth between Sikeston and Benton. He was doing a Benton stand with his grandparents, right there in that house when it happened.

Shake took a deep breath, smelling the musky odors emanating from old Stinky Creek, the rancid little flow that still ran all along one side of the property. Shake and his cousins used to catch frogs down there. The malodorous black mud along the banks of what they called "the crick," always yielded fat worms that made the best bait for fishing out at Scott's Pond a mile or two on the other side of town. He'd walked that route many times as a kid with a cane pole over his shoulder and an old paint can full of worms swinging from his hand, a scene like something right out of Mayberry RFD when that old cornpone sitcom was running on TV. When he'd return with a stringer of bass, crappie, or bluegill, Grandma always fried them up for supper. Just like she always fried up the squirrels, birds, or rabbits they brought home from hunting in the woods nearby. She was the best game cook in the business according to everyone in the family. The kind of woman who always put little shot glasses by each table setting so friends and family could spit out the shotgun pellets that often remained in the meat.

On the trip up from Sikeston, Shake decided he needed to stop here, walk the ground, test his mettle, and confront the ghosts. He knew it would be a challenge, requiring a sort of courage unlike anything he'd ever had to display in combat or other dangerous situations. He was thinking about courage as he slowly approached the Benton house. There were so many varieties of it. For so many years since the last time he'd seen this house, he wondered whether his Dad had shown courage on that fateful day or just sad desperation.

He was breathing harder than he should as he rounded the corner of the house and passed Grandma's old birdbath in the side yard. She loved to watch the wrens, starlings, cardinals, and robins who pecked at the seeds she scattered and then fluttered through a quick dip in the water. See there, she'd tell him as she identified each new arrival, birds need to take a bath just like little boys. And then he'd be bundled off to scrub himself in her old claw-foot tub.

The screened-in porch at the back of the house had been modernized with storm windows, but the steps were still there. He was half expecting a bloody specter to rise and moan, but it was quiet here except for the drone of locusts and the occasional hiss of tires on hot blacktop. Shake stood looking for a moment, swallowing bile that rose in his throat. He'd been digging for worms down by the creek when he heard the shotgun. Too close to the house for hunters, so he ran to investigate. And right there on those steps, when he was barely 12 years old, wearing a brand-new pair of white Converse All-Star basketball shoes, he found something that scarred him more deeply than anything before or since. The shotgun was his Dad's old 16-gauge double barrel and it had done deadly work. Shake's father was splayed out across those steps with one side of his head missing and that old shotgun resting nearby. A pool of blood formed and dripped off the steps onto Shake's new shoes. For some reason, he would never understand, he knelt right there and removed the blood-stained shoes. He threw them over a fence and then walked barefoot down the road looking for someone who knew what to do.

Shake had experienced a lot of shock in his life including close-quarters fights, wounding, combat, cultural, and stress, but nothing like what he felt for years after that. Lots of people speculated about the cause of the suicide. Some blamed the divorce, some speculated it was the constant drinking, others said it was something that his Dad had discovered during a visit to the VA Center in Cape just before he killed himself. Maybe diagnosis of a terminal disease? None of that mattered to Shake. To him the why was obvious and personal. Somehow, he felt it was his fault. Or if not entirely his fault, at least it was something he could have prevented. Maybe if he'd been a better son—or better something—to give his father a thing to be proud of, a reason to go on living, watching a solid boy grow into manhood. And then he stopped speculating about it as life and other traumas pushed the painful memories to a deeper place in his mind.

He turned his back on those steps and walked over to a fence where he'd tossed those Converse All-Stars so long ago. Right over there his Uncle Kenny had kept those two beautiful bird dogs—Queenie and Jack—that Shake had loved as a kid. They were gone, of course, long gone along with anything else that tied him to this place and this house. *Somebody will eventually buy this place,* he thought, walking back to his truck, and they'll be happy here. There are no ghosts except in my mind.

Cape Girardeau

His phone buzzed as he was programming it for best route to Cape Girardeau. It was Sarah.

"Hey, Shelly. Where are you?"

"Just about to leave Benton, Sarah."

"Did you go by the house?"

"Yeah, I did. It was…well, it was interesting."

"You OK?"

"I'm fine, Sarah. Just wanted to take a last look. I don't think I'll buy the place if that's what you're asking."

"Oh, good Lord, no. I just wanted to be sure you're not all depressed."

"I'm fine, Sarah. What's up?"

"I've been rummaging through the albums, Shelly, and I found this great picture of your Dad and Uncle Kenny. I emailed it to you just a second ago. Anyway, they're posing with a huge old gar fish that they apparently caught somewhere in one of the bayous. They had it mounted and gave it to a friend who hung it over the bar at Schindler's Tavern. You know where that is?"

"Rings kind of a vague bell…"

"Well, it's a little joint in New Hamburg. Been there forever. Local hang-out that your Dad and Uncle Kenny frequented. They used to have turkey shoots every Thanksgiving."

"It's coming back to me. I think my Dad took me there one year. He won a turkey as I recall. Brought it home and Grandma cooked it up for Thanksgiving Dinner."

"That sounds about right. Anyway, my brother tells me that dang old gar fish is still hanging up there. Got a little plaque with your Dad and Uncle Kenny's name on it. You might want to run by and get a picture or something. Brother says if you go be sure to have 'em make you a baloney-burger."

"How far is it?"

"Just four or five miles from Benton. Run up 61 and look for a sign that says State Road A."

"Maybe I'll take a look. Thanks. I'll be back by with the boat in a couple of days."

New Hamburg made Benton look like a thriving metropolis. State Road A ran right through the middle of the little burg and appeared to be the only street. If there were any houses in the area, they had to be out of sight behind the Feed Store, a hardware and farm-implement outlet and his destination. He parked and took a look at Schindler's Tavern. He'd probably been about 10 or 11 when he'd last seen it from the front seat of his Dad's 1950 Buick Roadmaster.

He walked around to the rear of the place, and memories came flooding back. There was a canvas awning stretched over a long table that had numbers painted on it. From one to five, designated shooting lanes. Downrange there were stacks of haybales that served as backdrop for shooters who fired at targets pinned to the bales. Three rounds, no scopes allowed, and tightest shot-group won what was being raffled, usually a turkey or choice cuts of venison, depending on season. His Dad was a crack shot, always had been, and he won a Thanksgiving Turkey Shoot with three .22 caliber shots that could be covered with a dime. Shake rode back to Benton with that big meaty bird resting on his lap.

He checked his phone and found the photo Sarah sent. His Dad and Uncle Kenny, looking decidedly as if they'd been celebrating for a while with beer bottles in hand. They were smiling and pointing at a huge gar, probably a good five feet long, that was mounted on a finished board. *Has to be a joke,* Shake thought as he climbed the steps toward the tavern's front door. Those damn alligator gars were every local fisherman's bane. Couldn't eat a gar as the fish had more bones than meat. They were bottom feeders who just sucked bait and wasted effort. Every time they went fishing and hooked a gar, Dad or Uncle Kenny would cuss, kill the thing and toss it on the banks for the birds to scavenge. Stuffing and mounting a gar this size had to be some kind of joke.

Schindler's was a breezy little joint lit mainly by natural light and neon signs. Stag beer was apparently the local favorite. Off the main room, there were a couple of screened porches that looked well-used. Apparently, the joint drew crowds occasionally. Inside, there were a few tables opposite a long bar, the kind of country elbow rest that featured honest beer and blood stains plus a brass footrail. Just one customer at the bar, a stumpy little man in bib overalls, no shirt, and greasy John Deere cap. He smiled brightly revealing a couple of missing incisors and pointed at a stool.

"Make y'sef to home. Marlene's out back. She be back directly." He spoke with a throaty growl that reminded Shake of Billy Bob Thornton's character in *Sling Blade*. He nodded, slid onto a stool and looked up at the gar hanging over the bar. It was still there, ugliest damn fish he could remember seeing. He turned to his fellow customer and pointed.

"Know anything about that gar up there?"

"Onliest thang I know is it's been hangin' up there long as I can remember. Cain't for the life of me unnerstan' how come somebody to mount one of them damn old gar fish." He shook his head and hit at his beer mug. "But there it is…damned if it ain't."

Marlene was a fairly good-looking brunette wearing a Schindler's Tavern t-shirt—Save Water Drink at Schindler's—who emerged from a back room wiping her hands on a towel. "Sorry," she said moving down the bar toward where Shake sat. "I was in back scrapin' the grill. Getcha something?"

Shake ordered a Stag and asked if the kitchen was open to make a baloney-burger. Marlene's eyebrows lifted. "You ain't from around here," she said, "so how come you know about baloney-burgers?"

"World famous!" He grinned and winked at her. "I've got family used to live in the area and the word about Schindler's fabulous baloney-burgers has spread."

"Shoot," Marlene laughed and plumped a beer mug down at his place. "I know that's a damn lie, but I'm glad to hear it. I'll get you a burger directly the grill heats up. Won't be too long."

"Would you mind if I came back behind the bar?" He pointed at the mounted gar. "I think my Dad and my Uncle caught that fish and brought it by here years ago."

"Sure," Marlene said and lifted a little section of the bar that gave access. "I been here five years and I always wondered about that fish. It's big but it's a damn *gar*. Who'd mount some trash fish like that?"

"You had to know my Uncle and my Dad," he said stepping onto the duckboards behind Schindler's sturdy bar. "I don't know for sure, but it was probably some kind of inside joke." He borrowed a bar towel and scrubbed at the little brass plate under the fish. His Dad and Uncle's names were there. The date was 1955. Beneath that it said, "Fisherman's Luck." He took a few snaps with his phone while Marlene went to the kitchen to make his burger.

"What's it say up there?" His neighbor at the bar was looking at the gar with renewed interest.

"Just my Dad and Uncle's name. Looks like they caught it in 1955. It says fisherman's luck."

Bib overalls snorted into his beer and followed with a wheezy laugh. "Fisherman's luck, all right. That's what you say around here when you go out after bass and get skunked. Maybe they was just wantin' to show how they caught *somethin'*…even if was just a damn old gar fish."

"Well, it's big enough. I don't think I've ever seen a gar that size."

"Oh, shoot fahr, we got 'em bigger'n that around here back in them bayous. I heard a fella say one time they caught one was a good six feet. Folks mostly kill 'em if they catch 'em. Damn things gobble up all the good eatin' fish."

The baloney-burger was surprisingly good, a beef patty fried with a slice of baloney on top and served with fresh onions and pickles. Shake kept looking up at the fish while he chatted with Marline and Mr. Sling Blade, both long-time New Hamburg residents. She said she'd gone to Sikeston High School before she married the guy who ran the hardware store next door. She might know his cousin Sarah but she wasn't sure. She did know that New Hamburg was originally just Hamburg, "named after some place in Germany," when it was founded back sometime right after the Civil War. She took his phone and swiped around a bit.

Sure enough, Schindler's Tavern had a Facebook Page. Marlene said they didn't do too many turkey shoots nowadays, but they did sponsor a golf tournament called the Cow Patty Classic.

Mr. Sling Blade was an ardent fisherman and recommended a place called Honker's just outside the Cape city limits where Shake could park his truck and launch the boat without much trouble or expense.

Wittenberg

On the fourth day of organized calisthenics, Desmond stood at the front of their group and led them through a series of exercises that had become the routine for their outdoor period. Jambon was at the back of the formation, keeping a close eye on Marco who was on guard duty that day. The Nigerians finished a long set of jumping jacks followed by push-ups. Marco watched them struggle, laughing at some of them who were having trouble with the unfamiliar exercise. Then he walked off, lit a cigarette, and pulled out his phone. Jambon gave the prearranged signal, and Desmond ordered all the men to begin running in place.

Everyone in the little clearing was doing their best, legs churning and arms swinging back and forth. Desmond shouted for more speed, his own legs pumping like pistons until he caught Jambon's nod. And then he spun and took off, running hard for the parking lot at the front of the building. Jambon followed immediately. They never slowed despite shouts from Marco to stop or he would shoot. Jambon knew that was unlikely. Bullets would damage valuable property. He ran hard, his leg muscles already loose from the exercises, and caught up with Desmond in the parking lot. He pointed and both men headed toward the dense woods that surrounded the facility.

"Go that way," Jambon shouted to Desmond once they were on the main access road. "I'll go this way. Don't stop until you find someone to help!"

Jambon ran harder than he'd ever run before with no idea where he was heading. He could hear the barking and howling of dogs, but that just gave him an extra burst of speed. He ran, panting and gasping until he found himself facing a huge river. There was a tall island out there in the middle of the river. Jambon Imbasa dove in and started swimming.

Cape Girardeau

outheast Missouri State University was a sprawling campus that dominated a good portion of Cape Girardeau. It had a rustic collegiate charm, and Shake kept thinking that it reminded him of the mythical Faber College from *Animal House* as he drove around looking for a convenient place to park his truck and trailer. He finally found a student lot with a friendly attendant who pointed him to an open slot at the rear near some parked RVs. He even provided a campus map and marked out the way to the library.

The public records section of the library contained a large section on SEMO history. Shake paged idly through some musty old compilations, reading the occasional snippet that caught his eye. He'd never known that Cape Girardeau derived from Jean Jacques Girardo, a French fur trapper that established a trading post in the area around 1730. There was more interesting stuff, but it was too easy for him to slip down a research rat-hole, so he moved to a collection of early university athletic material from the period 1919 to 1946 when SEMO was Southeast Missouri State Teacher's College. And there, in a big compendium of sports team photographs, was his Dad, crouched in the old knuckle-down lineman's stance, wearing number 11. His face was locked in a determined scowl under an old leather helmet. Dad was listed as an outstanding right end on a SEMO eleven that went 8-1 for the 1931 season in the Missouri State Athletic Association. The boy had some beef on his frame and looked like a guy who could throw in a solid block or blow through tacklers if he was carrying the ball. Shake made note of an address that promised copies of the photos for a nominal fee and headed to the library's help desk for directions to the Civil War material.

A pert student librarian told him the stacks were open only to students, or prior-approved researchers. Shake was neither, but he noted a little Marine Corps emblem pinned to her blouse and thought he might be able to play the Marine card. She was engaged to a guy who was just then up at Quantico, undergoing the Officers Qualification Course, she said with a grin when he produced his retired ID card. They planned to get married when he returned after commissioning. And maybe she could make an exception since she was about to become part of the Marine Corps family.

She called up a history major who worked at the library. He knew a great deal about the Island No. 10 naval battle that took place in 1862 near the river loop at New Madrid, but not much about Tower Island or the Confederate Vessel *Natchez*. He did, however, know where to look.

Much of what Shake found in the archives was a repeat of what Sarah had shown him earlier. He did get the count of the slaves who were either landed or revolted and escaped—both versions were indicated—and he did get the name of the captain of the CV *Natchez* which sailed from New Orleans in early March 1862. It checked. He was Captain Fielding Woody and his cargo included 500 bales of unprocessed cotton, some bundles of tobacco, a "quantity of arms and ammunition," and 20 negroes. The boat was scheduled to make port calls at Memphis and then Cape Girardeau. Likely that quantity of war materiel aboard *Natchez* was what drew Union attention.

New details about the fight indicated the *Natchez* was intercepted by two armed vessels—the USS *Carondelet* and USS *Benton*—both part of the Union Navy's Mississippi River Squadron, the Yankee version of a brown water navy operating on inland waterways. There were some line drawings of ironclad gunboats, and they looked formidable for the time. He could see cannon muzzles poking out of apertures in the superstructure and a brace of smaller carronades on the open deck spaces. The *Natchez* was described as heavily damaged after an inconclusive couple of hours of fighting and maneuvering before it escaped south. No surprise that none of the slaves were named. One account said only 10 of them volunteered to serve in the Union Army. The rest were apparently ferried upriver and released. No indication of where or what happened to them after that.

The only other useful bit of information Shake found was a couple of warnings from river mariners saying that waters around Tower Rock Island were notoriously tricky with strong currents and rapid whirlpools at certain high-water times. A quick hit on the Missouri State Fish and Game website told him the Mississippi running in the area he wanted to visit, was at high water. He left the library intending to be very careful, especially with a borrowed boat.

He stopped into an outdoor sporting goods store on the outskirts of Cape and did a little shopping for what he planned as an overnight stay on the island. He had a good amount of camping gear in the back of the truck, but he bought some aluminum foil and a folding grill that would do well over a campfire. He picked up some mosquito repellant plus a jar of what the clerk told him was guaranteed catfish bait. Shake had his little Zebco rod and reel in the truck, and he thought it might be a treat to catch and cook a fat river cat for dinner on Tower Rock Island. While he was pawing through a rack of maps, looking for one that featured a fisherman's schematic that would give him water depths and temperatures, he spotted a special sale on .45 ACP ammo. It was just standard 230-grain ball, probably reloaded range brass, but it was dirt cheap. Shake had his favorite Kimber Custom CDP pistol in a hide-out rig under the driver's seat of his truck. Maybe he'd just burn through a few cheap rounds somewhere out on the river. It had been a while since his last range session, and he liked to keep his pistol skills sharp.

The clerk knew all about Honker's launch site and gave him directions after he'd run Shake's credit card. It was just coming onto noon when he left the store. He planned to be on the river in another hour or two and at Tower Rock Island an hour or so after that.

ΔΔΔ

He paid for services and parking then backed the boat trailer into the water. It was a good rig, easily maneuvered by one man. He got the boat launched and tied up and then drove the truck and trailer to a designated parking spot. He dug his pistol out from under the seat and stuffed it and the new box of ammo into his pack. He had what he needed once he strapped his old sleeping bag and the collapsible rod-reel combo to the outside of the pack. It was a light load, but he didn't think he'd need much. It was just a little overnight outing, a camping trip to get a feel for the fight at Tower Rock Island and do a little fishing.

A dock hand was working in a line of rental boats when Shake got back down to the water. He was lean, deeply tanned, and rock hard, fussing with equipment, arranging it all around the boat. He looked like the kind of guy who knew the river. He was talking to a couple of men, one white and the other black, who did not look like they knew the river or ever had much to do with rivers of any kind. They had the requisite casual clothes and work boots, but it was different from the hand's faded jeans and ratty t-shirt. Their outfits looked fresh from J. Crew or some other preppy empo-rium. And the white guy of the two had lots of ink on his arms, full sleeves. The tats were faded and sun-bleached, but Shake rec-ognized a few of them even at a distance. Military of some kind. They were bunched around an aluminum skiff with a Mercury outboard at the rear. The gear being loaded didn't look like what you'd expect from a couple of amateur fishermen on vacation. No rods, reels, or tackle boxes. He noted two gun-sleeves going into the boat, not long enough for shotguns or rifles—just about right for an M-4 or something like it.

Shake idled around his boat, waiting for a chance to talk to the dock hand about conditions on the river. He got it when the two men walked away toward the little store near the ramp. As they turned, sun glinted off something shiny suspended around the black man's neck. Fairly elaborate whatever it was. Probably a badge, he speculated and walked over near the skiff. He smiled at the hand who was cramming a dip of Copenhagen into his lip.

"Couple of fishermen heading out?"

The dock hand shrugged and worked at his dip before he spit into the water. "Couple of guys want a little boat ride, that's all. Why you askin'?"

It was Shake's turn to shrug. "Just looks like a lot of gear…"

"Ain't no concern of yours, is it?"

"Nope. Just wanted to ask you about Tower Rock Island."

"Ain't much to know. You plannin' on headin' over there?"

"Yeah, just want to take a look at it."

"Well, ain't much there anymore. Sometimes when we got a drought and the water is real low, people can walk out to it. Water's high right now so ain't likely to be anyone around."

"I hear there's some rough water out there."

"Yep. Eddies and whirlpools and current's runnin' right strong now. You know how to handle your boat?"

"I think I can manage." Shake saw the two dudes heading back carrying plastic bags. He nodded and headed for his own boat tied up nearby. "Thanks. Sorry if I bothered you."

He was shoving his bass boat away from the shoreline when he heard the Merc fire up and watched the trio in the skiff turn north upriver. As the dock hand hunched over the motor to steer, his t-shirt pulled up at the back. There was a semi-auto pistol shoved into his jeans.

As Shake started his Evinrude and turned the boat in their wake, he had about half decided that the two passengers in the skiff were likely cops of one kind or another, maybe Feds. They ran to that type. Probably out on a hunt for some fugitive or jailbreaker. Probably a good move to bring his own pistol along this time.

Tower Rock Island

Jambon Imbasa was exhausted as he sat slumped around the small fire he'd made just below the island crest. The swim to this refuge was relatively short, but he had to fight a strong current all the way. He'd learned to deal with wild water swimming in the ocean off Lagos beaches, and that experience was his salvation in dodging the men who chased him through the forest. Now he had to calm down, think clearly, and decide on his next step. Somewhere on one side or the other of the big river that flowed around the island he had to find someone in authority, the American police, or anyone who could help him rescue the others. If he managed to swim onto the island, he could manage to swim off of —as soon as he regained some of his strength.

He tended the little blaze carefully, sitting naked with his wet clothing suspended over the flames on a rack of branches. He didn't want his pursuers to see a pillar of smoke rising from the island, so Jambon fanned the flames with his hands and glanced nervously up at the sky, ready to extinguish the fire immediately if it threatened to betray his presence on the island. Certainly, people visited here, he knew. He'd found the stone circle of a campfire site and a discarded box of wooden matches that allowed him to light the lifesaving fire, but as far as he could tell from his initial exploration, the island was deserted.

Jambon heard the sound of motors then and climbed to the top of the island where he had a clear view of both sides of the river. There was a boat approaching. Just one man in it and he was steering directly for the island. A plan began to take shape. It

might be someone from the clinic looking for him. He would
have to be very cautious if the man landed on the island. Jambon
scrambled back down to extinguish his fire and shrug into his still
damp clothing.

ΔΔΔ

The skiff ahead of Shake was making good speed, and in less than
an hour it had disappeared, turning left into some little fork that
ran off the river on the Missouri side. Shake kept his speed down,
in no hurry, enjoying the riverside sights. It was peaceful and relatively deserted. Most of the structures and domiciles along this
stretch, either in Missouri to his left or Illinois to his right, were
inland, on higher ground and hidden by verdant stands of tall wil-
low, birch or sycamore trees. Folks who lived close to the Mississippi, had learned long ago that the river could turn from a placid
stream into a raging monster in times of bad weather and floods.
Levies built by riverside communities or the Army Corps of En-
gineers could only do so much. Smart folks built inland on high
ground, where they stood a better chance of keeping rampaging
water out of their living rooms.

Shake trundled along, basking in sunlight reflecting off the
brownish water and let a hand trail over the side. He closed his
eyes and inhaled deeply. The smell was so familiar, a peaty admix-
ture of dank earth and the leafy scent of riverside plant life. Most
of the city smells, the cloying affluent of industry and internal
combustion engines, were absent here.

Ahead, just off the starboard bow of his bass boat, Shake spotted the looming shape of Tower Rock Island. His map said the
nearest little burg was a place he'd never heard of called

Wittenberg over on the Missouri side. He steered for the islet, planning to approach on the Illinois side. The big pile of limestone looked lower there, probably offering a place where he could land the boat. That's when he heard gunfire.

ΔΔΔ

Marco saw the black man dart from his right to his left, leaving the cover of one tall sycamore and heading for another on the edge of the cottonfield. He slammed the M-4 carbine into his shoulder and triggered a three-round burst. Wood chips flew, but he missed the escaped man who took off running deeper into the stand of trees. It was dark in there, and the bastard was fast. Marco fired a couple of more shots hoping to halt the man and took off in pursuit. *Go ahead and run, kafir; you'll just die tired.*

Samuel came charging into the trees from the opposite direction as Marco dropped to a knee and locked the red-dot reticle of his ACOG sight on the fleeing man's back. He fired a double-tap that drilled into the man and slammed him to the ground.

"Dammit, Marco! I said to run him down, not kill the bastard!"

"The little *kafir* runs like a fucking cheetah. We'd never have caught him."

Samuel Imshana just shook his head and walked to where the escaped man was crawling painfully, leaking blood and still trying to put distance between him and his pursuers. Marco followed and pinned the man to the ground with a boot in the middle of his bloody back.

"Desmond Amara," Samuel said, kneeling to grab the dying man by an ear. "Where is Jambon? We know he was with you." Desmond Amara just groaned and shook his head.

"He is about done," Marco said. "Might as well finish it." He aimed his carbine at the back of the man's head, but Samuel shoved at it with an angry swipe of his hand.

"The job was to keep these people alive, Marco! This is going to be difficult to explain."

"He was a dead man to begin with, Samuel. What's the difference?"

"The difference is a lot of money. The difference is a loss that we will need to explain to the people paying our keep. You get that?"

"I get it. I also know if the bastard escaped and reached whatever kind of authority they have in this place, we'd be in worse shape. I told you that exercise business was a bad idea."

"I'll handle it from here. You don't say anything. Understand?"

Marco shrugged. "So what now?"

"Now we get rid of him and see if we can find the other one before it gets dark."

Samuel Imshana flicked the safety off his carbine and fired a kill shot into the back of Desmond Amara's head.

ΔΔΔ

Someone was shooting at something a way downriver. The pops echoed off the water and carried easily in the still air. The sound was familiar and unmistakable to Shake's veteran ears. It was semi-auto stuff—larger than a handgun, smaller than a shotgun—and it was coming from the Missouri side where he'd seen the three men in the skiff disappear. There were about six shots, Shake decided, fired as double taps, so maybe the guys in that boat *were* cops and maybe they'd found a fugitive. Or maybe it was just some over-anxious squirrel-hunter. Curious, but it didn't much matter. It was a long way off and no factor in what he had planned for the rest of the afternoon and evening.

The strong eddies and whirlpools on the eastern side of Tower Rock Island were easy to see. Tree limbs and other debris floating downstream marked the dangerous spots. He steered around two of them, watching cottonwood branches and some old plastic water jugs dance in circles, pushed by strong currents. After he got a good feel for the water's behavior, he found a little inlet and steered for it. The boat bounced a bit, fighting crosscurrents, but it carried him to the island where he was able to nose up on a muddy bank. He uncoiled some plastic line and cut it into two lengths, knotting each of them to one of the bass boat's mooring eyes. Then he grabbed a couple of steel tent pegs and stepped over the side into ankle-deep water. He tied one stretch of line to a solid cottonwood tree about 10 feet up the bank and then sunk a tent peg into the earth nearby, wrapping the line securely around it. Probably overkill, but Shake was headed up to the top of the island, and he didn't want his borrowed boat to disappear in strong downstream current while he was away from it.

The climb was steep and tough. Tower Rock Island was about 80 or maybe 100 feet high at its peak. The rocky ground was mostly porous limestone that broke away easily underfoot. It took him an hour or better to make the ascent, working his way around loose patches of shale and sidling through thick scrub vegetation. He wondered how those slaves handled the climb so many years ago. Surely, they'd want to get up high, away from the musket rounds and cannonballs flying around down at water level. And like as not, they had made the climb barefoot. Tough guys. *Field hands or domestic servants?* Shake wondered as he neared the peak. He'd read somewhere that while slave labor was employed in Missouri's cotton fields, many of the slaves in the state were domestics, what the old racist rebels called "house niggers." That made him wonder if there had been any women among the slaves who escaped the *Natchez*. Probably. The research he'd seen didn't specify.

If Tower Rock Island could be said to have a peak, Shake was standing on it. The view up and down the river was panoramic and spectacular. There was not much traffic or activity. The only thing he spotted was a couple of fishing boats miles away to the south. No tugs or barges in sight, but it was still early. He turned to face south, looking downriver, and closed his eyes, imagining himself at the helm of the CV *Natchez*, standing beside old great, great uncle Fielding as he spotted Yankee gunboats approaching. Probably one headed for the Missouri side of the rock and another making for the Illinois side. The *Carondelet* and the *Benton* spoiling for a fight.

So Cap'n Woody didn't have time to turn and run. *He'd probably muster a few men with muskets topside*, Shake thought, or to man any deck armament he was carrying. Nothing he'd read indicated the *Natchez* was rigged as a warship, but they probably carried something for self-defense since they were making runs around the edge of Union territory. He turned north, looking upriver, imagining the Federal Captains giving the order to man battle stations, running the cannon inboard to prime charges in the muzzle-loaders. They didn't have much traverse, so the helmsmen would have to steer the boats and bring broadsides to bear. He saw how they might do that, turning to port or starboard against the flow of the current.

And that provided the chance old Cap'n Fielding Woody was looking for, Shake imagined. While the Yankees maneuvered, he steered the *Natchez* into a hull-defilade position right over there. Shake pointed toward the Illinois aide of Tower Rock Island. He's probably already taking incoming at that point, some balls skipping off the water and a few hitting home. Probably some wounded already and certainly a panic among the slave passengers.

And either they revolted, knocked out a few of the armed sailors, held others at bay until they all escaped and made it to the island. Or the captain, wanting to distract the attacking Yankees and get the hell out of cannon range, ordered them released and put ashore. He kind of hoped the latter was the case. He looked back toward the Illinois side of the island where his boat was moored. Either way, they'd want to get out of the line of fire and maybe set up somewhere they could signal the Yankees and get rescued. Maybe one of the slaves was standing right here and waving his shirt or something so the Union sailors could see them easily through a telescope.

And down below, Cap'n Woody had turned the *Natchez* downriver and was making his escape while being chased by Yankee cannon fire. Did the Yanks give chase? Maybe the runaway slaves saved Cap'n Woody's Confederate ass, if they distracted the Union skippers into maneuvering to pick them up instead of chasing the *Natchez* back downriver. Guess we'll never really know exactly what happened.

Shake took a last look, turning north and south, imagining this stretch of the Mississippi roiling with gunpowder smoke and overlaid with clouds of steam from straining engines. Water churning with spouts and splashes where balls went long or short of target. And the *Natchez*, splintered and shattered topside from gunfire, beating the river into froth as it fled to the south. It was a different kind of fight from what he'd experienced, but lives were on the line, an assigned mission hung in the balance, and Shake had no trouble imagining what was going on in the minds and the hearts of the men involved. The techniques of deadly combat change, but the gut-wrenching fear is always there, always the same no matter if it involves broad axes and bows, cannons and muskets, or M-16s and AK-47s. That aspect has never changed— and never will.

The irregular rock formations at the top of the island didn't offer much flat ground for a campsite, so Shake descended to what he'd call the military crest and began to scout for a piece of level ground. He found it about 30 feet below the crest line, and it looked like someone else had found it also. There were ashes inside a rough circle of stones, and the ground underneath the ashes felt warm. He stood looking around, wondering if someone else might be on Tower Rock Island. He'd spotted no one on the climb, and he couldn't hear anything carried on a gentle breeze that might suggest another human presence.

Shake laid out his camp, tucked the Kimber into a holster and strapped it onto his belt, and then picked up his fishing gear. The sun was crossing its zenith now and moving west toward the horizon. Catfish bit well in the early morning and late afternoons. He'd find a good spot near the water and see if the miracle bait he'd bought in Cape worked as advertised.

He didn't need a bobber on his line to indicate a bite. He was after catfish and when one took your bait, you had to just feel for the tug. If you were holding onto the pole, you could tell it was a cat. Crappie, bluegill, or smallmouth bass hit hard and ran. River catfish just swallowed bait and swam away slowly, tugging your line with them. He was sitting with his back up against a cottonwood on the south side of the island. He was still contemplating the riverboat battle, holding the little rod loosely in one hand and tossing pebbles with the other. His line was baited and rigged with shot that would keep his hook on the bottom. He'd felt a few nibbles, probably bluegill, and was about to reel in and check his bait when he heard a snap to his rear. It sounded like someone or something had stepped on a piece of deadfall. Out of reflex, he stood with his left hand resting on his holstered pistol.

He could see nothing much inland through the thick brush and overgrown trees. There was another snap and the sound of something moving through the scrub. Shake buried the handle of his rod in the mud and weighted it with a rock. He drew the Kimber and slowly moved inland to search for whatever it was that made the noise. Making a slow semi-circle to cover the ground about 20 meters from where he'd been fishing, he saw nothing. If some tourists or locals had landed on the island, he'd have seen them from up on the crest, or at least heard their boat. Nothing, and there was no way to spot footprints in the tangle of rocks, vines, and vegetation that covered the ground. *Maybe an animal,* he thought, *a feral dog or fox.* He hadn't seen any wildlife other than waterfowl on his climb, but there were stories about huge river rats big as beavers. Whatever it was, it was gone or hiding out of sight. Shake holstered his pistol and went back to his fishing spot willing himself to relax. Whatever it was that made the noise, it was unlikely to be any kind of serious threat.

There was something on the other end of his line when he picked up the rod. He held it steady for a little while, watching the water. The line was moving steadily downstream and when he jiggled the rod, he felt hefty resistance. *And that's Mr. Catfish.* He smiled and gave the rod a smart jerk to set the hook. The fish felt fairly good in size, and he had to walk up and down the shoreline a bit, reeling line in slowly, letting the fish play as it wished. After a while of slowly recovering line, he saw the black shadow in shallow water. It was a big flat-headed river catfish, probably about 18 inches and a good five pounds or better. Just what he wanted.

Shake landed the fish and let if flop for a bit. Removing the hook from a catfish that has swallowed bait can be a delicate operation, and he didn't have the needle-nose pliers he generally used for that chore. Cats have three very sharp fins, one dorsal and two ventral, that can open painful wounds in your hands if you don't know the trick. He picked up the fish carefully, gripped it tightly, and slid his hand along its body from the mouth backward, pressing on the fins with his palm and fingers to keep them pinned. That left Mr. Catfish defenseless, and Shake was able to retrieve the hook. He gutted his catch quickly and cut off the head, tossing the offal back into the water and washing the gut cavity carefully in river water. Catfish don't have scales. You need to peel their surface skin off carefully to keep from damaging the flesh you intend to eat. He'd take care of that once he had a fire going at his campsite. It was growing dark. Suppertime.

With a fire started and his ancient cast-iron skillet warming on the new grill, Shake poured in a light layer of corn oil and went to work on his meal. He peeled the skin off the cat carefully, working from front to rear of the fish. His old Marine K-Bar that he'd carried since he was a corporal was razor-sharp and easily sliced long strips of flesh from the cat's central skeleton. He cut them into chunks, rolled it all in an envelope of aluminum foil filled with a flour and cornmeal mixture, and tossed the battered chunks into the skillet. There was a lot of meat sizzling, and Shake didn't imagine he would eat it all. *Leftovers for breakfast in the morning,* he thought, as he put his old coffee pot on the fire alongside the skillet. *Coffee and catfish for breakfast. And ain't we just livin' large like old Huck Finn?*

The catfish chunks were delicious. Maybe it was just something issued with every guy's man card, but eating something you caught or killed just made it taste better. He ate what he wanted, wrapped the remaining fish in foil and sat by the fire for a while, drinking coffee and thinking about lots of things that he'd seen or heard over the past week. A few holes in the family blanket had been patched. A few lingering images had been confronted and either reinforced or corrected. Maybe even an old ghost had been exorcised during the stop in Benton. All in all, not a bad trip down memory lane. He'd expected more landmines than he actually encountered.

There was a huge white moon rising over the river. It seemed so close he might be able to reach out and touch it. If you held your head at the right angle and squinted, it was easy to make out the pattern of dark spots, craters and convolutions that ancient stargazers had declared was the face of the man in the moon. He walked up to Tower Rock Island's crest, thinking about slaves, and recalling a virulent time, a time that should have been joyous and triumphant, as humans first set foot on that moon.

He was mostly at loose ends. Which was not a bad way to be at a major Marine Corps base, assuming you were senior enough to avoid shit details and smart enough to keep a low profile. Shake had no problem in either area. He was what the Marine Corps called a transient, unassigned and awaiting orders. As a Staff Sergeant, he didn't have to hide and slide, dodge and duck like more junior transient Marines at the facility. In the Marine Corps, Staff NCOs were assumed to be self-motivated and busy with productive things at all times, so he mostly got a nod and pass from the people roaming the transient barracks looking for idle bodies to flesh out working parties.

His wounds, from an AK round that tore a chunk out of his right thigh, were healing nicely although he still had to concentrate through some pain to avoid limping. A week earlier, the Docs had reluctantly deemed him fit for return to duty. They didn't really think he was ready, especially when he told them he intended to go back to the combat zone, but they had their hands full with other wounded Marines who were clamoring to avoid that at all costs.

The transient barracks where Shake lived was crammed with junior Marines back from the war which had flared into deadly action again in 1969 following the brutal fighting during Tet the previous year. The papers and TV were calling it a "mini-Tet" and it was producing both a steady flow of casualties and more virulent anti-war protests on college campuses and practically everywhere else around the country. Some of that was spilling over into Camp Lejeune, where crowds of disgruntled Marines were waiting for discharge, either as a result of wounds suffered in Vietnam or expiration of their service contracts. After what they'd experienced in Vietnam, the Marine Corps and the U.S. Government writ large couldn't move fast enough or as efficiently as they'd like to get them out and back to civilian life. It was a tense time at Camp Lejeune, for those reasons and a couple of others that were only remotely related to the war.

Shake tried to maneuver around all that, be the grey man among the turmoil. He was neither angry about the war nor anxious to avoid further service in it. With his medical clearance chit in hand, Shake submitted a request for return to combat duty in Vietnam. That raised more than a few eyebrows since he'd already completed a couple of combat tours and had three Purple Hearts on his record. Shake had to work his bolt a bit, call in some favors from senior Marines he knew. As he told the Master Sergeant, an old buddy who was running the Personnel Section, Staff Sergeant Davis was a professional Marine. And professional Marines belonged where the fighting was, where their leadership and experience could help accomplish the missions and save lives. The buzzwords worked wonders with the Master Sergeant, himself a pro festooned with long service hashmarks and campaign ribbons. Shake's request was working its way up the personnel pipeline with favorable endorsements.

Now all he had to do was mill around the transient barracks until orders arrived and he could get the hell out of Camp Lejeune, running for Southeast Asia like a scalded-ass ape. He didn't like what he was seeing among the Marines at the base, particularly among the black Marines. Dr. Martin Luther King, Jr., a well-respected leader in the American Civil Rights movement, had been assassinated by a whack-job white supremacist in April, just three months earlier, and many black Americans, including a sizeable contingent in uniform, were spoiling for some sort of retribution, some decisive action they thought appropriate in a racist America. Many black men in uniform, some returned veterans, some slated for assignment to Vietnam, and others just unhappy with their lot in life, had formed cliques determined to voice their frustrations.

Shake didn't consider himself racially prejudiced although he'd come to the Marines from a segregated area of the country and from a family that held decidedly racist views. All that nonsense was gradually wiped from his psyche when he began to serve and live alongside black men. Admittedly, it had taken some time, some practical experience watching black Marines perform in service and in combat, to erase early childhood canards, but he'd long since concluded that skin color was just a genetic accident. A Marine was either good or bad, depending on how he behaved and how he performed. He didn't buy into the philosophy that all Marines were green and skin color was irrelevant. He'd seen the results of segregation, poor education, prejudice, and preferential treatment. He knew it was a factor. Still, he'd done his best to help disadvantaged men, advance their careers, and forcibly discourage hints of racial discord where and when he found it.

That left him a little confused and angry about what he was seeing at Camp Lejeune and elsewhere in the country he served. In some factions he'd encountered around the base, just being white was an indictment. It was hard not to take it personally. The tension was palpable. Shake knew in his heart that he was standing too close to a big pot that was about to boil over and when that happened people were going to get hurt. In his view, if the country exploded into racial violence—prompted by the killing of Dr. King, violent encounters with Freedom Riders in the deep south, or the war in Vietnam—progress in the Civil Rights movement was going to hindered rather than helped. And that was one of the many reasons he wanted to go back to Vietnam. Service in a combat zone, where lives were on the line constantly, where warriors of all colors and mindsets, had to cooperate and guard each other's backs, made more sense to him than the race-based animosity he was seeing in America.

Even the monumental events in space, a moon landing mission that was just then reaching culmination, didn't seem to be sufficient distraction. He headed for the base bowling alley right after evening chow. He planned to watch the American astronauts on the Apollo 11 mission land on the moon for the first time in human history. Walking past a crowd of Marines milling around outside the EM Club, he noted that all of them were black, some sporting non-regulation Afros. He heard some shouting and saw a few fists raised skyward toward a bright full moon. Hopefully that was just excitement over what was about to happen when Neil Armstrong and Buzz Aldrin attempted to land the Eagle lunar module on the surface of the moon.

The bowling alley was crowded with Marines drinking beer, all gathered around a couple of TV sets in the lobby area. Shake heard a few diehards rolling balls out on the alleys, but everyone else was glued to Walter Cronkite's narration as the landing attempt was taking place. He bought two lukewarm beers and found a place where he could see the screens. There was a digital artist's rendition of the mission running as Cronkite tensely and tersely described how the Eagle was descending toward the moon's surface. Then it switched to a grainy video transmission from the Eagle's onboard cameras. There was a wild roar as Armstrong's voice crackled in his first transmission to Mission Control in Houston. *The Eagle has landed.*

There were cheers and shouts mixed with counter arguments for silence so the crowd could hear what came next from the very first humans to set foot on a planetary surface that was not mother earth. Shake had finished one beer and started on another when Armstrong carefully descended the ladder of the lunar module. *That's one small step for man,* he said over the ping of recorders and the hiss of his breathing inside the helmet he wore, *and one giant leap for mankind.* An awestruck silence descended on the crowd of Marines, but it didn't last long. It was followed by some mumbles, and then it swelled into a roar. They were in a military bowling alley on a base in North Carolina, but everyone in the crowd around the TV sets was at that moment imagining themselves thousands of miles away in the airless reaches of space. A literally breath-taking historical moment for all Americans had just passed. All of them in the bowling alley, elsewhere at Camp Lejeune, and all across the country would likely remember where they were and what they were doing on that day at that instant.

Shake finished his beer amid the chaos, thinking he might find somewhere a little quieter to watch the rest of it. There was so much shouting and cheering that Uncle Walter and any further transmissions from the men on the moon were silenced. He walked out of the bowling alley heading for the Staff NCO barracks where a friend kept a personal TV set in his room. He'd pick up six beers at the package store and drop by to watch the wonders of the moment being transmitted live.

But he never made it further than the EM Club where the crowd he passed earlier was now a shouting, chanting mob. Black Marines were in a brawl with MPs. Senior Marines, white and black, were wading into the turmoil. He heard sirens and voices on bullhorns shouting threats. As more military police trucks screeched up to the area, smaller groups of black Marines broke off and began running into the dark. Shake found an MP officer he knew and asked if he could help.

"It's out of control," the captain told him. "We got people trashing buildings and running riot all over the base. Best thing to do is get somewhere and hunker down until we can get a handle on this."

He was nearing a block of enlisted barracks when he walked up on a bloody fistfight between three black men and two white men slugging it out beneath one of the standing lights in the nearby parking lot. The white guys were losing badly, retreating toward the barracks under a barrage of boots and fists. When he saw one of the black men pluck an Afro pick from his hair and began stabbing at an opponent with the pointed handle, Shake waded into the melee. He grabbed the nearest black man and used a hip toss to send him to the deck. The man hit the ground hard, flat on his back and stayed down trying to recover. Shouting for the white men to run for the barracks, Shake spun to confront the other two angry Marines. The partly healed wound in his leg was throbbing painfully, but he ignored that as the other two ran toward him with fists cocked.

Shake ducked under a roundhouse from the first man to reach him and drove his elbow into the man's solar plexus. The man staggered backward gasping for breath just as his buddy aimed a vicious kick, trying to sweep Shake's legs from underneath him. Catching the man's leg in mid-kick, Shake twisted and shoved. The second attacker fell backward on top of his buddy.

"What the hell are you doing?" He shouted, backing away to a point where he could see all three men. "You people knock this shit off and get back to your barracks!"

"Fuck you, honkey!" One of the black men untangled himself and got to his feet, breathing hard and staring at him through blood-shot eyes. He raised a fist. "We ain't takin' no mother-fuckin' orders from you cracker assholes no more."

"Listen up…" Shake decided he needed to be calm at this moment. They were Marines, very angry and upset, but Marines nonetheless, and they'd seen he was willing to fight. Hopefully they'd respond to authority. "My name is Staff Sergeant Davis. I don't know your names and I don't want to know them, assuming you knock this stuff off and get back to your barracks with no more trouble."

"I fought in motherfuckin' Vietnam, dude!" The black Marine that Shake had wrestled to the ground stood and advanced. "I ain't afraid of you or the motherfuckin' Marine Corps."

Shake faced him and took a step forward. "You fight along-side any white Marines over there? Or were you in some lash-up where only splibs did the fighting? My experience was we all fought together over there."

"It ain't the same." The black Marine sidled toward his buddies and they stood shoulder-to-shoulder staring at Shake. "That was The Nam, dude. This here is The World."

"And this here is the world we gotta live in until things get better. Nothing is gonna improve with you people rioting and tearing up the place. You all know that and so do I. If you've got a bitch, and I expect you do have an honest bitch, it ain't with the Marine Corps. We can work it out together, just like we did in The Nam. If you're just out to raise hell and beat up on some cracker, you can start with me."

"That's bullshit! How we gonna make it any better if we don't protest?"

"This ain't protest, dude. This is chaos, a bunch of pissed off, frustrated guys doing all the wrong things. You want change, fine. I'm all for it. But it ain't gonna happen this way."

The fight had gone out of the men he was confronting. Shake recognized that from long experience with violent encounters on and off the battlefield. He knew these men might find another mob and continue the rampage, but right now they were unsure. It was the best he could do. "Take my advice and call it a night," he said. "People are gonna get hurt, jailed or killed if this shit continues. Be Marines; don't be part of that."

The three black men glanced at each other, nodded, and trotted off into the dark. Shake entered the barracks to see what he could do for the men who'd taken the beatings. It was another mob scene with white Marines carrying improvised clubs and standing in clumps around windows and doorways. Whistles sounded and senior men from the unit housed in the barracks descended, shoving and pushing men back towards their squad bays. There wasn't much an outsider could do to help, so Shake wandered back to his barracks room. Camp Lejeune was in full riot control mode and stayed that way for most of the rest of the month.

When the worst was over a week later and Shake checked out with orders back to Vietnam in hand, the casualty count was one killed and 16 injured in one form or another. That was a good deal fewer than many others who faced court-martial, punitive discharge or jail time. His return to a line outfit and combat operations in mid-Summer, just in time for another Vietnam monsoon season, seemed like a respite, a return to things he understood and could influence for better or worse.

Tower Rock Island

S hake walked back downhill to his campsite, idly wondering if any of the angry black Marines he'd encountered at Camp Lejeune during that turbulent time many years ago might be descendants of the slaves that found their freedom right here on this rock in the middle of the Mississippi River. As he stretched out on his sleeping bag, he could see the moon shining through the trees above him, its size, shape, and brilliance unaltered by space missions. It was a comfort. Like most other people who lived a lot of their lives outdoors, he had a great appreciation for the beauty of the sky. He always tried to make time to look up, appreciating various colors and clouds above him in different parts of the world. And night skies, full of brilliant stars when he was in the field and could see them clearly beyond ambient city lights, always pleased and humbled him.

He'd sleep well under the moon and stars as he usually did but not before he did a little reading. That had become a bedtime ritual over the years. Whenever possible, Shake was in the habit of reading himself to sleep. Bedtime was when he could read slowly, absorbing and contemplating. He saw no reason to surrender that just because he was sleeping on Tower Rock Island. He rose and rummaged through his pack for the dog-eared paperback copy of Joseph Heller's *Catch-22* that he'd carried around the world. Heller's absurdist takes on military life and dark humor brought him to love and laugh with Yossarian and the other characters from an Army Air Force bomber squadron based in Italy during World War II. Serve a little time in the lunacy of war and you came to realize that there were a lot of Catch-22s, and they were both real and ridiculous.

He found the book but couldn't locate his flashlight. He searched through the rest of his gear until he remembered that he'd left the light in the boat. A quick dip into *Catch-22* seemed irresistible and he certainly had time to kill, so he carefully made his way down to his boat.

His reliable little Surefire flash was just where he'd left it resting on a pile of life vests. He snapped it on and checked the boat's mooring. All secure and nothing in sight nearby. He swept the beam across the water and spotted a couple of bullfrogs. Their amphibian eyes shown like beacons when the light hit them. He started back uphill listening to their bass croaks, remembering a story his Uncle told about hunting frogs with Shake's Dad when they were boys. Their technique involved one man sweeping a light across the water to spot frogs and the other snatching at the illuminated quarry barehanded, then plopping the newly caught croaker into a gunnysack. You had to be quick or the frog would escape. As Uncle Kenny related it, Shake's Dad was stretched out to make a snatch when he discovered that what he was about to grab was not a frog. It was actually a cottonmouth water moccasin with mouth open and fangs exposed. *Bet you never knew your Dad could walk on water.* Uncle Kenny loved to tell that story.

The climb up was easier with a light to pick out his path. Shake opened the book and settled in to read a bit. As he nestled into his sleeping bag, he noticed something was wrong. His coffee pot was missing…and so was the little foil packet that he'd made to protect the catfish leftovers. He slid back out of the bag, grabbed his pistol and swept the light over his camping gear. Nothing was missing that he could spot except the old stained coffee pot and the fish. An animal might have made off with the catfish, but he knew of nothing on four legs that drank coffee. And that meant there was likely someone else on Tower Rock Island. He checked his pack but discovered nothing missing. Whoever had visited the campsite while he was making the trip to the boat and back was hungry and thirsty, but he wasn't a thief beyond that. There were enough items of value in the pack and elsewhere in his gear that a person was unlikely to pass up if he was after valuables of any kind. He could just let it go, but he didn't think he'd sleep very peacefully if he did that. And that damned old stained and dented coffee pot had been around the world with him a time or two.

Shake extinguished his light, used a snap-link to hang it on his belt, and went into stealth mode. He began to make a slow cautious sweep of the area, working a grid pattern from high ground to lower. After about half an hour, he found a small clearing and took a knee to assess the area. Someone had been here. There was a pile of pine boughs cobbled together into a rough bed. He could smell the sharp tang of urine. A moonbeam slashed through the trees and pale light glinted off something lying in a tangle of roots. Shake approached it cautiously, following the muzzle of his pistol into the clearing. It was his coffee pot, cold and empty. He didn't want to use his light just yet. He had good night vision and there was no advantage in alerting the culprit that he was being pursued. He spotted a few newly broken branches on the other side of the clearing but nothing else. Whoever stayed here, the coffee and fish thief, was long gone. He reassembled the coffee pot and set it down where he could find it later. Then he slowly maneuvered downhill, assuming that his visitor would move away from the scene of the crime.

He was just above the spot where he'd moored his boat when he heard splashing and mumbling. He began to scramble toward the sound. Last thing he needed was for some bastard to steal his boat. And it looked like that was about to happen when Shake broke cover and snapped on his light. There was a black man, a relatively small and skinny guy in torn jeans and what was left of a pink oxford shirt standing in the boat, struggling to fit himself into one of the orange life-vests. Shake spotted a shiny amulet showing through the unbuttoned shirt. He was reminded of the thing he saw on the black cop back at Honker's boat rental. The man spotted the pistol trained on him and raised his hands. He stood there, rocking in the bass boat, blinking in the beam of the flashlight and looking as if he was about to cry.

"Please, sir…don't shoot me." It was English with a distinct foreign accent, a little British and a little Caribbean lilt. Shake didn't recognize it immediately, but the man was not a local.

"Just step out of the boat and keep your hands up where I can see them."

The black man did as instructed, looking terrified and clumsy as he stumbled onto dry ground. Shake kept the pistol pointed at him and moved closer, staying just out of arms reach.

"OK, pal. Who are you and what are you doing here?"

"My name is Jambon Imbasa," he said. The name and pronunciation made Shake think he might be African, and the man confirmed that with his next words. "I am from Nigeria. I am trying to escape…"

"Escape from what?"

The man looked to be about 30 or possibly a bit younger. He was not in great shape, thin and so terrified that Shake decided he was unlikely to make any move that couldn't be handled easily.

The stranger kept glancing around as if he was expecting someone else to appear any second.

"You can put your hands down now." The man did so and rubbed at his shoulders as if trying to massage away some pain. "And you better tell me what you're running from."

Shake expected to hear some made-up tale about being jailed for a crime the guy didn't commit and making a break from detention. He was thinking about the cops he'd seen at the boat launch site and wondering if the man trembling in front of him might be the fugitive they were after. The answer he got surprised him.

"I was taken from a ship near the city of New Orleans," he said. Along with nine other Nigerian people. We were promised work in the U.S. but the men who put us on the ship in Lagos lied. When we got off the ship, we were put into a truck and driven a long way. I escaped along with another man, but they still have the others."

"Where's this other guy?"

"I don't know, sir. We went different directions to throw off the guards. I don't know where Desmond Amara is—and I really don't know where I am."

"You're on a little island in the middle of the Mississippi River." Shake kept his light on the man who kept his own eyes on the muzzle of Shake's pistol. His experience told him the guy was telling some version of the truth as he knew it. It was a strange story, and Shake decided he wanted to hear the rest of it.

"Did you take my food and coffee from the campsite?"

"I did, sir…and I am truly sorry. I was so hungry. It's been two days since I've had anything to eat."

"Well, all you had to do was ask, Mister…what did you say your name is?"

"Jambon, sir. Jambon Imbasa, my people are the Ibo of Nigeria."

"Well, you're a long way from Nigeria, Jambon."

"Some call me Jim, sir."

"OK, Jim. I'm curious how a man from Nigeria winds up here."

"It's a very bad story, sir, very sad. I think it unlikely that you will believe it."

"Let me be the judge of that, Jim. We'll get you something to eat and you can tell me about it."

ΔΔΔ

Shake used his light to point the African upslope. When they reached the campsite, Shake nodded at a flat rock near the fire. "You sit there, Jim. I'm going to put my gun away. If you do anything stupid, it comes back out and I'll shoot you."

"I will do nothing like that, sir. I just want to reach the police. I must find the others and rescue them."

Shake dug out some dried rations and mixed them with water from his canteen. He handed over a bag of chow and a plastic spoon. "It ain't fine dining, but it'll fill your belly while you tell me your story."

"Where to start…" Jim tucked into the food, cramming mouthfuls and looking around all the time as if he expected a threat to emerge from the dark beyond the campfire.

"The beginning usually works best. Take your time and tell me about it."

"Yes, from the beginning." He paused, thinking. "About six weeks ago, a man came to our village which is north of Lagos. He was an Ibo, same as the rest of us in the village." Jim held up the amulet suspended around his neck. Shake could see it was some sort of an animal, like a lion or other big cat, hammered out of polished brass and surrounded by small gemstones. "He wore one of these to identify himself as Ibo—so he would be welcomed, so we would trust what he said. This man claimed to work for a company, an American company that was looking for laborers to work in hospitals. If we were otherwise qualified and agreed to come, we would be given permits and paid well. We were having troubles with the Boko Haram bandits, so many of us wanted to leave. We had to take tests before we were accepted for employment."

"What kind of tests?"

"Medical tests, sir. They wanted to take blood samples and be sure none of us who wanted to go had the HIV in our system. That is very prevalent in my country. Only myself and nine others were cleared. We packed up and were taken by bus to Lagos where we were to board a ship."

"And none of you suspected it might be some kind of scam?"

"I don't know, sir. The medical tests seemed like a thing that would be required for people who wanted to work in a hospital. My cousin is a midwife and she said that kind of thing was quite normal. When you are poor and desperate, when you have the Boko Haram kidnapping and killing people all around you every day, you accept many things that you might otherwise question, sir."

Shake poured some water into a cup and handed the man a granola bar. "So what happened next?"

"The ship departed Lagos. We were fairly well-treated during the voyage. The man who said he was Ibo and one other, a white man, gave us papers and helped us to fill them out. None of us had passports or any other kind of papers, but the men said all that would be taken care of when we reached America. I should have known it was too good to be true, sir."

"So you arrived in New Orleans. What happened then?"

"Nothing was as promised. We were taken off the ship before it landed at the docks in New Orleans. It was at night and we were put into a smaller craft. We went into some swamp lands and spent the night there. We were all complaining, asking questions and being eaten by mosquitos. The men had guns and they forced us to remain silent until a big truck arrived the next morning. We were loaded into that truck and driven for many kilometers. There was just a little food and water in the back of the truck, and they did not stop to let us relieve ourselves. It was a horrible journey, sir."

"Where did you wind up?"

"I don't know, sir. Somewhere not too far from here. We were taken into a building that looked like it might be a hospital. There were a few people in hospital clothing that examined us, and the air smelled of cleaning fluids. But we saw no other patients or doctors. We were kept in a locked room and always with guards around when we were fed or taken to the bathing facilities. We were made to bathe every day, much emphasis on cleanliness. They stuck needles in us and took our blood all the time. No one ever explained why. No one would tell us anything. Many of us thought it was a prison and we were being locked up for entering this country without proper papers."

"Nope. We don't do that kind of thing in this country, Jim."

"I should have known that, sir. I am an educated man. I had some university schooling in Lagos."

"Yeah, I suspected you might be. Your English is very good. Go on with your story."

"After about one week, two of our group tried to escape. They were caught and taken someplace away from the rest of us. We didn't know where or what might happen to them. But they did not return. And then they began to give us pills to swallow, twice each day. They were strong things that made us very sleepy and weak." Jim just stared at the campfire and shook his head as if he was trying to get rid of an awful image. "Another man and I were taken on a cleaning job. We had to scrub a large room with lights, beds and some machines that we were ordered not to touch. When I went to the toilet…I saw into another room. It was horrible, sir."

"What did you see?"

"The two men who were taken away earlier, sir. They were laying on low tables…and they were dead. They had cuts on their bodies." Jim drew a series of lines across his stomach and around his lower back. "I could not believe it, but I had some idea of what they might be planning for the rest of us. They were cutting out parts of our people. And we were trapped in that place. I have heard that a person's lungs and kidneys and other things could be sold and put into others who are sick. Is that true?"

"I'm guessing it is, Jim, given what you saw. And you think that's what they had in mind for the rest of you?"

"I think so, yes sir. And my friend Desmond agreed. We were looking for any chance to escape. I told the Ibo man Samuel Imshana that we needed some air, sunlight and exercise or we would all get sick. I thought that if he allowed us outside, there would be a better chance to escape. We hid the pills in our mouths and did not swallow them anymore. On the next day, they took us outside for exercise. That became the routine. One day when the guard was distracted, Desmond Amara and I ran into the woods. They came after us with dogs, but I kept ahead of them until I reached this big river. I was able to swim to this island, but I didn't know what to do next. I needed to get help, to rescue the others, but I have no idea how to do that. And then you arrived with your boat."

"Assuming you got my boat, what was your plan?"

"To find the police, sir. To find someone who would help us."

"And where were you going to take the police once you convinced them to help you?"

Jim dropped his head into his hands. "I don't know, sir. I haven't been able to think. The place where they are holding the others must be around here somewhere. I must search until I find it and then bring the police."

"And maybe I'll give you a hand with that, Jim…in the morning. Come with me."

Shake led up to the crest of Tower Rock Island. "Look around, Jim. Did you get into the water on that side of the river?" He pointed at Illinois. "Or from this side over here?" he asked indicating the Missouri side.

"From that side, sir." Jim waved a hand at Missouri.

"OK. You're gonna sleep for a while and I'm gonna do some thinking."

Shake sat by the fire watching the Nigerian toss and turn on his sleeping bag. He was fairly sure at this point, assuming all this guy said was true, that the two men he'd seen back at the boat launch were not cops after all. They were likely the two men Jim described, kidnappers out looking for a couple head of their human herd who managed to escape. It all seemed a little farfetched, but he didn't think the man was lying or making up some wild story to cover illegal entry to the U.S. If that was the case, he'd surely come up with something less fantastic and gruesome.

Shake had certainly heard of organs harvested either from volunteers who could spare a kidney or other more vital organs from people who indicated they'd be donors after death. You read about that stuff all the time. There were probably thousands of terminally ill people waiting for suitable donors and transplant of organs like kidneys, hearts, lungs, and other parts from suitable donors in short supply. If you could provide those organs there were big bucks to be made and likely few questions asked in some circles. Anytime big bucks were available, there were always slimy people willing to meet demand, laws and human decency be damned.

But were there assholes in the human race evil enough to start an organ farm chopping up innocents kidnapped from Africa? Probably. Unfortunately, there probably were assholes like that. And why not right here in the heartland, remote and centrally located to buyers from north, south, east, and west? Lord knows he'd seen enough other horrible and gruesome crimes against mankind. Why not a little black-market organ farming among people that no one was going to miss or get overly excited about in this country?

In the morning, he intended to investigate. *This is not the kind of thing that should happen in the country I love, in the country I fought for,* Shake decided. A little recon would provide a plan of action, he thought as he leaned on his pack and shut his eyes. If what Jim said was accurate, that facility couldn't be far from here.

And if he found it as described, Shake intended to bring all the law he could find on that side of the Mississippi down on it. Bastards who would do something like that needed to be killed, captured, or stopped in whatever way was most convenient. If he somehow managed to find that organ farm, he intended to bring the Missouri State Police plus every redneck gun-toting sheriff's deputy he could muster to smash the operation.

D
r. Anton Vanderhoek checked to be sure the subjects were properly anesthetized. Not that it mattered all that much. And the two assistants he'd brought with him from Johannesburg were trained and mostly reliable. Still, they sometimes did sloppy work. He couldn't tolerate that. Organs must be properly excised, stored and transported if his team was to collect the promised fees.

Using a white maker, Dr. Vanderhoek began to draw incision guides on the first of two subjects slated for the day's operations. White markers were necessary for work on subjects with such dark skin color. He'd learned that little trick doing surgery in his native country—before the incident which cost him his license to operate in South Africa. That incident also cost him his commission as an Army surgeon and a criminal conviction. He'd had a year to contemplate it all in a minimum-security prison, but he did not regret the chance he took.

A very senior officer in the South African Defense Forces needed a heart transplant. And there he was operating uselessly on a woman who was near death anyway. Dr. Vanderhoek and his SADF surgical assistants made the logical choice, a choice that would set them all up for life when the hefty fee they were promised was paid. In practical terms, it was easy, safe and very lucrative—until the family complained. The police got involved. A year in prison for all of them and revocation of medical licenses. What a travesty. What a waste of talent. But Dr. Vanderhoek and his team had recovered nicely from all that. This offer of work in America was a Godsend.

"Both kidneys and heart from this one," Dr. Vanderhoek said to one of his assistants as he marked the subject's skin and glanced up at the tray of instruments nearby. "Heart valves separately and then the entire organ. We'll do that first and then come back for the skin and bones. What about the other one?"

His chief assistant, a female who handled anesthesia and had lost her credentials along with the doctor, checked her list. "Lungs," she said. "And there is a request for the liver if it is viable."

"Have you got the containers prepared?" Dr. Vanderhoek looked over his surgical mask at his second assistant, a physical therapist and fellow convict, who was in charge of the containers used to ship the organs. "We will require one of the special ones for the heart."

The assistant pointed at a row of hard plastic containers. Each was sterilized and marked *Human Organs for Transplant*. "All ready, Doctor. The truck is standing by outside."

"And so we begin." Dr. Anton Vanderhoek snapped on an overhead light and picked up a scalpel. The men he was operating on would be dead shortly. There was no avoiding that unfortunate consequence. But it didn't bother him very much. If you had the proper perspective, it was simply a matter of give and take. As a soldier and a physician, he understood lives would be prolonged or saved by this work. One man dies, but perhaps two or three others would live.

And in a few weeks, Dr. Vanderhoek and his surgical assistants would never have to do this work, or any other kind or work, ever again.

Tower Rock Island

At dawn, Shake left Jim sleeping and retrieved his old coffee pot. He'd miss the catfish for breakfast but no reason to go without coffee. When he got back to the campsite, Jim was awake, sitting cross-legged on a rock and looking frazzled. Whatever sleep he got had apparently not refreshed the man very much. No wonder. He had friends that might be chopped up into marketable body parts any time now.

Shake made coffee, poured some for himself, and then handed a cup to his new friend. He still had some reservations, but a night of thinking it over had brought him to a few decisions. He was going to look into this thing, help the man and the others being held captive where he could. What he needed most was information. No use going to authorities with this kind of fantastic story until he had information that could lead to action. Time was the enemy right now, time and a lack of concrete information.

"So here's what we're gonna do, Jim." Shake finished off the coffee and started to break camp. "We're gonna take my boat and cruise downriver for a little while. I think I know a place to start looking." He was hoping to find the little tributary where he'd spotted the three men in the rental boat turn off yesterday. "If you see anything you recognize, you just sing out. Understand?"

"I think we should go to the police, sir."

"We will, but first we need to know where to send them, right? So we're gonna do a little reconnaissance. I'm a pretty fair hand at that kind of thing."

Jim helped with the packing and followed Shake downslope toward the boat landing site. "I see the markings on your pack, sir. You were a soldier?"

"Something like that, Jim. I was a U.S. Marine…for a lot of years."

"Were you in the war?"

"Which one?"

"I don't know. America has had a lot of wars."

"That's a fact. I was in the one in Vietnam and the beginnings of the one in the Middle East."

"I feel better now."

"Food and sleep will do that for you."

"No, sir. I feel better now because I have a soldier helping me. Soldiers in Nigeria are no good, but American soldiers are very good."

"Some of them are. I hope I'm one of the good guys."

"You are, sir. Many people would have just ignored me or maybe killed me."

Jim was a bit on the naïve side but no sense in disabusing him or educating him about how things work in this country. There would hopefully be time for that later. If what he suspected was true and if they could prove it, Shake had no doubt Jim and his buddies—if they were still alive and intact—would receive humane consideration from immigration authorities. The current administration was getting properly tough on illegal immigrant freeloaders these days, but what was happening to these innocent Nigerians had to be a special case.

They untied the boat and shoved it out into the current. Shake cranked the motor and steered around the whirlpools to the Missouri side of Tower Rock Island. Then he turned downstream and poured on the gas. The river was busier at this early hour. They churned past a tug pushing barges upstream and a couple of speedboats involved in what looked like a waterborne drag race, creating huge wakes that threatened to swamp the bass boat. Closer to shore, there were a few fishermen in little skiffs trying their luck and visibly bitching about the speedboats.

After about a mile, Shake slowed and began to look for the inlet where he'd seen the rental boat turn off. There were a number of them, and they all looked about the same, just little gaps in the shoreline where water from inland streams flowed into the big river. He motored on another half mile. Jim didn't recognize anything. He hadn't been watching for landmarks with dogs on his heels. Shake suspected they were having trouble because of the perspective. He'd been headed in the opposite direction when he saw the guys in the boat ahead of him make their turn. He plowed around to reverse direction and headed back upstream. He seemed to remember an old cypress tree hanging out over the water. One of the men in the bow of the boat had to shove some of its branches out of the way when they turned.

He spotted the cypress hanging over the inlet after about 30 minutes of cruising. The weeping branches were hanging low on the water. It looked like the spot he wanted. Shake steered the boat toward it, keeping the motor at low idle and making as little noise as possible. Jim shoved the branches aside and they entered the stream. There was nothing in sight except a few cottonfields glowing white in the sun on one side and flatlands on the other beyond the trees that lined the bank. The stream they were negotiating twisted and turned. Shake kept the Evinrude at trolling speed searching for a landing but didn't see anything that looked like it might have recently been used. They made a sweeping left turn around a bend and he spotted a crumbling old wooden dock with a little fishing skiff tied up to it. The boat was well used and sun bleached. It looked nothing like the aluminum boat he'd seen earlier.

Probably shouldn't be looking for the boat from Honker's, Shake thought. It was a rental. They'd have taken it back by now. Shake decided to take a little walk, and the dock provided a convenient place to moor the bass boat. They tied up and negotiated the rotting boards leading to shore. Maybe look for a country road. They walked inland from the stream. If they're using a truck to transport people, they'd need a road.

Shake helped Jim over a distinctive split-rail fence bearing a rusted sign that advertised Red Man chewing tobacco. Ahead of them was a path that skirted the cotton field. They'd gone less than a quarter mile when a growl from a patch of woods to their left halted them abruptly.

"Y'all kin just freeze right where yer standin'."

Shake saw a rugged looking man in jeans and a sleeveless shirt standing in the shadow of a tall cottonwood. He had a well-traveled and sweat-stained Bass Pro cap jammed on his head and wisps of white hair curling around his ears. He was small, but the shotgun he was pointing at them was not. The man stepped cautiously out of the shadows and squinted at them. The shotgun never wavered.

"This here is private land. Yer trespassin'."

"Didn't mean to be." Shake shrugged and smiled. "We're looking for something and thought it might be around here somewhere."

"How come you to be packin' a pistol?" You some kind of law?"

"Nossir. We're just looking around. If we find what we're looking for, a pistol might come in handy, that's all."

"What's yer names?"

"I'm Shake Davis and this is…uh, Jim."

"And what is it yer lookin' fer that might require shootin'?"

"My friend here escaped from some men who kidnapped him. We thought they might be around here."

"Coupla fellers come by here yestiddy said they was lookin' for a black man that stole some money and run off. That be yer friend there?"

The little man came a bit closer and dropped the muzzle of the shotgun into a low-ready position. That marked him as ex-military in Shake's estimation, and he got confirmation when he spotted a faded tattoo on the man's sun-bronzed forearm.

"You a Marine?"

"Was one…long time ago."

"Well, there ain't no such thing as an ex-Marine." Shake pointed carefully at the Eagle, Globe, and Anchor embossed on the sheath of his K-Bar and then extended a hand. "Retired Chief Warrant Officer, Marine Gunner type, Semper Fi."

The man slung his shotgun over a shoulder like an experienced squirrel hunter and took Shake's hand. He stared at the hand Jim extended for a moment and then took it. He jerked his head toward the wood line. "Let's get over inta the shade. I don't mind helpin' out another Jarhead."

"I didn't catch your name, sir."

"That's cause I didn't give it. Name's Woodrow Cheeley. Most call me Woody. This here's my cotton patch and all that…" He swept a hand across a field to their right. "That's my land. And

I run a few cows on property over yonder." He waved a hand in the other direction.

Woodrow Cheeley had a nearly new Chevy Silverado parked on a gravel road that ran along his fence line. He opened the driver's door and perched on the seat, motioning for Shake and Jim to approach. He uncorked a half-pint bottle of Four Roses and took a healthy swig. "Family farm but ain't nobody left 'cept me—and it's a hard dollar, believe me. I been here since nineteen and seventy-three when I got out of the Corps." He laughed and hit the half-pint again. "Never got up as far as you did, Gunner. But I made some mighty good friends."

"Ever get to Vietnam?"

"Naw, they was windin' down over there by the time I finished trainin' and I was just a truck driver. Got as far as Okinawa though. Hell of a party over there. I wound up makin' PFC. Three times as I recollect."

"Well, Chesty Puller said you ain't a real Marine unless you been busted a couple of times."

"Old Chesty Puller." The farmer laughed and shook his head. "I ain't heard that name for a long time. Guess you really are a Marine. Nobody else would know about that."

"You said a couple of guys came by here yesterday?"

"Yep. One white man and one black one. Never give their names and I never ast. Black guy was a foreigner of some stripe or other. White guy wasn't from around here, that's fer damn sure. Talked like they was cops, or bounty hunters or somethin' like that. They was carryin' little black rifles, you know? Kind of like an M-16 but shorter with all sort of gadgets on 'em. I didn't want no truck with 'em."

"Did they say what they were doing here?"

"Like I said before, they claimed they was huntin' a black fella that stole some money and run off. I didn't buy it, and I didn't much care for their attitude either. I ain't one of them people that's prejudiced like some others around here, you know. Learned better than that in the Marine Corps." He nodded at Jim and made a little toast with his half-pint. He didn't offer to share. "Anyways, they took off after a bit and then later on, I heard gunfire..." He jerked a thumb at the field across his fence. "By the time I got over to take a look, they was long gone. If they shot somethin' or somebody, I never could find no trace of it."

"Any idea where they went?"

"They come up here on one of them rental boats from down to Honker's. I recognized that pissant Deeter works down there. They took off the same way they come. I got a picture of the damn boat." He pulled a cell phone out of his back pocket and began to fiddle with it. "Wait just a minute 'til I find it."

"You get cell phone service around here?" For some reason, Shake was surprised to see the man with a modern iPhone.

"We're fairly far out in the sticks, Gunner, but we ain't complete bumpkins." He handed Shake the phone. "Here, take a look at this."

No question it was the rental boat, and Shake could clearly see the three men in it. He spread his fingers to enlarge the shot and showed it to Jim.

"Those are the men," he said. "That one is Samuel Imshana, the one who came to our village. The other one with the tattoos is Marco, the man we met on the ship."

Shake sent the photo to his email address. He was getting an idea about how they might get a bit more information.

"Where you from, Mister?" Woodrow pointed at Jim.

"From Nigeria, sir."

"Where's that? Africa ain't it?"

"Yes, sir. On the west coast of Africa."

"You talk jist like that other fella that come by here. You know him?"

"I know him, sir. He's one of men who kidnapped me and the others."

"Bet yer glad you busted out away from them dudes."

"Yes, sir. But I'm very worried about my friends."

"Can't say I blame you fer that. Assholes that would kidnap folks is the kind of assholes need killin' if you ast me."

"Gotta find 'em first, Woody. You know anything about a hospital or a little medical facility around here?"

"Nearest hospital is down to Cape. Ain't nothin' closer." He thought for a moment. "I heard something about a new vet clinic over by Wittenberg. Supposed to be part of the university. Neighbor told me it ain't open fer bidness yet. I don't know anything about it, but we could use a place like that for cattle and other critters around here."

"You mentioned the man from Honker's, Woody. Do you know him?"

"I know him—and so does the sheriff, that's fer damn sure. Name's Deeter Manson. Used to know his Daddy before he died…God rest him. That kid'll steal you blind and he's into them damn drugs too. Don't turn yer back on him."

Shake shrugged out of his pack and dug around in one of the side pockets. Somewhere he had a Marine Corps challenge coin, a nice piece of work he'd picked up at a swap meet down in Texas with the EGA on one side and a depiction of Chesty Puller on the other. He found it and handed it to the farmer.

"We'll be going now, Woody. Thought you might like to have this."

"Ain't that something!" Cheeley turned the coin over and examined it with a beaming smile. "I surely appreciate that. Y'all just come back anytime…and good luck to ya."

They walked back to the boat and Shake checked his phone. He had two out of three bars, so there was a cell tower somewhere in the area. He wanted to make a call before they got out of range. The time differential didn't work out for a call to Chan, and he didn't want to wake her. He'd call later in the day from Cape. He scrolled through his contacts and punched up the number for Mike Stokey.

"Hey, Brother! How you doing—and where the hell are you?"

"I'm on the road, Mike. Decided to make a swing by some old stomping grounds while Chan is overseas. What are you up to? You guys leave for that cruise you were talking about?"

"Next week, Shake. We're packing now. Up and down the Rhine for ten days. I'm probably gonna be a full-on wino by the time we get home."

"If you've got some spare time, I need a favor."

"If I miss this cruise, I'll be shot at dawn."

"Shouldn't take too much time, Mike. You still tight with that FBI guy there in Vegas?"

"Ron Keene? Yeah, I see him once in a while. He always asks about you."

"Give him a call. I want to know what he and the Feds know about illegal organ harvesting. You know, if there's any file on people who cut folks up for organs that they can sell for medical facilities, stuff like that."

"Jesus, Shake. What the hell are you into?"

"Long story, but I'm thinking there's some people around here might have kidnapped some Africans—specifically Nigerians—and they're cutting them up to sell organs, maybe some kind of ghoulish black-market thing."

"I'll ask Keene, but you know he's gonna want more information."

"Just see if he knows that such things happen, Mike. If I turn up anything concrete, I'll fill him in completely."

They launched the boat, heading back toward Cape Girardeau. Jim seemed a little less anxious, as if they might be onto a trail. "Where will we go now, sir?"

"We're going to a boat dock in Cape Girardeau, Jim. I want to have a talk with Deeter Manson."

Las Vegas

That's what Shake said on the phone, Ron. Some kind of illegal deal where they harvest organs to sell for transplants. Is that really a thing?"

"Unfortunately, it probably is…"

Mike sat under a sun umbrella at a downtown Starbuck's sipping iced coffee. Across from him was Renaldo Keene, an FBI Agent and former active-duty Marine. Keene had been an MP in the service, stationed for a while on Okinawa where he met Shake and Mike. After his training at the Quantico academy, Keene's FBI star rose rapidly. He was cited for superlative work with organized crime task forces and had become somewhat of a guru on the subject. Now he was approaching mandatory retirement age. As a Nevada native, Keene asked to do his last couple of years in the Las Vegas field office.

"Damn, what some people won't do to make a buck."

"You'd be surprised, Mike." Keene plopped a manila folder bearing the FBI shield on the table. "I dug into it after you called. There are some notes in here you can read later, but the bottom line is that it's probably happening. Nothing huge as yet, but there's damn sure some unscrupulous doctors, you know, people who run medical service outfits or clinics that specialize in organ transplants."

"Yeah, but it can't be a very steady market, can it? I mean transplants require a lot of cross-matching and things like that to be sure the person getting the new organ doesn't reject it."

"It used to, Mike, but there's been some significant progress in anti-rejection drugs lately. What that means is people who need a transplant don't need to get the organ from a relative or someone completely compatible genetically. It's entirely possible right now for people to undergo successful transplants of organs from complete strangers."

"And there's your market."

"Right. So, the honest medicos have stepped up appeals for donors, but the demand will always exceed supply. And the money involved is huge. Did you know a single human body can provide raw materials for products that can sell for a couple hundred thousand?"

Mike just shook his head and examined his hands. "Hard to believe. One human meat-sack plus parts and you've got maybe a quarter mil."

"There it is. Big bucks. So then assholes get involved, and suddenly you've got a flourishing business, both above and below law enforcement radar. Basically, organ trafficking is just the business of selling organs for transplant. All legal and above board, right? Organs from volunteer donors or organs harvested from dead people, however ghoulish it sounds, is a legal market."

"But there's not enough of that to meet demand…"

"Uh-huh. And here come the profiteers. All they need to do is find someone who is not gonna be missed, someone homeless and desperate, or somebody from a foreign country. Give 'em a little money and a lot of promises, dope 'em up and start hacking out organs. Donor's dead but nobody's the wiser. The bad guys run the waiting lists and offer the organs for sale to the highest bidder."

"Don't the people who are buying or doing the transplants question any of that?"

"Records aren't hard to falsify, Mike. I mean, there's a thing called the Declaration of Istanbul which condemns organ trafficking and profiteering. Some surgeons have signed it. Others either never heard of it or don't care. Anyway, the FBI and other law enforcement agencies are aware there's likely some criminal activity, some middlemen who are making a killing—you should pardon my choice of words—from illegal organ harvesting and sale."

"Shake told me he thinks it might involve some people kidnapped from Nigeria. Does that sound reasonable."

"Don't see why not." Keene shrugged and sipped at his coffee "I mean you've got desperate people, some of whom are willing to pony up huge bucks for a viable transplant organ. So who cares where it comes from, right? You want to avoid a lot of legal hassles; you get your viable organs from someplace where no one asks a lot of embarrassing questions. You go to someplace where people are desperate. Why not a little shithole country like Nigeria?"

"That's a long way to go for organs that you've then got to get here to America before they…what…rot?"

"Think like a criminal involved in something like this, Mike. It's not likely you're gonna find some place in Nigeria or elsewhere in the third world where the appropriate operations can be safely done. So you pull in your supply in bulk. Bring them here to the States on some bullshit pretext. Then you pay some surgeon millions to do the work and you take the organs to market with phonied up documents. Won't be long before you're rolling in dough."

"Well, Shake seems to think he's onto something like that in Missouri."

"Tell him to email me with what he's got." Ron Keene handed Mike his card. "Contact's on there. If he is nosing around, he needs to pass it onto us or the local authorities. Guys who would do this kind of thing are already killers. We don't want Shake to wind up on a slab minus all his insides."

Cape Girardeau

The manager at Honker's said he didn't give a damn where Deeter Manson was. And he didn't care if he never saw the guy again. When Shake asked about him after he and Jim docked and recovered the bass boat, the ramp manager told them Deeter had been fired earlier in the day for pocketing boat rental money and a long list of other misbehaviors.

"He come back here yesterday after taking a couple of guys on a trip upriver. He only give me part of what was owed for the rental. When I asked him for the rest, he told me to stick it up my ass. That was it for Deeter. I never should have hired that crooked sonofabitch anyway."

"Any idea where I might find him?"

"Ask the sheriff. If that don't do you no good, you might drop by a joint called Pedro's out on the highway. He hangs out there every night with a bunch of other assholes selling drugs to college kids."

Shake paid the man to keep the boat and trailer for a while, promising to make up the difference if he didn't retrieve it the next day. Then he shopped around a bit at the little store. He returned to the truck with a new khaki shirt for Jim. The ripped jeans the man was wearing would have to suffice for a while. Mike called while they were getting ready to leave Honker's. Shake listened, nodding occasionally and looking over at Jim in the passenger seat of the truck. What he heard from Mike, what a seasoned and experienced FBI man speculated, convinced him that Jim's story was true.

"Thanks for the intel, Mike. I don't have enough right now, but I'm hoping to shortly. Nearest Feds are probably in St. Louis, but I'll take it to the local Sheriff. Or I think there's a Missouri Highway Patrol Barracks in Sikeston right near here. They work like a state police force."

It was nearly noon. Shake called his wife to check in and reassured her he was OK, and he'd be home in time to pick up Bear. They had some time to kill and that was making Jim nervous. He was silent as Shake drove to a little burger joint for lunch. When he got Jim into the clean shirt and pointed at the restaurant, the Nigerian was reluctant to leave the truck. He said he wasn't hungry which Shake knew was just a stall.

"I'm still thinking we should go directly to the police, sir. We should not waste time."

"Give me just a little more leeway, Jim. I think that Deeter guy, the one in the boat with the other two, probably knows something about where they might be keeping your friends. I'm gonna check that out. If my plan works, we'll go to the cops and we'll know exactly where to send them."

"But it's been almost three days since I escaped, sir. They may have already started work on the others."

"I know that, Jim, and I'm hoping we're in time with the police, but let's do it my way for a while." Shake didn't think time was as pressing as Jim did. From what little he understood about the process, transplant organs for sale needed to be carefully preserved. The people holding Jim's Nigerian friends would not want to carve anyone up too soon, before they knew what was needed, located a willing buyer, and could arrange a sale. They'd want to market fresh meat, likely wait and do the cutting at the latest possible moment, going for the organ required as they located the right middleman to arrange delivery. He didn't share that thought with Jim, but he might later. Especially if the cops were slow in making a move.

If Jim wasn't hungry, you wouldn't know it. He ate two huge burgers, a basket of fries and drank two milkshakes. "I love American food," he said licking his fingers. "There is a place in Lagos that sells American food, but I could never afford it."

"We'll get you some more for supper." Shake dropped some bills on the table and stood. "Meanwhile, I need to do a little shopping."

At the sporting goods store he'd visited earlier, Shake bought what he wanted: a pair of channel-lock pliers, some heavy-duty zip-ties, and a folding lawn chair. He took a look at Jim's ratty thongs and stopped by the footwear aisle. Jim was a fairly small man, but he had a pair of gunboats for feet. They rummaged through a ton of boxes before Shake found a pair of size 13 off-brand sneakers. Jim was a little wobbly as they headed for the check-out counter, but he was grateful.

"Very fine shoes, sir. I will repay you as soon as I'm able."

"Don't worry about it, Jim. We might have to do a little heavy work in the near future. I don't want you falling down on me."

They stopped at a roadside station where Shake topped off the truck with gas and bought some cold sodas and a couple of sandwiches. The joint had an ATM near the entrance. Shake entered his pin and withdrew $200 in fresh twenties. Then he walked out to the truck and tossed his purchases onto the front seat. Jim was biting on his lip as he eyed the sandwiches.

Shake realized he really didn't know much about the man he was trying to help.

"You a Muslim, Jim?"

"No, sir. I am a Christian—most Ibo are."

"That's good. They only had ham sandwiches."

They found Pedro's Bar about a mile outside the Cape city limits. It was a ramshackle structure with several adjoining patios and just the right rustic look to attract a wide range of customers. There was a brace of Harley's parked outside, so some of Pedro's afternoon patrons were apparently bikers. A tall sign at the entrance to the parking lot advertised live music nightly. A group called Ozark Ramblers was on for tonight beginning at 7 p.m. Shake told Jim to wait in the truck and began to walk about the place, looking for an area that would do for what he had in mind. He found a couple of big propane tanks about 50 meters from the parking lot. It would do. He returned to the truck and parked it behind the tanks. The sun was setting over a grove of sycamores to the west. It would be full dark in a couple of hours.

"Eat your sandwich, Jim. And tell me about yourself. We've got some time to wait."

They sat quietly side by side in the truck. Jim did most of the talking. He was 25, unmarried. He'd won a scholarship sponsored by the Catholic church that supported him through a year at a university in Lagos. He wanted to be a teacher one day if he could manage to finish his education. While he was in Lagos, Jim's father, an Ibo elder, was killed in a Boko Haram raid. His mother had been wounded in that raid and died a short while later. Jim was called back to assume the mantel of leadership that was generally passed down in families.

He spent too much of his time trying to get medical help for the people in his area who were spread out in a loose confederation of family and clan affiliations. HIV was a scourge in Nigeria. Rural populations were particularly hard hit, but Jim's immediate family had not been affected. Treatment for that illness and many others that plagued his people was hard to come by, and many died from lack of care. There were international medical organizations available to help rural populations, but they stopped coming when the Boko Haram guerillas stepped up their attacks.

For years the Muslim jihadis operated mostly in northeastern Nigeria with cells in bordering countries like Chad, Niger, and Cameroon. When the Nigerian military, under international pressure to do something about the situation, finally moved on Boko Haram, smaller bandit groups separated and headed south. Jim's village was right in their path and being Christians, they were priority targets. The village had been raided a number of times. Females were often kidnapped to serve as sex slaves. Those who could not escape were often forced to swear allegiance to Islam. Any opposition or resistance meant death.

It was a sad story, but it did serve to give Shake a little insight about why Jim and the others involved might fall for a scheme like the one that was pitched to them. When you're desperate and seemingly helpless, when you're given a shot at leaving all that behind, you don't ask a lot of questions. It might seem too good to be true, but there's always a chance it wasn't.

I'm assuming money is not the problem here." Arthur Solano carried a delicately etched glass half full of single-malt scotch across the well-appointed room and handed it to Dr. Ephraim Warren, DVM, PhD, Director of Veterinary Medicine at Southeast Missouri State University. "My records indicate the agreed upon sum has been transferred to the account you specified."

"It's not that at all, Arthur." Dr. Warren sipped his drink and tried to remain calm, despite jet lag and jangled nerves. He hadn't wanted to make this trip at all, but shortly after he spoke with the contact in St. Louis saying he wanted to shut down the operation, Arthur Solano had called personally saying they needed to meet, immediately and in person, to discuss the situation. And a man like Arthur Solano, the financial power behind a consortium of businesses and medical research facilities around the world, got what he wanted.

"Then why don't you tell me what's got you so upset."

Solano picked up his own drink, eased onto a couch across from his visitor, and crossed his legs. He was in his mid-70s but still slim and fit with a full head of silver hair. He'd be right at home in any corporate board room, but Arthur Solano operated only in shadows. He was strictly a financier. He left the details to others who would risk high-level business profiles.

"Any problem with the surgeon from Johannesburg? I'm told he's a top man, very discreet—and well paid, I might add."

"That's not it, Arthur. Have you heard about the incident with the men who escaped?"

"I did hear that one of your research subjects was killed. Is that what you're talking about?"

"Yes, it is." Dr. Warren gulped at his drink. Research subjects? Is that how he thinks of them? Of course, he could afford euphemisms. He kept his hands clean and his conscience—if he actually had one—uncluttered. "Arthur, that operation was always designed to be short-term and transitory. I had no idea it would last this long, or become some sort of criminal enterprise…"

Arthur Solano raised a hand to interrupt. "A criminal enterprise, Dr. Warren? You knew what was involved when we discussed it, did you not? The men running the operation do what's required to maintain security. That kind of thing sometimes requires drastic measures. And security measures are certainly in *your* best interest."

"We have no more time, Arthur. I need to shut it down immediately. There are procedures when a new facility is opened for research or operations. Inspections are required for any new off-campus facility. I can only hold that kind of thing at bay for a short time."

Arthur Solano nodded and smiled reassuringly at his guest. The whole idea had been a bit wild. But most advancements in business seemed like outlandish schemes at first. You simply had to have the courage to experiment. And the operation in Missouri was just an experiment to see how things might play out, assess the risks versus the rewards. In this case, potential profit had been phenomenal so far and risk to him personally was minimal. A veterinary research operation at a major university? Perfect cover but, as usual, these risky ventures depended on the reliability of the people involved.

"You're the man on the ground, Doctor. Let me make a few calls and we'll move the operation elsewhere. Will that make you happy?"

"We've got to be very careful, Arthur. It needs to be cleaned up thoroughly."

"Leave it to me. There are competent people who can handle all that."

"I have your assurances?" Dr. Ephraim Warren set his empty glass on the coffee table and stood to leave. He had a lot to do and a flight to make.

"Of course you do, Doctor. We'll shut down as soon as possible. Thank you for coming to see me. I've got a driver waiting to take you to the airport."

"I don't suppose there will be much need for further contact."

"Probably not." Arthur Solano rose and walked toward the door. "You've been paid for your assistance in this matter. And I'm satisfied that our business is concluded."

When the academic left to catch his flight, Arthur Solano called his man in St. Louis and ordered the Cape Girardeau operation closed, sanitized, and moved. There was a medical research clinic in Ames, Iowa that looked likely to cooperate. It was simply a matter of finding the right contact and offering the right sum of money. No sense in rushing things back into operation. They'd find the right cover to continue this business in time. And the market was certainly lucrative enough to pursue.

Haste makes waste, he thought as he mixed a nightcap. And waste creates risk. Meanwhile there was little to worry about with the Missouri operation. Who would believe such an outlandish story even if it was reported and police were prompted to investigate? It would all be gone without a trace by then. And certainly Dr. Ephraim Warren, DVM, PhD, was highly motivated to cover his own ass. On the other hand, Arthur Solano decided as he sipped his nightcap, Dr. Warren might become a liability. He'd think it over tonight. His man in St. Louis could easily arrange for the good doctor to suffer a fatal accident—perhaps a heart attack or a fatal stroke.

Cape Girardeau

J ust before full dark, the bikers who had been idling at Pedro's Bar took off in a cloud of dust and gravel. Shake watched carefully from a look-out post he'd established closer to the building but didn't see Deeter Manson aboard one of the departing hogs. As the sky grew darker and crickets began to chirp, he watched a steady stream of cars and pick-ups roll in and out of Pedro's parking lot. Some middle-aged locals, usually couples in western attire, and a steady stream of younger people arrived. Many of them emerged from vehicles with SE Missouri State campus decals. He didn't know what the max customer load was at Pedro's, but the place would be edging up on it shortly.

Deeter Manson showed up at the wheel of a beat-up Toyota Land Cruiser just about the time the Ozark Ramblers launched into their first set. The group playing inside was third rate at best, alternating between bad covers of Willie and Waylon and a few older rock numbers. What they lacked in talent they made up for in volume. *Just right,* Shake thought. Hard to hear anything over that racket.

He returned to the truck and fetched his pistol stuffing it under his shirt at the small of his back. He led Jim around to the back of the truck and pointed at the lawn chair. "Here's the plan. You set up that lawn chair over there under that tree and then stay out of sight. Got it?"

"Yes—but what will you do?"

"I'm gonna bring Deeter Manson out here and find out what he knows about this operation. He might know where your friends are being held, or at least he might know how to get hold of the guys that were with him in the boat." He picked up the channel-locks and the zip-ties. "Put these on the ground next to the chair. This is gonna get ugly, Jim. But you just stay out of sight and let me handle it."

∆∆∆

Pedro's was a zoo by the time Shake got inside and let his eyes adjust to the gloom. The only bright spots were on the stage where the band was playing, and back behind a densely packed bar. Tables and the few booths were also crowded, and the small dance floor was full of line dancers doing their version of close-order drill. If there was a Missouri ban on smoking in public places, Pedro's management were scofflaws. What little air was circulating in the place smelled of tobacco smoke, cheap perfume, and stale beer. It took a while for Shake to fight his way through the crowd at the bar. He spent that time staring into dark corners looking for Deeter Manson. He finally spotted the man perched on a stool just outside a hallway that was marked as access to the restrooms.

Manson was holding onto a bottle of Michelob, so Shake ordered two of those when he reached the bar. Then he milled around, bobbing a bit to the music. Just another guy out for a little fun, maybe looking to hook up with a woman. He kept an eye on Manson who was talking to a couple of guys. They didn't seem like Manson's type, probably looking to score some dope. The manager at Honker's said Deeter was a dealer. He didn't look like the kind of man who was into the heavy stuff. And you didn't try to peddle crack or smack in a joint like this. Probably got a stash of grass somewhere. Probably out in his vehicle.

When the two men left, Shake walked over to the spot where Deeter had cocked his stool back on two legs, leaning against the wall. He offered one of the beers.

"Remember me?"

Deeter looked at him, squinting in the gloom but made no move to accept the beer.

"Ain't you the dude asked all the questions at Honker's?"

"Yep. You want this beer or not?"

Deeter dribbled Cope into the bottle he was holding. It was apparently his field-expedient spit cup. Then he accepted the beer from Shake and nipped at it.

"What're you doin' here? Get tired of Tower Rock?"

"Nice place to visit, but I didn't want to stay long. Anyway, I was wondering if you could point me in the right direction."

"Right direction fer what?"

"I'm told this part of Missouri produces dynamite weed."

"You a cop?"

"Nope. I'm not a cop, and I avoid cops whenever possible. See, I buy good stuff for some serious people and they're always looking for local sources."

"Get the fuck away from me, man." Deeter let his stool fall back on four legs and shook his head. "You're a fuckin' cop."

"You been around long enough to know I'd have to tell you if I was. Otherwise it would be entrapment, right?"

Manson thought that over for a while, sipping at the beer and then shook his head. "I ain't interested."

"This help change your mind?" Shake pulled the cash from his pocket and used a thumb to reveal it was all twenties.

"How much?"

"Couple of hundred here. More out in my truck. Deal is two hundred for a reasonable sample. I like what you got, and we make a deal for a regular supply, we get into the big money."

"Where you from, man?"

"St. Louis—and I represent some serious players."

Deeter drained his beer and stood. "Follow me."

Shake followed him through the crowd and out the front door of Pedro's. Deeter headed directly for the Land Cruiser which beeped and blinked when he hit the remote. "So maybe I sell you some shit. Then what?"

"Then we go over there somewhere…" Shake waved in the direction of the propane tanks. "And we roll one up. If it's good shit, you get the two hundred, and we make a deal for a steady supply. You handle that?"

"Probably could. Depends on the deal, right?"

Deeter opened the rear cargo door of the Toyota, shoved some fishing gear out of the way, and fiddled with a little compartment over a rear wheel well. He emerged with a Ziploc bag and stuffed it into the pocket of his jeans. "This is primo shit, man."

"Let's go find out." Shake walked beside Manson heading for the propane tanks. In a short time, with Deeter talking all the way about his ready sources, a couple of cousins who ran a greenhouse somewhere in the woods south of town, they were in the dark away from standing lights illuminating Pedro's parking lot. Shake reached for his Kimber and poked it hard into Deeter's ribcage.

"Motherfucker, you said you weren't a cop!"

"I'm not, Deeter. Just keep on walking."

"Then you don't need no fuckin' gun." They were standing in the clearing behind the propane tanks now and Shake could see the lawn chair open and ready near a tall sycamore.

"I think I do, Deeter, at least for a little while."

Shake used the barrel of his pistol to slam Deeter Manson in the side of the head just above the right ear. As the man lurched forward under the force of the blow, Shake grabbed his arm and twisted it into a come-along hold. Then he frog-marched Deeter Manson over to the lawn chair and slammed him down into it.

ΔΔΔ

"I'm gonna kill yer ass, man! You can count on that." Deeter Manson sat strapped into the lawn chair with his wrists and ankles zip tied. Blood seeped from a small cut above his ear, but it was already clotting.

"I don't think so, Deeter. But what you *are* gonna do is answer some questions." Shake picked up the channel-locks and tapped Deeter on the back of a hand. "And every time you don't answer me, anytime I think you're bullshitting, I'm gonna crush one of your fingers. You know crushed bone in hands and fingers is very hard to repair, so you don't want that."

"I'll have the cops on your ass for this shit."

"You can try—but as I understand it, you don't have the best reputation with law enforcement around here. Might be they'd just think you got what an asshole like you deserves. Let's get started." Shake clamped the channel-locks down on Deeter's right index finger and took a gentle bite, just enough so the man could feel the serrated jaws biting into his flesh. "Tell me everything you know about the two men you took upriver the day I saw you at Honker's."

There was some thrashing and cursing at first but that ended promptly when Shake used the pliers to crush the first joint of a finger. After that, it got easier. Early questions didn't reveal much that Shake didn't already know or suspect. It started about a month ago when two men showed up at his house while Deeter was looking for work. Said they found him through a buddy he'd been in jail with a while ago. The black man was an African and the white man was from someplace back east, had tats, full-sleeve up and down both arms. Good money if Deeter could drive a truck from Bayou Lafourche up to Cape. They drove him down to Louisiana in a rental car where they picked up the truck out in some swamp. The white man rode in the cab of the truck with Deeter during the trip. It was a white box truck with signage that said it was from some outfit Deeter couldn't remember exactly. He thought it had something to do with veterinary service supplies.

The man who rode with him didn't say what was in the cargo bay. Deeter figured it was people from what he could hear. He didn't care, but Deeter thought it was probably wetbacks or maybe smugglers on the run from the law. He was told not to ask any questions, and he didn't. They met the black man at a truck stop just outside Cape where Deeter collected his fee. He never saw the two men again until the day they showed up at Honker's. Cash deal for Deeter to take them upriver in a rental boat. According to Deeter who whined loudly as Shake increased the pressure on his right middle finger, the men were looking for "a couple of niggers that run off" and they knew where to start looking. All that checked.

"What happened after you took them upriver?"

"They told me to wait in the boat after we tied up at a little dock. I don't know what happened after they disappeared into some fuckin' cotton field." Deeter was breathing hard against the pain. Shake increased the pressure slightly.

"I'm starting to detect bullshit here, Deeter. Better go over it again."

"Jesus, man! That fuckin' hurts like hell!"

"I imagine it does, Deeter. And it can get worse. What happened next?"

"I swear to God, I don't know, man. I heard some shots over in the direction of that cottonfield. Next thing I know the two dudes come hustling back carrying a fuckin' corpse—a black dude. They dumped him in the boat."

"Better." Shake eased up on the pressure a bit. "Where's the body?"

"Bottom of the river, man. Them dudes wrapped it in a poncho, tied it up with ropes and dumped it over the side. Used the boat anchor and a couple of cement blocks to weight it down. Told me to keep my fuckin' mouth shut, and they'd have more work for me later. Them dudes are badass, man. They told me I ever say a fuckin' word, I'm gettin' the same treatment as the dead nigger."

"You got eight fingers left, Deeter, so let's be real careful and tell the truth. Where are those guys now?"

"I don't know, man. No shit, I don't know."

Shake increased the pressure and a glob of bright blood spurted out from under Deeter's fingernail.

"Goddam, man! OK. I seen the damn truck that I drove one time. It was out by that new vet clinic up near Wittenberg. Always figured they hung out up around there. I swear to God, man. I don't know no more!"

"I don't think you do, Deeter." Shake walked behind the lawn chair and wrapped Deeter Manson in a sleeper hold. In less than a minute, the man was out cold. Shake was using his pocketknife to cut away the zip-ties when Jim emerged from the trees.

"My friend Desmond Amara is dead."

"It appears that way, Jim. He might have been talking about someone else that escaped, but I don't think so."

"At least he was not cut up for body parts." Jim walked over and looked down at Deeter Manson who was sprawled on the chair drooling. "Is this man also dead, sir?"

"No…just damaged a little bit." Shake rolled the unconscious man out of the chair, folded it and handed it to Jim. He pocketed the channel-locks and picked up the scraps of zip-tie.

"That must have hurt terribly, sir, what you did to him."

"Yeah, I expect it did, Jim. With a guy like that you don't get answers by asking polite questions. Now we know where to start looking for your friends."

"Now we go to the police?"

"That's the plan. You'll have to tell your story and I'll back you up. We won't mention how I came by the information, but now we know where they can start looking."

Before they headed for his truck, Shake peeled off five twenties from his roll and stuffed them into a pocket of Deeter Manson's jeans.

Sikeston

It might have been better to hole up somewhere and wait for morning, but Shake was beginning to understand the time crunch that Jim was feeling. And the state university element—if their facilities were being used as some sort of cover—was disturbing. He drove to Honker's where a sleepy night man accepted a twenty to open the gates and let him hook up the bass boat and trailer. He was headed for Sikeston, so it seemed like a good idea to drop off the boat with Sarah on his way to see someone at the Missouri Highway Patrol office there. His initial instinct was to take the story to the county sheriff, but this all seemed like something that should be reported to a higher authority.

During the drive he thought over what he'd discovered from Deeter Manson, filling in blanks in the pattern and trying to decipher how something this gruesome and complicated might work. If Southeast Missouri State University was somehow involved in all this, things would get complicated in a hurry. Hard to imagine a prestigious state school with a sterling reputation, wouldn't be aware. Goons with guns aren't your standard campus sight even at remote facilities. Somebody would visit or check, wouldn't they? Maybe the veterinary medicine thing was legit. Jim had mentioned cows and dogs at the facility. Maybe there were vets operating on something besides animals and nobody's the wiser. It seemed like a stretch but if someone relatively high up on the academic food chain, maybe somebody running the vet school, was providing cover, they might get away with it. For a short time anyway…enough time to make serious money, clean up the mess and revert to legit operations.

Troop E of the Missouri Highway Patrol had a facility on US 60 about a mile west of the I-55 major artery around Sikeston. Shake pulled into a parking spot next to a couple of MHP cruisers and led Jim up to the door. He glanced up at a camera mounted over the entry and found a button to press for the attention of someone inside. It was nearly midnight and Shake knew the night watch standers would have to wake someone up once he dropped his bombshell.

A female in a crisp blue uniform shirt was seated at a desk behind a plexiglass screen. They had to talk through a system of speakers and amplifiers.

"My name's Shake Davis. I'm visiting up from Texas and I want to report a major crime."

The woman glanced at them expressionless. Major crime didn't seem to impress her a bit. "Do you have some ID, sir."

"I do…" Shake plucked his military ID and driver's license from his wallet and deposited them in a little sliding drawer. He pointed at Jim. "He doesn't. That's part of what we want to talk with you all about."

The desk officer glanced at Shake's ID but made no move to return the documents. And what's your friend's name, please?"

"I am Jambon Imbasa…from Nigeria."

No reaction except for a slight lift to the woman's eyebrows. "And what is the nature of your complaint, gentlemen?"

"Listen," Shake said, "this is going to sound a little goofy, but I assure you it's serious. I believe there's an operation up near Cape where men like Jim here are kidnapped and cut up for their organs…you know, organs that can be sold for transplants? He escaped and met up with me. We need to make a report and get someone up there to rescue the others."

"What others?"

"There were originally ten Nigerians brought here aboard a ship bound for New Orleans. They were promised good work…hospital work…in this country. When they got here, they were taken at gunpoint to a place up near Cape Girardeau. I think that's where the operations are taking place. Can we talk to a duty officer or an investigator? I'm not sure how that works with you guys."

The woman pressed a button on her desk. A uniformed officer in full rig including a Smokey Bear hat and Sam Browne belt with holstered pistol appeared at her shoulder. There was a brief conversation that prompted the uniform man to glance at them a couple of times. He was smiling and nodding as if he was listening to a joke.

"OK, Mr. Davis. You and your friend have a seat over there." She pointed at a row of plastic chairs. "Officer Donnelly will stay with you until I can get hold of the Lieutenant."

The uniform officer buzzed through a door on one side of the desk and led them toward the chairs. He stood at parade rest but there was a smile on his face as he looked them over.

"So she's gonna call an officer?" Shake asked.

"Lieutenant Sundstrom is the Troop Duty Officer. He'll be in shortly. You can tell him all about your…uh, situation." The trooper swallowed a chuckle and cleared his throat. Shake slumped in his chair and closed his eyes. This guy was going to drink free for a week telling this night watch story. Hopefully, Lt. Sundstrom would take it a little more seriously.

Wittenberg

"e're gonna move." Samuel Imshana punched off the call and tossed the phone on his bed.

"When?" Marco Sanpere was just stepping back into the room from the shower he badly needed after four hours of toil on a bobcat, digging deep graves out in the woods that surrounded the facility.

"Soon as we can get it cleaned up and get the *kafirs* loaded. He's sending two men down from St. Louis to give us a hand. He said to be sure there were no more escapes or fuck ups."

"Wasn't my fault. I told you we should never have taken them outside. Fuckin' PT session. That was bullshit and you fell for it."

"It was designed to keep them healthy. We keep the *kafirs* locked up in the dark like fucking mushrooms, and they're gonna get sick."

"Who gives a shit? They're all gonna be dead soon anyway."

"Regardless, we are going to have to move the ones who are left. Should be easier this time. Fewer to deal with and the Doc is gonna knock them out for the trip."

"Did they say where we're going?"

"To be determined. Said we'd get orders by the time we're ready to roll."

"Can't say I'll be sorry to get out of this dump." Marco flopped down on his bunk and stared at the ceiling.

"We've been in worse and making a lot less money. Remember Chad—or Djibouti?"

Marco extended his right arm and stared at one of his tattoos. *Legio Patria Nostra.* The Legion is our Fatherland. "A legionnaire goes where he's sent, *mon ami.*"

"And a smart ex-legionnaire makes good money doing it."

L t. Walter Sundstrom of Troop E, MHP, was a tall, lean man, nearly bald and deeply tanned. He wore rumpled civilian clothing and looked like he'd just been jostled out of a sound sleep. He led Shake and Jim toward a room at the rear of his headquarters, glancing at the documents he'd gotten from the Desk Officer.

"You're from Texas, Mr. Davis. What are you doing in our lovely state?"

"Kind of an old home week, Lieutenant. I was born and raised around here. I came up to take a look at a few places and visit some relatives."

"And a retired Marine…seems like you guys are all over the place." The tone suggested Lt. Sundstrom would be happier if that were not the case.

"You serve?"

"Yep. Army airborne. I made a couple of sandbox deployments then got out and went back to college. Knew a few of you guys when I was in Afghanistan." Shake didn't like the way he said it. It sounded like knowing a few Marines was not the highlight of the man's overseas experience. The Marine card was not likely to be much help tonight.

Sundstrom led them into an interview room. There was the standard two-way mirror on one wall and a recording device on the table. Sundstrom sat on one side and motioned for Jim and Shake to take the chairs on the other side. "I'm going to record our conversation. That's SOP so we've got everything clear and on the official record. You folks got any objections to that?"

They had none. Lt Sundstrom started the recorder, gave his name plus the date and time. "Now, give us your full names and addresses. Just talk to me in a normal tone."

"Shake Davis from Lockhart, Texas."

"Jambon Imbasa…and I am from Nigeria…a small village near Ibadan."

"As I understand it, Mr…uh…

"Please call me Jim."

"OK. As I understand it, Jim, you have no passport or visa. Is that correct?"

"Yes, sir. When we left Lagos, the men who offered us the job said we would not need passports. They gave us papers to fill out and said that was all that would be required."

"So, your legal status is essentially undocumented alien…"

"Lieutenant, excuse me." Shake leaned forward on the table. "Jim's legal status isn't the issue here. We need to tell you about why he was brought here with the others who are right now being held captive somewhere up near Cape Girardeau. And I think I can tell you where to start looking."

"Let me direct the line of questioning, Mr. Davis. We'll get to all that in good time."

Lt. Sundstrom's good time was about a half an hour later after he'd pressed Jim about how, where, and when he'd illegally entered the United States. At last they got around to the story of illegal organ harvesting. Jim did most of the talking with Shake filling in to keep the timeline relative to Jim's narrative. Shake showed him the picture of the three men in the boat and sent it to an official email address Sundstrom provided. It took another hour to get through it all. Sundstrom looked alternately bored and speculative. He nodded or shook his head a few times, but made no notes and only asked a few questions, mostly about what Jim had seen at the facility. He wasn't quite ready to believe that the whole gory operation could be occurring at a vet facility sponsored by SEMO.

"OK," the Lieutenant said at about two in the morning. "I think I've got what we need for now."

"What happens next?" Shake had the distinct feeling that no immediate action was forthcoming from the Missouri Highway Patrol in its capacity as a state police force. In fact, it felt to him like he'd just spent two hours talking to a bureaucrat masquerading as a cop.

"Well, you've made a formal report, that's now in the form of an official complaint. We're bound to look into it. I imagine first steps when the investigators get the report will be to make some calls and nose around a little."

"My people might be dead soon." Jim was antsy and sweating. He was rapidly beginning to think either the police didn't believe their story, or they would be too slow in looking into it.

"Jim, you're from another country, so I don't expect you to understand, but we can't just go busting into places, especially places like a state university facility and start accusing people of running an illegal organ-harvesting operation. I'm not saying I don't believe what you say you saw, what you've related to me here, but you said yourself you're not sure where you were. Mr. Davis thinks it might be a university vet facility, but he's not sure. We have laws in this country. We have procedures to follow. We'll look into this. I can assure you of that." He turned to Shake and nodded. "I'll need a number where I can reach you. Are you planning on heading back to Texas?"

"Yeah, I guess so, once we get this thing cleared up. I'd like to think you guys will do something before Jim's friends are carved up like fucking Thanksgiving turkeys."

"You're going to have to leave that up to us at this point, Mr. Davis. Leave your contact information at the desk and then you're free to go."

That wasn't good enough. Not for Shake or for Jim. The state of Missouri and some ex-Army bureaucrat might want to cross all t's and dot all i's before they made a move to stop this murderous operation, but that wasn't Shake's style. The police powers might want to be sure before they made any moves, but Shake was sure, and he stood to leave fully intending to make a few moves of his own.

"Let's go, Jim."

"You can go, Mr. Davis. But your friend will have to stay with us. We'll be putting in a call to Immigration and Customs Enforcement. They'll hold onto him for us while we investigate his story."

"I'll take responsibility, Lieutenant. No need to lock him up."

"Not possible, Mr. Davis. There are protocols and procedures to be followed. He goes into ICE custody where he can be reached as required."

And there stood the law enforcement brick wall firmly reinforced with red tape. He borrowed a scrap of paper, jotted down his mobile phone number and handed it to Jim. "If you need anything, borrow a phone and call this number." He shook Jim's hand and pulled him close to whisper. "I'm on this thing. Don't worry."

Jim looked into Shake's eyes for a long moment, reading in his new friend's hard expression what had to remain unsaid. Then he pulled the Ibo Leader amulet from his neck and handed it to Shake.

Shake caught a couple of hours of much-needed sleep in his truck at a roadside rest stop north of the city. A bright sun glaring through the windshield woke him, and he checked his watch. Nearly 0930, and he needed to get moving. He really didn't have a decisive plan of action. What he knew was that the cops were going to be too slow and too cautious to get anything done in the very near future. And if something wasn't done in that very near future, more innocent men would die, carved up for their innards. Something that lurid, evil and inhumane actually taking place right here in rural Missouri? Closest comparison Shake could make—and it wasn't a very good one—would be the old days of illegal abortions, something he always thought of as taking place in the dark, dingy and crime-ridden shadows of big cities. He checked his watch again. Time to find out—and past time to do something about it. He started the truck and began to search for a quick breakfast.

The priority as he saw it, sitting at a truck-stop eating stale pastry and drinking bad coffee, was to rescue the Nigerians. He wasn't the law. He was happy to leave the investigation, apprehension, and prosecution to them, if and when they eventually got around to it. But that might be too late for Jim's Nigerian friends. He needed to conjure up and execute a rescue mission.

And as always with that kind of mission, reconnaissance was vital. If he intended to rescue those guys, get in and out with them alive, he needed to know about where they were being kept. He felt certain it was the vet clinic facility near Wittenberg, but he needed to confirm that. And if he did, he needed details on the layout, guards, and everything else that might prove to be a significant mission obstacle. What about equipment? What would he need? And when he determined that, where would he get whatever he needed? And he was only one man facing…what? How many guards beside the ones Jim mentioned?

Shake stared out the truck stop window and saw a wizened little man in faded khakis climb out of rusting pick-up. The guy reminded him of Woodrow Cheeley. And that's when the first piece of the puzzle fell into place. He gulped his coffee and headed for his truck.

Woody's Farm

He drove for an hour on Missouri 177 until he was southeast of Perryville. Wittenberg was just a few miles from where they'd had the encounter with Woodrow Cheeley, and he was fairly sure the stream on his right was the one they'd explored with the bass boat. He drove down a few farm roads with gravel rattling off his fenders before he found familiar ground. A cottonfield on his left, long split-rail fencing—and there was the Red Man sign. He parked the truck and began to walk. On the other side of a cottonwood stand, he heard the growl of a laboring engine.

Woodrow Cheeley was steering a muscular John Deere tractor and towing a disc harrow over a field, churning up long rows of loamy soil. As he made the turn at one end of the field, Shake saw sunlight glint off a bottle. Hoping he wasn't about to ask a very big favor from a chronic drunk, Shake vaulted the fence and waved until he caught the man's attention. Woody waved back, shut down the tractor, and climbed off. He was wiping sweat with a shop towel when he joined Shake in the shade of the cottonwoods.

"Glad to see ya come back by, Gunner. I been lookin' for an excuse to get off that damn tractor."

"You gonna put more cotton in here, Woody?"

"Naw, I'm thinkin' corn this year. Cotton in the piddly little bit I grow ain't worth shit no more."

"Woody, listen…we don't know much about each other, but I'm hoping as a Marine, you'll trust another one who needs a big favor."

"Well, I ain't got no money to lend if that's what yer about to ask. But I can give you a bite to eat and a drink of whiskey if you're of a mind to tell me about it."

They drove back down the road in Shake's truck until they turned off on a path that led to Woody's house. It was an impressive place for a site so far out in the Southeast Missouri boondocks. It was two stories of solid timber and looked well-kept despite a front yard littered with rusted farm implements. Woody kept a pair of bird dogs in a pen on one side of the house. They were pawing the fence and whimpering with their tongues hanging out. Woody waved and smiled. "Them two are Hank and Hilda," he said. "Best pair of pointers in Perry County." Next to the dog run there was a big garage that doubled as a workshop that Woody said made him relatively self-sufficient. He was a man who believed in owning little that wasn't necessary and fixing what you owned when it inevitably broke. Inside the house, they walked past a few Marine mementos that Woody had mounted in his living room near a gun cabinet that contained a couple of revolvers hanging from wooden pegs and a good selection of rifles and shotguns.

"Looks like you do some hunting, Woody."

"Oh, yeah. Deer tag every year, and I got some nice quail and pheasant on the property. Saves me from doin' too much bidness with them damn robbers at the grocery store."

They sat across from each other in a roomy kitchen lit by sunlight that gleamed through a bay window. Woody served plates of cold fried chicken and potato salad. He poured sweet tea from a jug when Shake declined whiskey. They ate for a while, and Shake complimented him on the food.

"Had to learn to do some cookin', Gunner. Lost my wife about ten years ago," he said. "We never had no kids. Wasn't for lack of tryin'. Jist luck of the draw, you know? Anyway, she come down with kidney failure. Had to do that dialysis all the time. Docs said she needed a transplant, but we was never able to get all that worked out before she died."

"That brings me to what I need, Woody. You remember Jim, that guy was with me when we first met?"

"Yep. One that said he was kidnapped, right?"

"That's it. He was being held with some other Nigerians until he escaped. I'm gonna try to rescue his friends."

"Sounds like a job fer the cops."

"I went to the Highway Patrol down in Sikeston. I don't know whether they believed the story or not, but they ain't gonna do anything about it in any kind of hurry. And I'm worried that by the time they get around to it, those other men might be dead. There's men cutting them up to harvest their organs and sell them for transplants."

"Sheeeit-fahr, Gunner! You mean to tell me there's people that would do somethin' like that, to reg'lar live people? Just cut 'em up and sell their insides?"

"There are those kinds of people, Woody. A pal of mine in the FBI said it's becoming a racket, lots of money involved."

"And yer thinkin' there's somethin' like that goin' on around here?"

"Yep…and I'm pretty sure it's up at the new vet clinic you mentioned. Anyway, I'm gonna take a look. And that's where you can give me a hand."

"What have you got in mind?"

"Recon mission, Woody. Couple of old Marines out on a snoop and poop. I need a man who knows the area and can guide me, somebody with a little combat training that can watch my six."

Woody toyed with a chicken bone and sipped his whiskey. He looked away and stared out the bay window for a few moments. "You'll recall I said how I was a truck driver in the Marines, Gunner. I didn't have much trainin' in the combat stuff."

"You're a Marine, Woody. That's all I need to know. If we find those guys where I think they are, I'll handle any rough stuff. I just need to do the recon so I can make a plan."

"Well, I ain't goin' if it's gonna be half-assed."

"What's that mean?"

"It means if I he'p you out on this, I'm gonna be all in or not at all."

"Woody, these people holding the Nigerians are bad-asses, and they won't have any second thoughts about killing anyone who tries to interfere. I can't ask you to take that kind of risk."

"You ain't askin', Gunner. I'm volunteerin'. I never got to Vietnam, but I always figured if I did, I'd be a fair hand in combat. Never had no chance to test that out. Now I do. You want PFC Woodrow Cheeley on this mission, it's got to be all in."

"Let's do the recon first. Then we develop the plan."

"Copy that, Gunner. I been by that place a time or two. It's about two miles on the other side of Wittenberg."

"So you know the terrain?"

"Damn straight I do. I go deer huntin' up around there every year. Now first thang we got to figger is its new construction. They still got bobcats and buildin' materials stacked all around.

It's set right in the middle of a little clearing. There's chain-link fencing and a road runs off the county line right up to the building. I seen a couple of trucks but never no people. We best make an approach from the west so's anyone lookin' out will have the sun in their eyes…" Woody paused to hit his bottle of Four Roses. Shake reached across the table to grab his hand.

"Woody, we can't do something like this half-drunk."

Cheeley looked at him and then at the bottle in his hand. "Force of habit, Gunner. I like this stuff—but I don't need it." He walked to a kitchen cabinet and stowed the bottle behind a stack of dishes. "Dry as a popcorn fart 'til we get this thang done, Gunner. My word on it. Then we'll come back here and have us a snort or two."

He had no night vision aids, so Shake decided to make his initial recon in the late afternoon that day before the sun set. He liked Woody's idea of approaching from the west with the sun at their backs. They'd take Woody's Silverado as close as seemed safe before dismounting. He didn't know if there was any sort of roving patrol on the grounds, but if someone spotted the parked truck, it would have local license plates. Woody had a pair of serviceable 7x50 binoculars that would be useful on the approach and a hefty set of bolt cutters that would chew through the fencing when Shake moved in to get a closer look. Shake had his phone charged to take pictures as required.

Woody came clumping down the stairs wearing jungle boots and an old set of Marine Corps camouflage utilities. The uniform was a pattern that Marines adopted late in the Vietnam War and wore for a few years after before adopting the marpat uniform like the one Shake dug out of his pack for the recon mission. Woody had obscured the high points of his face, nose, chin, and cheekbones with a camo stick that he handed to Shake.

"Nice work on the camo, Woody," Shake complimented as he looked into a mirror and obscured his own prominent features. "Training pays, right?"

"You can take the boy out of the Marines but you cain't take the Marines out of the boy." Woody unlocked his gun cabinet and stood contemplating his collection of weapons. "What do you think, Gunner. "Shotgun or rifle?"

"This is recon, Woody. I'm hoping we don't have to do any shooting at all. After we see what we're up against, we can make a decision about what we need for a raid on the place."

"That don't answer my question."

Shake walked over to examine the guns on display. There was a scoped deer rifle, a nicely appointed Winchester Model 70, and a Marlin lever-action, but those were too much gun. He pointed at a Remington 870 Wingmaster 12-gauge pump shotgun. "What kind of rounds have you got for the 870?"

"Everthang from birdshot to buckshot. That there's my favorite scattergun."

"Let's take it. And load it with birdshot. I don't want you to shoot at all unless we've got to defend or cover our exfil. No need to blow a big hole in somebody and have to explain it all later to cops."

Woody selected the shotgun and rummaged in a nearby ammo can for the shells he wanted. Shake checked his Kimber .45, loaded an extra magazine, and then did a quick inventory of their gear. It was coming up on 1600. Time to hit the road to their rolling point for the recon.

Wittenberg

They parked Woody's truck near the road leading to the vet facility. There was a thick stand of sycamore and cottonwood trees ahead of them in an easterly direction. A bright hot sun was setting at their backs as they moved into the woods. Woody said the facility was about 300 meters on the other side of the dense thicket. He led the way, weaving easily and silently through dense underbrush, like an experienced deer hunter—or a trained Marine. After 100 meters, Shake stopped worrying about Woody's competence.

Twenty minutes later, they were at the edge of a clearing and got their first look at the vet facility. There was a small patch of cleared ground between the tree line and the chain-link fence that appeared to completely circle the area. The fencing was marked in several places. A couple of the metal signs advertised a Cape Girardeau construction company, others indicated the land was property of Southeast Missouri State University, private property, no trespassing. Shake glassed the building. It was single story, concrete construction with a big central AC system and what looked like a generator or maintenance shed set off to one side. The exterior was unpainted, and there were stacks of construction materials, bags of concrete, and stacks of cinder blocks scattered around the grounds. A bobcat was parked to one side of the building, and what windows Shake could see on this side of the building were set up high, about eight feet off ground level. They waited and watched for 20 minutes, but there was no one in sight.

A starter growled from somewhere to their left front, and Shake heard a truck engine roar. He tapped Woody on the shoulder and pointed in that direction. "Got to be the main access road over there," he said. "Let's get a look at that."

They maneuvered through the woods until the main entrance to the building came in sight. There was a larger sign proclaiming that the site was a SEMO State University Veterinary Medicine Research Facility Annex. A big truck was parked next to a black Ford Escalade near the entryway which appeared to consist of a concrete sidewalk leading to a pair of glass doors covered by a corrugated aluminum awning. Next to the truck and the SUV was a smaller van with a driver at the wheel. That was the vehicle they'd heard start. The big truck was vanilla white with rental markings from Avis. The step van carried signage that indicated it belonged to an outfit called Carteret Medical Supply Company of St. Louis, MO. Shake used the binos to get a closer look at the driver, a Hispanic guy in a blue uniform shirt who was smoking a cigarette and looking bored.

The glass doors opened, and a smallish woman in surgical scrubs emerged carrying two containers that looked like picnic coolers. The driver waved and got out from behind the wheel of the van to slide open an access door. The woman chatted with him for a while as they loaded the containers. She was blocking Shake's view of what was being loaded into the van, but he kept the glasses on them hoping for a better look.

"Looks like some kinda nurse or somethin'." Woody lay prone next to Shake cradling the shotgun. "What's in them coolers?"

"Can't see clearly…" Shake shifted the binoculars when he saw the doors open again. A man, also in scrubs, emerged and headed for the van. He was carrying a large envelope tucked under one arm with another similar container in his hand. This time Shake got a good look. The container was marked in vivid red: *Human Organs for Transplant.*

"Bingo." He handed the binoculars to Woody. "Far as I know, vet clinics don't ship human organs."

"I'll be goddamned!" Woody whispered. "Looks like you was right on the money."

"Roger. I'm thinking this is the place. Now we've got to figure out how to get in there and find those guys they're holding—if any of them are still alive."

When the step van departed, they made a slow circuit of the facility perimeter staying out of sight inside the wood line. There were at least two other doors that looked like access points. Big metal oblong industrial doors with no visible handles on the exterior. Probably a push bar on the inside, Shake figured, the kind of thing that would need to be pried open absent an explosive breeching charge which he did not have. On the far side of the building they noted two dogs in their pen. Both were asleep in the shade, but Shake led them farther away to give the animals a wide pass. On the back side of the structure he spotted an oblong window that stood partially open about six feet above the central HVAC unit they could hear humming from their position in the woods. "We'll make one more circuit," Shake said, "but I'm thinking that window above the AC unit is the easiest access point."

When they reached the entry area, looking from the opposite side of the facility, the step van was gone. The white box truck was being loaded. The cargo door was rolled open, and there were several cardboard boxes stacked at the rear of the vehicle. As they watched, a man emerged from the building pushing a dolly stacked with what looked like electronic equipment. There were LED screens glinting and wires dangling as the man trundled his load toward the rear of the truck. He had a pistol holstered on a duty belt, some kind of semi-auto, maybe a Glock, and a little carrier for what Shake recognized as a stun-gun. It looked like one of the heavy-duty Vipertek models that Shake had used in nonlethal weapons training. That was one little bit of confirmation. Another was the sleeveless t-shirt that exposed a pair of sinewy arms covered by tattoos.

"Hello, asshole…" Shake whispered and handed the binoculars to Woody. "Recognize that guy?"

"Yep. That's one of the pair that come by my place. He's damn sure spent some money on skin art, ain't he?"

"Those are military tats, Woody. I recognize a few of them. I think our boy over there is a former member of *La Legion Etrangere*."

"Say what?"

"French Foreign Legion, Woody."

"What the hell's a guy like that doin' here?"

"My guess is he's hired muscle. What it means to us is he's a tough customer. Question is how many more of them are on payroll. Those Legion dudes are bad ass. I know from personal experience."

"We get to that drink of whiskey, I'll be wantin' you to tell me about that." The tattooed man at the back of the truck was busily loading equipment and boxes as Woody watched through the binoculars. "Cain't tell what all that stuff is, but I'd guess somebody's loadin' up to move."

"Looks like it—which means we need to crank up the schedule. How soon you think it'll be dark?" Shake pulled his phone, adjusted for a tighter frame, and shot several photos.

Woody rolled over to take a look at the treetops. "Maybe an hour, not much more than that."

"You stay here until it gets dark. Keep an eye on them and let me know right away if you see any of the black guys or if any of the vehicles move."

"Where you gonna be?"

"Around the back. I want to get another look at that window we spotted above the AC unit. Join up with me when it gets dark and we'll make our move."

Shake found his way around to the rear of the building and studied the ground. He could see a couple of sodium-vapor standing lights mounted near the roof of the building, one at each visible corner. They'd likely switch on by sensor once it got dark. If there were surveillance cameras, he couldn't see them. He was thinking about the pair of hounds penned up on the opposite side of the facility. They were a problem. Dogs didn't have to see something out of the ordinary to alert. They relied on their noses. The next step was to get a closer look, maybe get inside through that window, scope the building layout, find out where the captives were being held. With one or more military trained security types inside, just busting in and winging it was not a bright idea.

And if they were loading up to move somewhere, he didn't have much time to sort it all out and get it done.

ΔΔΔ

The standing lights came on as Woody slid in beside Shake who had just about decided on the next move. "Closed up the truck they was loadin'. That one and the Ford are still parked. Seen that tattooed dude and couple others. Everybody disappeared inside right after it started to get dark."

"So you saw…what? The tat-man, a man and a woman in surgical scrubs…"

"Yeah, and some other guy talkin' to the woman for a while. Big boy in khakis and work boots. Didn't see no guns on him, but he looked like the type would have one handy."

Shake just nodded, trying to get a headcount on the opposition. Tats, the man and the woman, another guy…plus the black guy who claimed to be a Nigerian. Five at least. How many others inside?

Woody eyed the open ground on the other side of the fence. "Them lights are gonna be a problem, ain't they?"

"Always a problem in night ops, Woody, but I haven't spotted any cameras. Likely they haven't mounted any yet. What's got me worried are the dogs."

"Them ones we seen on the other side?"

"Yeah. They start barking and raising hell and we're screwed. Somebody's likely to run a check on the grounds."

"Dogs don't bark when they're eatin'. I got me a sack of feed for Hank and Hilda that I keep in the truck. Let me go get it."

"What are you gonna do with that?"

"I'll set up over yonder while you make yer move on this side. I keep tossin' dog chow over the fence and they'll get to chasin' it. Even if they do get to barkin', a body would check on that side of the building and not on the back side where you'll be."

Shake waited an hour while Woody with his sack of kibble got into position. Then he picked up the bolt-cutters and crawled up to the fence. In a few minutes, he'd clipped enough links to let him crawl through. He was just outside the bright pools from the standing lights as he bent the cut portion of fencing back into shape and headed for the building. He'd be illuminated for about 20 meters, but he opted for speed over stealth and ran toward the HVAC unit. Standing on that would put him shadow and let him reach the open window.

As he climbed up on the unit, he heard the unmistakable hiss of running water. He stretched a hand up and felt steam seeping through the window. That's why they left it open, he realized. *It's a shower room, and that means there's somebody standing under it,* he thought as he carefully chinned himself up to take a look. There were two men standing slumped in the running water, both naked as he'd expected, and both were black men, looking decidedly docile and downhearted. He was peeking through an opening well above their heads. Unless one of them looked up, he was relatively safe. Shake was straining to hold himself in position when the black man Jim had identified as Samuel Imshana appeared.

"That's enough," he said tossing towels at the two men in the shower. "Dinner time."

The men who had been showering shut down the water and shuffled off out of sight. Shake dropped back down onto the AC unit to give his arms a rest. He waited 20 minutes. The dogs were silent, so Woody's scheme appeared to be working. He listened carefully for a few minutes more. Other than the hum of the AC unit he heard nothing. He chinned himself up to the window and got the leverage he needed to work his shoulders though the opening. There were pipes running along the ceiling, and Shake grabbed at one of them to pull himself the rest of the way into the shower room. He dropped to the wet floor and looked around. Two showerheads, tiled walls, and a drain in the floor. He crossed to the shower room door where he found what appeared to be a changing room with wet towels hanging from pegs and a door leading into a corridor.

He took a quick glance looking in both directions. The corridor was lit by neon tubes, and there were some more packing boxes stacked along its length, but the place seemed to be deserted. He drew his pistol and duck-walked into the hallway. Left or right? Didn't matter, but he heard the sound of silverware clinking on plates to the left and crawled toward the sound on hands and knees. There was a long window above some of the packing boxes. He shouldered in behind the boxes and determined he must be right outside some kind of mess hall where the prisoners were being fed. There was the low mutter of conversation and he risked a quick peek. Four black men were seated at a cafeteria table. Samuel Imshana and his tattooed buddy were keeping watch, discussing something on the other side of the room with their backs turned to him. He saw the woman in scrubs carrying a pitcher toward the table. She had a web belt around her waist over the scrubs. It looked like a British rig with a canvas flap holster covering something like a revolver. When she turned in his direction, he ducked back down out of sight.

Hoping dinner would last for a little while longer, Shake trotted back down the hall in the opposite direction. Through a series of doors, he discovered a couple of supply closets, an operating theater, and what looked like an admin office. A big screen TV was mounted on the wall of that office, but Shake didn't see anything that looked like monitors for a video security system. There was no one in any of the spaces. Dinnertime at the facility must be a communal thing. It appeared that he was in a main corridor, probably the artery that bisected the building. At the very end of the corridor he ducked into a room that was set up like a military squad bay with rows of beds along one wall. This had to be the barracks room where the prisoners were kept when they weren't eating, working—or being carved on in the operating room. The door was standing open, and he could see another of the oblong windows high above the beds. This one looked the same as the one in the shower room, but it was closed. He checked the door. It was wood, hollow frame with a key-lock set, and no knob on the inside.

He spotted a sturdier security door at the end of the corridor, a push-bar access with an illuminated exit sign mounted over it. Probably alarmed, Shake decided and hustled back toward the shower room. Jim had indicated six men remaining in captivity. Ten original captives, minus the first two that got cut up, minus Jim and his buddy that escaped. That should leave six remaining, but Shake had only seen four. So there were a couple more somewhere else, or they'd already been carved up for parts. As he pulled himself back through the window, he did a quick review. He'd seen four captives, two security guards, and two medics of some kind, a man and a woman, at least one of them armed, maybe one other unidentified man that Woody spotted out front. No telling about firepower if it came to a shoot-out. His biggest problem if he decided on a kinetic entry would likely be the ex-Legionnaire and the black man with pistols and rifles at least.

He had all the tactical information about the objective that he was likely to get. If there were reinforcements or barriers in another part of the building, Shake would have to deal with the surprises. Worrying a little less about cameras, he crossed the yard and slithered through the cut in the fence line. He charged through the woods, heading for the other side of the compound to pick up Woody. Now he had to make a workable plan.

We haven't had time to look into this." Captain George Selby, commanding Troop E of the Missouri Highway Patrol, shrugged at his visitors and thumped a finger down on the file folder siting in the middle of his desk. "We've just barely opened the file. How does the FBI get involved?"

"One of those lucky things, I guess." Special Agent Ken Warrior, a full-blood Chickasaw who was a Southeast Missouri native, just shrugged. "You know how it goes, Captain. We got a hit on a scanning program that alerts us about certain things."

"One of your officers…uh…" Special Agent Joe Huerta consulted his notes. "A Lieutenant Walter Sundstrom forwarded a spot incident report from last night."

"Yes, well as you know, that's SOP for state law enforcement agencies. Anything that might concern the FBI, such as kidnapping in this case, is automatically forwarded."

"Well, it worked as advertised, Captain. We got the alert and drove down here from St. Louis to take a look."

"Are you willing to declare jurisdiction here, Gentlemen? On something this thin?"

"That depends," Warrior said. "We'd certainly want to go over the full interview transcript and talk to the guys who made the complaint."

Captain Selby opened the file and donned a pair of reading glasses. "All I have for one of them—Mr. Sheldon Davis of Lockhart, Texas—is a phone number. Says here he was heading back to Texas so I have no idea where he might be right now." He jotted a number on a memo pad and handed it across the desk to the FBI agent. "That's the number he gave us. As for the man who was with him—Mr. Jambon Imbasa, an illegal alien from Nigeria—he's in a holding facility. We're waiting for ICE to take custody."

"Have you interviewed that man beyond the initial contact?"

"Not as yet. I'm waiting for ICE…and advice from the State Attorney General's office."

"Fine, Captain. Meanwhile, we'd like to talk to the man."

Captain Selby checked his watch. "It's just about seven. Can it wait until morning?"

"No, we'd like to do this right away, Captain. Can you take us to see the Nigerian?"

"Certainly. I'll get a cruiser and you can follow me to the holding facility. Just one thing before we go, gentlemen. There is some speculation in the interview report that this might somehow involve Southeast Missouri State or one of their facilities. We are very proud of the school around here, and we tend to tread softly around anything that involves them, their faculty or the student body. I'd hope the FBI would exercise the same sort of discretion."

Agents Ken Warrior and Joe Huerta in an FBI Tahoe followed Captain Selby's MHP cruiser toward downtown Sikeston. Warrior was driving while Huerta thumbed through a thick file.

"Seemed a little antsy about the university connection, didn't he?"

"Natural enough," Warrior shrugged. "I went to school there. The university is big bucks and lots of prestige for Southeast Missouri."

"We gonna tell him about the good Dr. Ephraim Warren?"

"Not until we've talked to the Nigerian and taken the case. No use opening that can of worms until we have to."

Agent Huerta heard a buzz and checked his phone for an incoming text. "Well, Dr. Warren isn't going anywhere in a hurry. They moved on the currency transfer thing. Found his account in Belize and froze it. He is officially broke except for pocket change."

"It's like a damn clown car sometimes. You know? One thing leads to another. New Yok organized crime is looking into Solano. That leads to Warren. Warren leads to the university and then some pissant incident report hits with a reference to kidnapping and mentions the school. Clown car, I swear."

"Good police work is what it is. Warren's dirty, probably on a lot of charges, but he's not a kidnapper, is he? So, what's the link here? What's Solano paying Warren to do? Cheat his kids into school like that Springer dude out in LA?"

"Whatever it is, it's worth seven figures. I don't think Solano is gonna pay that much for a vet from Southeast Missouri to vaccinate his poodle."

"What about that organ harvesting thing? Anything to that you think?"

"Un-fucking-believable," Agent Warrior shook his head and clicked on a turn signal to follow his lead into a large parking lot. "And Warren is a vet, right? Far as I know, vets don't operate on human beings. Let's see what the Nigerian has to say and focus on the kidnapping angle."

Thirty minutes after the FBI agents started talking to Jambon Imbasa, Ken Warrior excused himself and walked outside the holding facility in downtown Sikeston to make some calls. He spoke with his SAIC in St. Louis and got an official number for a brand-new case that involved kidnapping, human trafficking, murder, and illegal human-organ harvesting. Then he spoke with Captain Selby, notifying him that the case was now under FBI jurisdiction. He also asked for and made note of the Perry County Sheriff's personal number.

"Sheriff, this is Agent Ken Warrior of the FBI out of St. Louis. My partner and I are down here on a very serious matter that might require your assistance. I know it's late, but can we meet as soon as possible? Yes, sir. Tonight."

Wittenberg

S o how's this thing work with you guys? The two men from St. Louis sat in the cafeteria staring at Samuel Imshana. "We gotta be cleaned up and gone before noon tomorrow."

"It's just a matter of loading the last of the equipment boxes. We've had them cleaning and sanitizing all day."

"We gonna have any trouble with the passengers?" The larger of the two St. Louis visitors was a big man who had the flattened nose and ridged forehead of an ex-boxer.

"We'll handle them." Samuel nodded and stretched. He didn't much care for the new men's attitude, and neither of them had been much help with the grunt work and site sanitizing that had gone on all day at the facility. "I don't expect any problems. The doctor will medicate them before we start. They should sleep most of the way."

"We was told you had a couple of 'em run off." The smaller of the St. Louis visitors seemed to be in charge of the reinforcement detail, and he clearly resented the assignment. "What about that?"

"We handled it." Samuel made a fist and extended a finger like he was aiming a pistol.

"You got one of them. What about the other one?"

"Very likely also dead," said Samuel. "If he survived, he's no threat. If he was, we'd have had a visit from cops by now."

"Well, security sucks around here from what I seen so far." The smaller man picked up a clipboard and examined it. "I don't want no problems on the road. You got the truck all set?"

"Four cots in the back for the passengers. My partner and I will ride in front. We follow you."

"And we take the medics with us in the SUV. They disappear when we get to the place in Iowa. You guys are on until we get word otherwise. That the way you see it?"

"That's my understanding." Samuel rose as the bigger man reached for a small overnight bag. "We've got a couple of cots set up for you in a room just off the lobby. We'll begin the last load out at six."

"What about them dogs outside?"

"We called a guy. He's gonna pick them up before dark tomorrow."

"OK. Who's on guard tonight?" The smaller man pulled a small S&W semi-auto from his belt and press-checked it.

"My partner is on right now. I relieve him in an hour or so." He checked his watch and held up a large keyring. "I'll make a last check, and then we'll leave them to sleep until we wake them up at five to see the doctor." Samuel rose and started for the cafeteria door. "Should go smooth and easy."

"Damn well better," the bigger man mumbled as he followed Samuel out into the corridor.

Woody's Farm

They were seated at the kitchen table, staring at a drawing Shake made to diagram what he'd seen on the recon. It wasn't much more than a series of double lines and boxes. What had him worried was what the building might contain beyond the corridor and the few spaces that opened off of it that he'd managed to check.

"Any chance a place like this has got a basement?"

"This is Southeast Missouri, Gunner. Water table this close to the Mississippi is about a foot below ground level."

"Right…but there's probably something on the other side of this corridor." Shake tapped a finger on the center of his drawing. "There's too much space I couldn't get to. What if they've got a platoon of goons situated somewhere beyond that main corridor?"

"We woulda seen some of them. If they wasn't patrollin' they'd be in there at that chow hall eatin', wouldn't they? You gotta figger with a deal like this whoever's runnin' it would want to keep the payroll small. Right? There ain't that many prisoners to deal with anyway. And the fewer people is involved the less likely you're gonna have leaks or problems with yer staff."

"OK. So the order of battle, the defense, is something like this. The black guy and the Legionnaire—handguns and the two rifles you saw when they came by here. And at least one of them, probably both, have stun guns. Then there's the two in scrubs that we saw. At least one of them, the woman, is armed with a pistol. I'm thinking that probably means the guy has one too."

"Well, you're the expert, Gunner, but seems to me some of that can be overcome by the element of surprise."

"Yeah. But that only works if they're all in the same place or close by. Otherwise, they've got time to regroup and react. What I don't want is a shoot-out with those Nigerian guys caught in a crossfire."

"Probably be asleep if we go around midnight."

Shake pointed to the square on his drawing indicating the barracks room. "I need to get in here where they're sleeping. Jim said they give these guys some kind of drug. It's probably some kind of tranquilizer. They dosed these guys twice a day, so it can't be a big dose. Most of it would have worn off if they've slept for a couple of hours. We go in late. Midnight is as good a time as any."

"Bound to be somebody standing sentry duty, ain't there?"

"That's likely. Assume he's somewhere in that main corridor where he can keep an eye on the barracks area—maybe in the cafeteria. I need to find a way to decoy him away from his post and take him out without shooting the bastard which would bring everyone else down on me."

"Lemme show you somethin'." Woody got up from the table and walked into his living room. Shake heard a drawer opening. Woody returned and tossed a heavy black leather sap onto the table. Shake picked it up and examined it carefully. It was about ten inches long, black leather with a palm loop on one end. It swelled into a heavy bulb at the business end. Inside that was stitched some kind of weight, probably a large slug of lead. "Picked that up on Okinawa. Some call it a blackjack. Cops used to carry them all the time. Comes in handy if yer losin' a fight. Guy out there showed me how to use it."

Woody took the sap, slipped his hand into the loop, and tapped Shake behind the ear. "That right there is what they call the mastoid bone. You whomp somebody right there with this thing and he's down for the count. I done it before and I can do it again."

"I'll be the only one going into the building, Woody. I need you on the outside ready to get us out of there in a hurry."

"You wantin' me to do the same trick with them dogs?"

"No, not this time. Let them bark if they want. Like you said before, maybe someone goes to check and that puts them on the other side of the building. One less for me to deal with inside."

"Yeah, them hounds looked to me like trackers. They wasn't no kind of attack animals anyway."

"OK, so I'm inside and ready to make the big run toward the entryway. If we make it out, we go with the plan. If I go down or don't show, you get the Nigerians in the truck and take off..." Woody squinted hard at that idea and shook his head. "Marines don't leave their buddies on the battlefield, Gunner."

"Marines accomplish the mission at any cost, Woody. You know that. We police up the bodies afterward. Let's just figure I get them out..."

"I been thinkin' about that part of it." Woody was frowning over the diagram. "We'd damn sure be better off if they was some kinda smoke screen. You know, kinda add to the confusion."

"How would we generate that? Start a fire someplace?"

"Remember me tellin' about how I was a truck driver in the Marine Corps?"

"Yeah. How's that help?"

"Well, I hauled a lot of ammo and stuff. Not all of that cargo got to where it was goin'. Gimme a minute." Woody went into his living room and Shake heard more drawer searching. He checked his watch. They needed to roll in the next half an hour, or sooner.

"Never thought I'd have much use for this…" Woody plopped a cannister on the table. "But I kept it around anyway." Shake immediately recognized an M-18 smoke grenade, this one had a colored marking band which indicated it would produce a billowing cloud of violet smoke for up to a minute or slightly more than that. Shake had tossed any number of the things when he was on active duty to obscure movement or mark landing zones.

"Damn, Woody. How old is this thing?"

"Figger I made off with it in 1973 or so. It's old, but them things got a pretty fair shelf-life, so I'm told. I'm bettin' it would still work."

"Maybe…" Shake hadn't decided whether or not to trust the old piece of ordnance when his phone rang. He pulled it out of his pocket and checked the number. Nothing he recognized. He checked his watch. Nobody he knew would be calling him at 2215. And he didn't have time for distractions.

"You ain't gonna answer that?"

"Don't recognize the number. Probably a robocall." He pressed a few keys to block it and went back to the planning.

Perryville

I got to tell you, gents." Maynard Katz, the Perry County Sheriff, sat facing the two FBI agents in his office. "This is the damndest thing I ever heard—bar none. I've been wondering about that place out there. Didn't know nothin' about it until the construction crews started work last year. I got hold of the university, and they told me it was some kind of research facility. They wasn't planning on opening it until next year sometime."

"I know it's hard to believe, Sheriff, but we're working on what we believe is credible information."

Sheriff Katz scrubbed at his unshaven chin. This wasn't the first time he'd been summoned from his bed in the middle of the night, usually for a break-in or a shooting somewhere, but he'd never heard of anything like an operation to cut people up and sell their organs. Not here in Perry County or anyplace else that he could recall. Things like that didn't happen in his little patch of the backwoods. On the other hand, he thought as he sat sipping coffee and contemplating the tale he'd just been told, assuming there was any truth to it, finding and then busting up a big-time crime operation would damn sure get some headlines, and he was up for reelection at the end of the year.

"I appreciate the FBI coming by rather than just barging in on a thing like this. Have you been in touch with the fella that made the initial complaint?"

"I've been trying." Agent Warrior held up his phone. "The number he provided just rings and then the call drops. No voice mail, no nothing. He might have blocked an unknown number."

"Probably halfway back to Texas by now." The Sheriff got himself more coffee and offered to top off his visitor's cups. "Maybe best if y'all let me round up a couple of deputies in the morning. We'll get us a warrant from the judge and then get on out to that place and take a look."

"We'd like to do that right now, Sheriff." Agent Huerta placed a hand over his cup. "We have probable cause and an imminent threat to health and safety."

"So you think we might could do this without a warrant in hand? Them university lawyers can be mean as pit bulls."

"The FBI will assume responsibility. Potential Federal crimes involved. You'd be acting on our authority, as a cooperating agency."

Sheriff Katz chewed on his lip for a bit and then checked his watch. "I only got one deputy on duty right now, and I don't want to pull him off patrol. How about I go along myself, and we'll see what's up over there." Sheriff Katz checked his pistol and headed for the door. When the agents wanted him to ride along with them in their Tahoe, the sheriff nodded and asked them to wait just a minute. When he returned and climbed into the rear seat, he was carrying a shotgun. He loaded it from a box of 00 buckshot as he directed Agent Warrior down the county line toward Wittenberg.

Wittenberg

They had emptied the back of Woody's Silverado and lowered the tailgate for easy access. Plenty of room for four or five men back there. They were on the road now, sitting silently, both mentally reviewing the plan they'd settled on before leaving the farm. Shake wanted to keep the whole thing as simple and straightforward as possible. In by the shower room window and out running like hell and leading the captives through the front door. He had the smoke grenade in a pocket of his trousers, but he still hadn't decided whether or not to add it to his scheme of maneuver. Like most raids he'd planned and conducted, what they needed to accomplish tonight broke down into three phases: approach, actions on objective, and exfiltration.

According to the approach plan, they would drive up to a rolling point, blacked out and as silently as possible. The truck would be parked as close to the facility entrance as seemed safe. Woody would dismount and leave the engine running, keeping watch on the entryway where Shake would lead the captives out of the facility. Taking them out a window and through the hole in the fence would take too much time that he didn't have. But the approach was the easy part. It was actions on objective that had him much more worried.

What if the Nigerians panicked? They might believe they were being spirited away to be shot or something. Lord knows they'd been through enough of that already. Shake had the Ibo amulet Jim gave him hanging from its cord around his neck.

Hopefully, the sight of that would encourage them to cooperate. He wasn't sure what else he could to do discourage time-consuming questions and encourage instant compliance.

And what if the cut in the fence that he'd made during the recon had been discovered? What if the guard force spotted it and mounted roving patrols? What if the shower room window was closed tonight? What if they closed it after shower hours every night? He'd have to execute a more kinetic entry. Shake had a sturdy Hooligan Tool tucked in his belt, a souvenir of his days on Marine Corps urban assault teams. That handy piece of gear could be used to pry, pound, or puncture his way through another entry point. But it would be noisy as hell. And if he was confronted with an armed guard force running to investigate, he'd have to rely on the Kimber locked and cocked in a holster on his left hip. A gunfight in that long corridor was bound to get someone besides an intended target wounded or killed once it was crowded with people running one way or another.

Some of that would depend on what the guard or guards did if they discovered him leading their captives on the run down that corridor heading for the front door and freedom. That made him lean toward trying the smoke grenade. It was after midnight, and Shake hoped for minimal guard force with most everyone else inside the facility asleep. There was bound to be some noise, but Shake was hoping to keep it to a bare minimum. Assuming all or most of that worked out according to plan, they had to execute an exfiltration.

Would the guard force give chase? Shake thought it was unlikely if they managed to clear the parking lot and make it to Woody's idling truck. If it looked like they were being chased, Woody was to fire a few rounds to discourage pursuit and then hustle back to the truck where Shake would be behind the wheel ready to jam his foot down on the accelerator. They had considered a plan to disable the vehicles in the parking lot, but that seemed like an unwarranted complication. An option was to have Woody shoot up the tires or put a couple of rounds through the grilles if the opportunity presented itself but that was a secondary concern. When they got the Nigerians out of the facility—assuming Shake was able to do that in the next hour or so—they would tumble them into the Silverado and tear ass back to Woody's place. From there they would bunker in and call the local law. It was well short of a great plan, but it was all they had.

"I got ol' Maynard Katz's number in my phone," Woody said as he turned off Route 177 heading for the facility. He didn't seem to have half the doubts Shake was feeling. "We get them boys rescued and he'll come runnin'. He's a good ol' boy and he'll have him some high-profile prisoners by morning."

"We let the Sheriff deal with bad guys if they run," Shake agreed. "Let the Sheriff and the Highway Patrol people handle all that pursuit and arrest stuff. We stay focused on the rescue."

"I hear you, but it just seems to me we might could rescue them fellas and wrap the others up for the law while we was at it. Once this thang gets out wouldn't nobody blame us for shootin' a couple of 'em."

"Don't get us into a gunfight, Woody. Just do it the way we planned."

Woody nodded, doused his lights, and slowed to a crawl up the facility entrance road.

ΔΔΔ

"How we gonna handle this, gents?" Sheriff Katz scrunched forward from his back seat to rest his arms on the front seats. "We're comin' up on the turn off. Might want to have us a little plan."

"Well, you said the place wasn't open for business, right?" Agent Ken Warrior had been thinking about the approach on the drive from Perryville. "Do you know if they have security guards or something like that?"

"I don't expect so. If they was hiring help around here, I would have heard about it. Unless we find the people you're after, I'd expect the place to be deserted."

"Probably best if we follow your lead, Sheriff. If it looks like nobody's home, we'll just inspect the grounds a bit. You know rattle a few doors, look through the windows, and see what we can see."

"On the other hand," Agent Joe Huerta said, "if the place looks occupied, we'll want to get inside for a look around. We'll wake somebody up and flash badges and creds."

"If there's some people there doin' what you think they're doin', it could get ugly."

"Probably best to stop short of the parking lot," Warrior said. "We'll walk up so we can assess the situation. Safer that way all around."

∆∆∆

When Woody was in place with his shotgun in a patch of woods facing the facility entrance, Shake gave the man's shoulder a quick squeeze. "Showtime, Marine. Let's do it by the numbers."

He made his way through the surrounding woods to the place where he'd cut the fence and watched the grounds carefully for a few minutes. The sodium-vapor standing lights were blazing, but he'd expected that. No one seemed to be on the exterior grounds. It was deathly still. Nothing from the dogs on the other side of the building. A slight breeze rustled the leaves in nearby trees, but it was the only sound he could hear beside the steady hum of the HVAC unit directly to his front. And the shower room window was still standing open to the night air. *Thank you, Lord, for small favors*, Shake thought and crawled toward the hole in the fence.

He was in full combat mode as Shake made his rush for the back of the building. As usual his senses were razor sharp. Sight, smell, touch, and that extra little undefinable thing, a mental acuity that had served him so well in past dicey situations, made him conscious of his surroundings in a way that went beyond the obvious. He would miss nothing, ignore nothing no matter how small from this point. He had that familiar and ultra-heightened situational awareness that was a blessing to combat trained and experienced men, that half-step edge that was the difference between survival and death.

The crossing through illuminated portion of his approach was quick and soundless. What gear Shake carried was strapped as tightly as his nerves. He forced himself to pause crouched beside the HVAC unit for a full three minutes. No sound at all. He could smell soap or maybe shampoo—maybe a whiff of coffee aroma wafting through the open window above him. He mounted the humming AC cabinet and slowly pulled himself up to peek over the sill and into the shower room. Dark in there, but he could see lights from the corridor through the open door. No shadows flickering from anyone moving through the light. If there was a sentry on duty, he wasn't actively patrolling.

Shake levered himself up to get his upper body through the window. It was a bit easier this time, and he knew where to reach for the overhead pipes. He dropped to the floor soundlessly and paused to recover from the effort, feeling in a leg pocket for the survival-kit signal mirror he carried. Lying flat on his belly near the door that opened on the corridor, he cautiously extended the mirror to get a look at what he might be facing. The tattooed Legionnaire appeared to be on watch. He was sitting in a plastic chair outside the sleeping area door, reading something on his phone. He angled the mirror in the other direction, but saw nothing beyond some boxes stacked near the door that led to what must be the lobby area and the main entry doors. That direction looked clear.

Tat-man would have keys to the sleeping area. He'd need to open the door every once in a while. He'd do that to spot-check his charges if he was diligent, but Shake couldn't wait. No telling when this guy might decide to take a look if that was even part of his routine. He moved back into the shower room and turned on a nozzle full blast. The hiss and spatter of water flowing onto the tiles should bring tat-man to check shortly. Shake pulled the sap from his back pocket and ducked into the shadows near the door. He heard footsteps approaching and saw a flashlight beam probing ahead of the man as he slowly stepped into the shower room. He held his breath and waited until the guard stepped further into the dark. Then he brought the heavy sap down on the part of the man's skull that he hoped was the right spot.

The tattooed man dropped the flash and fell to his knees, reaching out for the wall to steady himself. Shake hit him again, this time sure of his mark. There was a muffled grunt and the man fell forward on his face. Shake rushed to shut off the shower and then began to rummage through the man's pockets. Wallet, cigarettes, a lighter, a money clip—no keys. And just like so many other plans Shake had made and tried to execute flawlessly, this one was rapidly swirling toward the crapper. If the sentry on duty didn't have the keys to the barracks room, who in the hell did?

There was no time to investigate. And Shake had no idea how long he had until someone came to relieve the unconscious man at his feet. Tat-man looked like he was definitely down and out for a while. There was a trickle of blood from his ear and a huge swelling above that. Shake pulled the Glock out of the man's holster and dropped the magazine. He found a nearby toilet, raised the seat lid, and tossed both gun and ammo into the water. He was about to duck into the corridor when he noticed the stungun. He grabbed it and pressed the button. Green light, full charge. He stuck it in a pocket and pulled the beefy Hooligan Tool from his belt. Employed properly at just the right spot between the door and frame, the tool would serve to open the door, but it would be far from silent. No help for that now.

Shake pulled the Ibo amulet from beneath his shirt, letting it hang where it would be in easy view. Then he sprinted down the hallway for the barracks room door. The Hooligan Tool was relatively easy to slide between the door and frame at the spot where the key tumbler was located below the door handle. He had to bump it a few times to be sure it was seated but that didn't make much noise. The next step would be different matter and much noisier. Shake checked the hallway, took a deep breath, and jerked hard on the long end of the tool. The blade bit hard, bending the door frame as Shake leveraged the tool, inserted the blade more deeply and heaved again. Something inside the frame game way with a loud pop that sounded like a pistol shot. Progress.

Shake heaved again and heard metal snap. There was a squeal of tortured metal, but the lock set was still resisting. He put his shoulder against the door and bumped it hard with his full weight while pushing in the other direction with the lever.

There was a shout from the shadows near the other end of the corridor, and Shake looked to see someone peeking outside the cafeteria. Samuel Imshana with a coffee cup in hand. The black man dropped the cup and his hand disappeared. When it reappeared, it was holding a nickel-plated revolver. The first shot missed and thudded into the wall near Shake's right shoulder. He didn't wait for Samuel Imshana to correct his aim. Shake drew the Kimber, thumbed the safety off and tossed two unaimed shots down the corridor.

The dogs penned up outside the building set up an immediate clamor, barking and howling. He could hear shouts from another part of the building as he heaved his way into the barracks room. He shoved the door shut behind him. It was dark inside, but he could sense men moving on the other side of the room. Shake felt along the wall for a light switch and found it. Neon tubes in the ceiling blinked, buzzed, and illuminated. Four very frightened black men were crowded together in a corner. Shake holstered his pistol and held the amulet up for them to see.

"Jambon Imbasa sent me. I'm going to get you out of here. But you have to do exactly as I tell you. Can you do that?"

"We heard shooting." One of the men approached to take a closer look at the amulet.

"Yes, and there's likely to be more. But you'll be OK if you just do what I tell you to do." Shake wasn't sure exactly what that would be now that he was trapped inside the room with four terrified men and who knows how many fully alerted and armed people on the other side of the door at his back.

The men began to crowd around him now. They were in underwear and barefoot. "Where is Jambon Imbasa?" One of the men stepped forward and pointed. "That is his symbol."

"He gave it to me—so you'd trust me and do what I say. He'll be waiting for us once I get you out of here." Shake was thinking fast, thinking about the smoke grenade that was banging against his thigh, and hoping the damn thing would still work after years of storage in Woody's junk drawer. "Quickly, get dressed and be sure you've got shoes on. We may have to run."

Shake could hear voices from the corridor as the Nigerians scrambled to get dressed. Someone was shouting for him to come out with his hands high. At least they weren't trying to force the door. They knew he had a weapon and wasn't afraid to use it after the exchange of fire with Samuel Imshana. They'd wait a while and assess the situation. They'd take some time to plan, come up with something that would avoid damage to the Nigerians. These guys were valuable commodities as long as they weren't ventilated by bullet holes.

"Form a line here," Shake said pointing at the door. "Everyone holds on to the man in front of you. Just grab at his waist…" Shake demonstrated by shoving his hand inside one of the men's pants at the small of his back. "Don't let go and when I start to run, you follow me."

ΔΔΔ

Woody heard the gunshots. Just three rounds so far. Nothing more after that. Was Gunner Davis down inside there? He looked over his shotgun sights and spotted shadows flitting around—maybe a couple of men moving. Dogs raising hell and lots of yelling, but he couldn't understand what was being said. He was sorely tempted to leave his post, just get in there and see what he could do to help. But Marines don't quit their post until properly relieved.

He was trying to remember the rest of the general orders he'd learned back in boot camp when the entry doors swung open and two men emerged carrying pistols. They were looking around, in low crouches as if they expected an ambush or some other kind of surprise encounter. They crouched at the fenders of the SUV and waved at another man waiting for them inside. Woody saw the man dart out of the shadows and head for the Escalade. He didn't appear to be armed.

Looks like somebody's about to make a run for it, Woody thought, *and that ain't gonna happen on my watch.* First round in the chamber of his 870 was birdshot as ordered. But sometimes a Marine had to think ahead of the plan, look at contingencies, so Woody had loaded the rest of the magazine with 00 buckshot. And he had a pocketful of deer slugs to back that. He jacked the birdshot shell out of the chamber and pumped up a load of buck.

When the two men carrying pistols and the third guy moved to get into the SUV, Woody took careful aim and blew out both back tires with two quick shots. The armed men ducked, backing toward the entry doors and shoving the unarmed man in front of them. They winged a couple of rounds wildly into the woods, but they were all wide and high. Woody changed positions anyway. It wasn't quitting his post. It was just repositioning his post, getting a better angle for flanking fire if it came to that. He settled in and reloaded the shotgun with slugs. If this is what combat is like, he could handle it.

ΔΔΔ

Shake pulled the door open slightly and extended his mirror, angling it around to get the best view of the corridor he could manage. Samuel Imshana was crouched low in the cafeteria doorway. It looked like he'd traded the little wheel-gun for an M-4. He was staring over an ACOG sight with the muzzle pointed at the entrance to the doorway. Another man darted across the corridor carrying a pistol. He disappeared into one of the office doorways across from the cafeteria. Shake studied the positions, trying to gauge the number of steps he'd have to make before engaging the shooters waiting for him. If that was the extent of the gauntlet they'd have to run, he wanted to be precise. Maybe they wouldn't fire wildly for fear of hitting the Nigerians, but he didn't know that. Could be Samuel Imshana and whoever else was in the building would figure the gig was blown at this point and just kill everybody in sight.

He heard a couple of shotgun blasts. Woody was on duty and probably shooting at a couple of squirters. Wish he'd let whoever was trying to escape just go. It would reduce the odds. Shake could see shadows flickering at the far end of the corridor that looked like a couple of men scrambling for cover. Two where he could see them in the hallway and maybe a couple of others—armed or unarmed?—at the other end of it. Odds were rapidly deteriorating from substandard to shitty.

ΔΔΔ

"Them first two was pistols. Last couple was a damn shotgun!" Sheriff Maynard Katz jacked a round into his own scattergun and walked to the edge of the road where the two FBI agents were huddled behind a tree. "Y'all hear them dogs? I believe the question about whether or not anybody's to home up there has been answered."

"What do you think?" Agent Ken Warrior drew his Glock 22 and looked at his partner.

"FBI help is a long way off," Agent Joe Huerta said. "You got anything we can call up right quick, Sheriff?"

"Like I said, I only got one deputy on duty tonight. Nearest SWAT is Perryville County, but it's gonna take some time to get them out and over here."

"Give them a call anyway, Sheriff." Agent Warrior flinched at another exchange of gunfire ahead of them about a hundred meters from their position. "Tell them to roll everything they've got Code 3—and tell them to bring an ambulance." While the Sheriff used his phone, Agent Warrior motioned for his partner to follow and slipped further into the woods on the side of the road. "Low and slow. We move a little closer and see if we can determine what's happening up there."

About 50 meters up the road, ex-PFC Woodrow Cheeley was in a firefight and having a hell of a time. The two pistol shooters made another run for a vehicle, trying for the rental truck this time and preceding their move with a barrage of ineffective covering fire.

"Well-aimed rounds win the fight," Woody mumbled into the stock of his shotgun. He put one slug through the open door of the truck which sent the man who had been trying to get behind the wheel limping back toward the entryway. A second round slammed into the truck up near the engine compartment. That drove the other two men scrambling back for the facility entrance behind their wounded buddy. Woody chased them with a slug that hit one of the entry doors as the men ducked through it. Plate glass shards scattered across the walkway. Woody couldn't see a target in the darkened lobby, so he pumped the 870 and shifted aim back to the truck. His next deer slung went into the vehicle's differential housing with a loud and satisfying clang.

"You ain't goin' nowhere in that vehicle." Woody waited for a bit, wondering what was happening inside with Gunner Davis and the hostages. If he didn't see something in a few more minutes, he intended to conduct a combat assault on a fortified position. He was fairly sure he remembered how to do that.

"Freeze right there!" Woody flinched but kept his finger off the trigger. The voice had law enforcement authority and he was sure there was a gun behind it. He scrunched around a bit trying to get a look at the man who was giving the orders. "FBI...I told you to freeze!" Yep, that's a cop of one kind or another. Unmistakable—and not a local—but at least it wasn't some asshole from inside the facility had the drop on him.

"Leave the shotgun on the ground and stand up slowly with your hands over your head!"

Woody did as he was ordered, turning around slowly to see two men half-hidden behind a tree with pistols leveled at him. A third man in uniform stepped up for a closer look.

"Goddammit, Woody!" Sheriff Maynard Katz glared and lowered his shotgun. "What the hell is going on here?"

ΔΔΔ

Shake glanced back at the conga line of frightened men behind him. All the shooting had made them more than a little antsy, pawing at the cement floor like a pack of ponies anxious to run. He figured from the determined looks on their faces that they'd follow where he led. What they wanted more than anything was to get out of this place. Given what they'd already endured, whatever happened later would be gravy. He dropped the magazine from his Kimber and inserted a fully loaded one in the well. With eight in the fresh mag and one in the chamber, he had enough for a little covering fire. He took a deep breath and turned to address the Nigerians as he would a squad of Marine infantrymen heading into a firefight for the first time.

"There's going to be some shooting in the next few minutes. The men outside probably won't shoot at you, but they will shoot at me. If I go down, don't stop. Don't stop for anything. Just keep running toward the end of the hall. There are doors there. Just push them open and run right through to the outside. I have a man waiting for you there. He'll take you somewhere safe and call for the police."

The first man in line behind Shake nodded. "We will go with you." Shake looked at the other three. They all seemed ready, anxious, and scared, but ready as anyone could be in a situation like this one. They didn't exactly look like soldiers steeling themselves, but they didn't look like helpless captives either. He turned back to the door and tried to visualize the run. Figure ten steps to the cafeteria entrance. Shoot right, across the body, just one round—another two steps and get the one on the left. Both hip-shots, just point and pull. They might be hit, or they might just duck the incoming. Didn't matter. Speed…violence…

impact. Don't give 'em time to think. He needed to channel General George Patton for this one: *l'audace, l'audace toujours l'audace.*

He levered the door a bit so he could get a good grip when it was time to swing it open. That elicited a couple of M-4 rounds that slammed into the stucco beyond the door. Shake checked his conga line a last time. They were all crouched and shoving forward. Nothing to it but to do it, Shake decided and dug out the smoke grenade. He pulled the pin and let the safety lever pop. On a two count he rolled the cylinder out into the corridor like a bowling ball.

ΔΔΔ

Woody had just finished a sputtering explanation of what was happening inside the facility when the Sheriff interrupted and pointed at the building. Huge gouts of bright violet smoke were pouring through one of the shattered front doors. In the sodium-vapor light it looked vivid and surreal.

"That there's my smoke grenade," Woody beamed. "Right shortly, Gunner Davis and four black fellas ought to be charging out the door." He reached for his shotgun, but Agent Warrior pinned it with a foot.

"No more shooting tonight, Mr. Cheeley. You just let us handle this from here."

The two FBI Agents took off in a running crouch headed for cover behind the white truck. "Do like they say, Woody." Sheriff Katz jerked a thumb over his shoulder. "Get on back to your truck and shut it down before you run out of gas." Sheriff Katz patted him on the shoulder and then trotted off to join the FBI men.

Woody didn't pick up his shotgun. He'd get it later. It was empty anyway, and he'd run out of ammo in the unexpected shoot-out. He reached under his camo blouse and pulled out the Ruger GP100 .357 Magnum he'd hidden in his belt at the small of his back. Woody was a law-abiding man, but he knew better than to run a gun dry without a back-up. He wasn't worried about his truck. It was full of gas. He slipped deeper into the woods and moved to his right where he could get a good angle on anybody the law-dogs missed.

ΔΔΔ

"Remember…don't stop for anything…no matter what happens!" Shake shifted the Kimber to his right hand, stuck it out into the corridor and triggered four quick rounds, hoping the wild shots would force the two shooters he knew about to duck. Then he shouldered the door open and bolted into the corridor. He was trying to be both fast and deliberate as he switched the Kimber to his strong hand and trotted into the dense cloud of violet smoke. The Nigerians were jostling him, pushing hard. It was difficult to breathe and impossible to see in the choking cloud that filled the corridor. He could hear the Nigerians behind him coughing and hacking, but he led on using his internal compass to guide the line straight ahead toward the far end of the hallway.

He heard a double tap from his left after he'd counted six steps. Shots were high, and he heard them hit the plexiglass of the cafeteria window. He increased his speed, feeling the tug at his waistline from the man immediately behind him. Shake counted four more steps before snapping the Kimber across his body to the right where he thought Samuel Imshana might be crouched with the M-4. He fired one round on the run…two more steps…and he fired again into the doorway on his left. He heard a scream, so that one had hit one of the shooters. Nothing from his right, so either he also hit Samuel Imshana, or the man had decided to make a run for it.

They were moving at a fairly fast clip, a jerky trot that caused the line behind him to bow and flex like an accordion with faster runners bumping into slower ones. Shake led on. Fifteen long strides…18…20. They should be nearing the lobby area. Suddenly, a form loomed up out of the violet cloud. A man holding a handkerchief over his mouth and nose with one hand and waving a big horse-pistol with the other. The gun looked like an old Webley, a weapon that could do significant damage at point-blank range. Shake juked to the right, feeling his shoulder impact the corridor wall. The abrupt stop caused the man behind Shake to stumble and fall, but Shake kept his eyes on the pistol swinging in his direction. The shooter was just a shadow in the smoke cloud, but Shake could see the pistol clearly. He batted at it with the Kimber and then extended his arm. When he felt the muzzle sink into soft flesh, he pulled the trigger.

The shadow slumped and the pistol disappeared. Shake reached for the man on the ground and pulled him to his feet. Some of the smoke was beginning to clear, and he could see the entry doors. Beyond those were bright yellow pools from the standing lights in the parking area. Almost home. He shoved at the Nigerians, pointing at the light and yelling for them to run. He wanted to be the last man out, to be sure there were no other shooters following down the hallway.

As the Nigerians scrambled past him, still holding onto each other, he counted. One, two, three—and four. Shake played tail-end Charlie and emptied his Kimber back down the corridor into the dissipating smoke. When the weapon hit slide-lock, he dropped the magazine and automatically reached into his pocket for a reload. It was instinctive, a move that had been drilled into him over decades of training. It was also a near fatal delay in this situation.

He felt a beefy arm wrap around his neck from behind and hot breath hissed onto the nape of his neck. The hot muzzle of a pistol was drilled into his right ear. "Drop that fuckin' gun! Do it! Right now—or you're a dead man!"

Shake let the Kimber fall from his hands. Whoever it was behind him had some muscle to back the gun he was pressing into Shake's skull. The arm wrapped around his neck felt like a boa constrictor. The man dragged him stumbling backward into the shadows of the lobby.

"How many outside?"

Shake could lie and claim he'd brought an army of cops. But that would probably result in a stand-off, a siege with him as a hostage inside the building when Woody sent the law. He decided on the truth. If this bozo thought he could make a safe break, Shake might maneuver him into a better position, somewhere he could do something besides just getting choked or shot.

"One man…in the woods out front."

"He got a gun?"

"Shotgun…"

"You lie, you die, motherfucker. You understand me?"

Shake just nodded the best he could as the man goosed him toward the entrance doors. Shake looked everywhere his restricted head movement allowed but the Nigerians were nowhere in sight. Hopefully, Woody had them in the truck and was long gone headed for the farm. That was the contingency plan if Shake went down or otherwise didn't make it out with the captives. But the guy who had him under wraps didn't know that.

When they had just reached the edge of the lights, the man jerked him to a halt and waved his pistol so it could be clearly seen by anyone waiting outside the building. "I'm coming out. Anybody takes a shot or fucks around out there and this dude dies!"

As they slowly shuffled out onto the concrete entryway, Shake carefully reached for his left trouser pocket and wiggled his hand into it. His captor didn't notice. The dogs were still barking themselves hoarse which was a handy distraction. The man was kneeing Shake in the back of the legs, keeping the pair moving forward. Shake could feel the man craning right and left, looking around, trying to spot the man with the shotgun. They stopped near the truck and Shake felt increased pressure from the pistol jammed against his ear.

"Tell your guy to come out with his hands up and empty."

"Woody! It's Shake…" He was choking and croaked as he tried to shout. He had his left hand on the stun-gun now, feeling for the switch to activate it. "Woody, come on out!"

Nothing. Woody was probably gone with the Nigerians as planned. Unless otherwise directed, a Marine follows the last order given.

"I think he must have taken off." Shake choked out the words and heaved as if he was having trouble breathing. "You're good, man. Ease up so I can breathe."

The tension in the man's arm relaxed just a bit. Shake craned back feeling with the back of his head to be sure of where the man was. Pistol on my right…Asshole's head on the left. Shake pulled the stun-gun from his pocked and jammed it hard over his left shoulder.

There was an intense blue flash. He heard the hiss and sizzle of an electrical discharge. The man behind him grunted and stumbled backward, but the shock impulse made him jerk the trigger. Shake felt a painful pop as his eardrum exploded and felt the searing heat of muzzle blast scalding his face. He could smell hair burning and realized it was his as he slumped to his knees and fell forward onto his face. Bracing hard against the macadam, he tried to crawl toward the truck. The pain was intense, but he knew the next shot would kill him. He heard that shot, but it was apparently not aimed at him. It came from up ahead in the dark, from somewhere on the other side of the truck.

Shake could barely raise his head, but he saw people running toward him, shouting something he couldn't distinguish through the searing pain in his head and the intense ringing in his ears.

ΔΔΔ

Woody leaned against an oak on the side of the building watching the pair cut through the chain-link fence. The cutters the black man was using looked just like the ones he'd loaned to Shake for the recon. He decided he'd wait for a while to make his move. Once the pair got through the fence and into the woods, he'd have the element of surprise and a dead drop on both of them. He had Federal JHP rounds in the cylinder and they'd make a truck-size hole, but Woody was hoping he wouldn't have to shoot. What he wanted was a couple of prisoners that he could turn over to his buddy Sheriff Maynard Katz who showed up to the party unexpectedly with a couple of Feds.

On the other hand, he was not about to take chances with people like these two. They were the kind of fuckheads that carved people up alive to sell their parts. That didn't merit much consideration or mercy in Woody's worldview. If the black fella unstrapped that little carbine from his shoulder or reached for the semi-auto on his hip, if the woman made a grab for the pistol she was wearing…well, Woody might have to turn a couple of corpses over to Sheriff Katz.

The black man tossed the bolt-cutters aside and pulled at a section of fence so the woman could duck through. *Right polite of you*, Woody thought with a grin, waiting for the pair to clear the fence line. They stood looking around, breathing hard, trying to decide which way to run when Woody stepped out from behind the oak tree with the muzzle of his Ruger GP100 pointed in their direction. He dropped into a solid Weaver stance, staring at them both over the sights, just so they'd know they weren't dealing with some bumpkin amateur.

"I got the slack out of the trigger here, y'all. You make any wrong moves and I'll ventilate both yer asses."

Woody's prisoners raised their hands, glaring at him. It was dark in the woods, and Woody wanted to be sure they understood their precarious situation. He stepped a little closer where some of the glow from the standing lights highlighted the silver matte finish of his big wheel-gun. The distinctive click the hammer made when he cocked it made the woman flinch.

"This is what we're gonna do," he said, flipping the muzzle at Samuel Imshana. "You drop that carbine off yer shoulder and toss it real easy in my direction." When that was done, Woody ordered the man to pull the semi-auto from his holster using just two fingers, a trick he'd learned from some cop shows on TV.

When he had the carbine and the semi-auto within reach, he turned to the woman.

"Your turn, missy. Unhook that pistol belt and toss it over on top of the rest." The South African scrub nurse did as she was directed. Woody was tempted to pick up all the ordnance, but he didn't want to lose focus fumbling with belts and slings. They could pick up the guns later after he had these two turned over to the law. He waved his muzzle toward the cleared strip on the outside of the perimeter fence. "Y'all just start walkin' in that direction." He pointed with his weak hand toward the facility entrance. "I'll be right behind with my finger on the trigger." He began to hear sirens screaming in the night. *Old Maynard Katz has called out reinforcements,* he thought with a grin. *He's about to get himself reelected in a damn landslide.*

After about 30 meters, they passed the hole Shake had cut during the recon. Woody chuckled. "Look over there to yer right," he said. "We cut that hole earlier. You woulda looked around a little bit, you could have saved yourselves a mite of work." His prisoners glanced at it, but neither appeared to share Woody's sense of humor.

ΔΔΔ

An EMT was dabbing salve on Shake's ear and the side of his head. There was an ambulance parked near where he sat propped up against a flattened rear wheel of the box truck. SWAT cops were swarming around him. One of them was leading a K-9 into the building. Another one had the two watchdogs on leashes and was walking them toward a truck. Radios crackled and lights on the roof of several police vehicles flashed in a steady rhythm. The strobing lights made his head hurt, and he closed his eyes, breathing deeply. He couldn't seem to remember anything after the shot that deafened him. Woody must have called in the law. Good man.

"He gonna be OK?" Shake opened his eyes and peeked over the EMT's shoulder where a man in a suit with a badge hanging from a lanyard around his neck was standing over him. The guy looked like an Indian, but the badge was the distinctive shield of the FBI. Shake wondered how the Feds got involved in all this. He tried to find out, but the question just came out as a half-whine, half-growl.

"Just relax," the EMT said as he began to wrap a bandage around Shake's head. He glanced up at the FBI man. "He's gonna be fine, but we need to get him to the hospital ASAP."

"Check. Just a few minutes here." The FBI man took a knee next to Shake and put a hand on his shoulder. "I'm Ken Warrior, FBI. You'd be Mr. Davis. Is that right?"

Shake cleared his throat and turned his head to spit. "That's me," he rasped. "The Nigerians OK?"

"Four of them made it out. We're taking them down to Cape where they'll be interviewed. They're gonna be just fine—thanks to you. That all there were?"

"Yeah. Four of an original bunch of ten. Is Woody...Mr. Cheeley...OK?"

A squatty figure in police uniform with a shotgun in the crook of an arm stood behind the FBI man and jerked a thumb over his shoulder. "Woody's over there somewhere," he said. "We run across him when we rolled up on this mess. He's good."

"We're gonna get you to a hospital pretty quick, Mr. Davis. Can you answer a question or two?"

"Yeah, but speak up." Shake shook his head trying to clear the constant ringing in his right ear. The voices sounded like they were coming from deep inside a well. "I'm a little deaf right now."

"No surprise there." The EMT stood to make room for the cops. "Lucky that was all the damage done."

"So far, we've got just two in custody, Mr. Davis. Can you tell me if there were any others?"

"I'm not sure how many there were when it all started." Shake closed his eyes and visualized the incident. "I knocked one guy out just after I got in—guy with full-sleeve tats on both arms."

"We got him." The FBI nodded toward one of the police vehicles. "And we got another one wounded in the leg, but there had to be more. Local police are searching the buildings and grounds, but we want to be sure we got them all."

"I shot at three of them. Pretty sure I got two. Don't know about any others."

The Sheriff pointed at a couple of nearby body bags. "That would be them two. Both nailed with .45 slugs from the look of it." He held up a plastic bag containing Shake's Kimber. "This your gun?"

Shake nodded.

"That works. But we didn't find no black guy other than the four you brought out."

"Can we go over the shootings, Mr. Davis? I'd like to get an initial reckoning before we get you to the hospital."

"There was a shooter on either side of the corridor when I popped the smoke grenade and we started the run for the exit. The black guy was on the right and another man on my left. I shot at the one on my right first. That was the black guy—name is Samuel Imshana. I don't know if I hit him. The guy on the other side was a little farther on down the corridor. He fired a couple of rounds at me. He missed. Guess I hit him. Another one came at me out of the smoke toward the end of the corridor. He had a revolver. I just pointed and fired." Shake's head was beginning to throb painfully again, and he shook it trying to stay coherent. That just made the worst headache he could remember even worse.

"Well, all that goes down as self-defense in my book." The sheriff seemed to be keeping score in a notebook he was holding. "Two down in the corridor, one down out here that Agent Warrior shot. That checks for body count. We didn't find no black guy."

"I think both him and the tattooed guy are former French Foreign Legion. And I saw a woman when I scouted the place."

"So that's at least two fugitives—black guy and a woman. We'll get them,"

"Hey, Sheriff! Look what I brung you."

The two lawmen stood. Shake craned around to look between their legs as a couple of the SWAT cops rushed to intercept a party that was turning into the parking area from the fence line. Woody was escorting two prisoners toward the cops. Samuel Imshana and a very dejected looking woman. They were quickly cuffed and stuffed inside one of the police vehicles.

"Those the two you described, Mr. Davis?"

"That's them…" Shake grinned and tried to stand. He waved at Woody who was headed in his direction, shoving the revolver into his belt.

"Hey, Gunner. What happened to you?"

"Long story, Woody. You did a great job, Marine. Nice work."

"Y'all can swap war stories later." The Sheriff grabbed Woody by the elbow. "Hope you ain't plannin' on gettin' any sleep tonight, Woody. Let's get down to my office for your official statements."

The EMT intervened, leading Shake toward the ambulance. Agent Warrior and another FBI man walked alongside. "We'll get you some medical attention, Mr. Davis and then I'm afraid there's gonna be a lengthy period of interviews and things like that."

"How long? I'm due back home in Texas."

"We'll make the initial stuff as brief as possible," Agent Huerta said. "But you'll likely have to travel and testify a few times. This thing is gonna get deep and heavy before it's all said and done. Is there anyone you'd like us to call or notify?"

Shake felt in his pocket for his phone. "Just my wife. She's overseas right now." He slumped next to an EMT in the back of the ambulance as the doors shut. He had no idea how to explain to her that a simple trip down memory lane wound up with him getting shot and suddenly becoming the star witness in a major Federal criminal case.

The flash burns weren't too bad. He'd have an ugly ridge of scar tissue on top of his right ear to compliment the others he'd picked up over the years, but the salve the doctors applied twice daily was working and the pain meds were fairly effective. He was concussed and shaky on his feet for a day or two, but that was stabilizing, and the Docs weren't overly worried about it. The headaches were diminishing despite raging tinnitus that constantly jangled through his brain. There was an ugly smudge of black powder burn that made an interesting contrast to his white hair, but that would grow out and disappear in time.

The real problem was his hearing. An audiologist said the eardrum was shattered, and he had some serious high-frequency hearing damage on top of what he'd already lost from years of gunfire and explosives during his military career. He'd likely wind up wearing hearing aids, but Shake had expected that anyway as he aged.

It took two overly long phone calls with Chan to explain it all, but she eventually settled down and accepted the situation. He begged her not to cut her trip short despite her initial response which was to rush home on the first thing flying out of Taipei. He'd be OK and the doctors said he could be released in a day or two. He'd head for Texas as quickly as he could get out of their care, drive home, and be in Austin to pick her up at the airport.

He met with the Sheriff and reps from the Missouri State Attorney General's Office almost immediately. Apparently, cadaver dogs had discovered five mutilated corpses in fields behind the vet research facility. Divers were looking for another body in the Mississippi near Perryville, but that one hadn't been found yet. The state authorities wanted detailed statements and background information on the actions Shake had taken during the raid. The interviews took longer than the doctors wanted to permit, but Shake waved off their objections and continued to talk into the recorders. He wanted to get it out, open, and over with as soon as possible. He was feeling used, abused, and homesick by the time they finished. The good news was that the State AG indicated there would be no charges filed against Shake for the shootings involved in the rescue. Those would go down as what the AG called self-defense by a citizen who was acting to prevent any furtherance of a gruesome crime.

The FBI was next. They were mostly interested in what Shake knew about the nature of the organ harvesting operation. It was terse but detailed. They had most of the story from the Nigerians who were being held in Federal custody. They'd be star witnesses in an upcoming, very spectacular trial. And that trial, according to Agents Warrior and Huerta who dropped by to check on him, was likely to be long, involved, and far-reaching. The Director of Veterinary Medicine at SEMO was a culprit as was a very high-level financier that they didn't name.

Other Feds told Shake at the end of their interviews that the case would be referred to the U.S. Department of Justice for final adjudication. Shake would likely be subpoenaed to testify at least once, maybe several times in a case this big and flashy. The Government would be in touch soon with their specific demands. Meanwhile, he was free to leave as soon as he was cleared by the doctors.

A gang of reporters crowded the hospital for the first two days. Shake wanted no part of that, and the Missouri authorities backed by the Feds generally handled all queries. They advised him not to give any interviews, and Shake was glad to comply.

Captain George Selby and Lieutenant Walter Sundstrom dropped by on the day he was due to be released. Both were apologetic, and Shake didn't press the issue with them. He asked Sundstrom if there were any military surplus stores in the area. Sundstrom knew of a couple, and he was glad to handle the little favor Shake asked. Sundstrom was back in an hour just as Shake was filling out final release papers in the hospital lobby. He handed over an oblong blue box and refused the payment Shake offered. "Ran into a guy who was a Marine," Sundstrom said. "He had just what you wanted."

Sheriff Maynard Katz showed up with a deputy to drive Shake out to Woody's farm so he could pick up his truck. The Perry County Sheriff was in a good mood. Nothing so spectacular had ever happened on his watch, and he was becoming something of a local hero. The deputy indicated Sheriff Katz was a shoo-in for reelection.

Woody was waiting in his front yard with Hank and Hilda running loose, about to break their backs with excited tail-wagging. Woody opened the door of the cop car and extended a hand to Shake. "You don't look so bad for a close-combat veteran," he said.

"I'm ready to roll for Texas, Woody." Shake draped an arm over the farmer's shoulder. "I just wanted to say thanks…for everything. It took two good Marines, but by God, we got it done."

"Damn sure did, Gunner. But me? I just done what you said."

"You did a lot more than that." Shake reached into his pocket and brought out the blue box. He opened it to reveal a Navy and Marine Corps Commendation Medal. "I thought you should have this, Woody. In official recognition of heroic service above and beyond the call of duty." He pointed at a blue, gold, and scarlet ribbon mounted above the medal. "And that's the Combat Action Ribbon. You damn sure earned that."

Woody just stared at the decorations. "Damn, Gunner. I don't know what to say."

Shake pulled him close and gave him a hug. "The accepted response on these occasions is just to salute and say thank you, sir."

Woody backed up a step, came to the position of attention and whipped up a very respectable salute. Shake returned it with a big grin.

"Very well, PFC Cheeley. Carry on."

"Aye, aye, sir!"

Shake dug the keys out of a pocket and headed for his truck. "You've got my number, Woody. Call me once in a while and let me know how you're doing."

Woody, the Sheriff and his deputy stood in the yard waving as Shake steered for the highway and home.

Lockhart, Texas

It took Shake four days to make it back to the Texas Hill Country. He got some beer and chow at the local HEB grocery and restocked the larders. He called the Sheriff to let him know he was back and drove to Austin to pick up Bear. The big dog leaped up to put his paws on Shake's shoulders and slobbered all over him. The minute Shake opened the passenger side door for him, Bear leaped into his standard riding position and barked. He knew when it was time to go home.

Chan was due back at the first of the week, and he wanted her to go along when he went to Washington to testify, but she declined. She knew when it was time to come home as well as Bear did. And Chan intended to stay there for a while.

The gruesome organ-harvesting story and the FBI's busting of the perpetrators, plus the arrest of several others behind the immediate scenes, was making headlines and leading newscasts everywhere. Hyperbole flew from news outlets in a blazing torrent. So far Shake's name had not been mentioned, and details of the rescue were spotty. The FBI and Missouri law enforcement were being given most of the credit, and they weren't sharing many details. Shake was to make several testimonial appearances in the next week or so. He was told he'd have to endure private sessions with investigators from the Attorney General's office, and there was some speculation that he'd be called on to testify before a Congressional committee.

He was noodling around on the computer, making notes to support that, when his phone rang. He didn't recognize the number and was about to let it go to voice mail when something told him to answer. If it was a nuisance call, he could just punch off and block it, but he had a feeling about this call.

"Mr. Shake? It is Jambon Imbasa."

"Jim! Where are you? How are you?"

"I'm told not to say where I am, but I am fine. We are all here together now. And we are being treated very well. I wanted to call and give you my most heartfelt thanks. My friends have told me what you did to rescue them."

"I'm really glad to hear from you, Jim. I was worried…"

"No need, Mr. Shake. We are all well, very well in fact. There is much good American food here. And people are being very kind to us."

"What's next, Jim? Will you stay here or go home?"

"We will be here for a while yet. The authorities are still interviewing us. And then we will go back to Nigeria. I'm told all that has been arranged. But none of us wanted to leave without telling you how grateful we are for everything you did. You saved our lives."

"I wish I could have done more, Jim. I really do."

"You will always be a hero, Mr. Shake, to me and to all my people."

"Which reminds me, Jim. I need to return that badge thing you loaned me. It's still hanging around my neck."

"Please keep it there, Mr. Shake. You are now one of us—a leader of the Ibo."

"That's very gracious, Jim. I'm honored."

"Come to see us some day, Mr. Shake. We will always welcome you."

About the Author

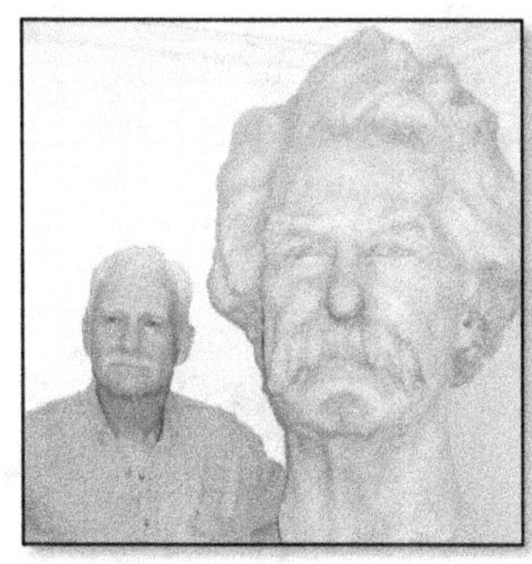

ale Dye is a Marine officer who rose through the ranks to retire as a Captain after 21 years of service in war and peace. He is a distinguished graduate of Missouri Military Academy who enlisted in the United States Marine Corps shortly after graduation. Sent to war in Southeast Asia, he served in Vietnam in 1965 and 1967 through 1970, surviving 31 major combat operations.

Appointed a Warrant Officer in 1976, he later converted his commission and was a Captain when he deployed to Beirut, Lebanon with the Multinational Force in 1982-83. He served in a variety of assignments around the world and along the way attained a degree in English Literature from the University of Maryland. Following retirement from active duty in 1984, he spent time in Central America, reporting and training troops for guerrilla warfare in El Salvador, Honduras, and Costa Rica.

Upset with Hollywood's treatment of the American military, he went to Hollywood and established Warriors Inc., the preeminent military training and advisory service to the entertainment industry. He has worked on more than 50 movies and TV shows including several Academy Award and Emmy winning productions. As a Missouri native, he has always been a Mark Twain fan who grew up with Huck Finn fantasies. He is a novelist, actor, director and show business innovator, who wanders between Los Angeles and Lockhart, Texas.

Gunner Shake Davis, U.S. Marine Corps, might be out of the active ranks, but he's anything but retired. Catch all his adventures by bestselling author Dale Dye in the Shake Davis series of scintillating novels.

And catch Shake's daughter Tracey in her own action-filled adventure in Sea Hunt—available wherever fine books are sold.

For these and other quality military fiction and nonfiction, visit
www.warriorspublishing.com